SPIKE'S LAST LIFE

VOLUME 1

THE POWER CRYSTAL CHRONICLES

NOEL ALVARADO

 Created with Vellum

For all the Spikes, Celestias, Ashleys, Jennys, and Marinas in the world. Thank you for standing up for basic human rights. The world will always need you even when it disappoints you.

For my Bubby Bear, who helped this story come to life in major ways. I'll thank you in other ways later. ;)

For those born from migrants, who live in fear everyday that their parents, siblings, or families will be torn apart but stay strong and accomplish great things. Keep accomplishing your dreams.

For my LGBT-QWUAH Family, I love y'all forever and always. If you can be one thing, be gayer out of spite.

People should not be afraid of their governments.
Governments should be afraid of their people.

ALAN MOORE - V FOR VENDETTA

GLOSSARY

Planets and Beings Mentioned:

Templite: An individual born of the planet, Tempus. Most Time Keepers are born from this planet.

Time Absorber: A Time Keeper, usually from Tempus (a Templite), that is placed in different forms of different beings from various planets in order to spy on said planet. (For example, a Time Absorber could be turned in to a bird in order to spy on Barretta. The bird would live its entire life on the planet sending back data to Tempus through their placenta pod data link. All information from cultural traditions to intel can be used by Tempus to plan an invasion.

Time Keeper: A being that can control Pulses and evolve abilities that mess with the fabric of time.

Epsilon: The second strongest planet in the galaxy. A planet of witches, warlocks, and warwicks. A coven of thirteen rules over the planet.

Witches: feminine magic wielders.

Warlocks: Masculine magic wielders.

Warwicks: the gender neutral magic wielders.

Lykos: The planet of wolves. Strongest planet in the galaxy. Formerly known as Necropolis. Colonized by Kairos.

Lycans: Wolves. Secondary forms are usually hybrid version of half-human half-wolf looking creatures. Their final forms are massive wolves.

Barreta: The planet of bi-pedal birds. Bigger planet usually uses its excess space to house refugees from different planets.

Barrettans: Weapon of choice: bow and arrow. They can also use their feathers as weapons. They will deplume themselves and allow the feathers to stab people.

Gamma-2: The lava planet of green rock type beings. Their planet is strong among the Neutralists and stays out of war affairs. They can decide to help when they want to. Tensions are strong between Barretta and Gamma-2 since Kairos pitted them against each other.

Venus: The planet of humans. Long ago, before the timeline wars, every beings originated from this planet. As the corrupt billionaires sold off and polluted resources, humans started to experiment with space travel to escape the low quality of life that was Venus. Centuries passed, humans scattered across the cosmos, and evolved in to different beings all together.

Crystalos: The planet of mirror beings. Terrifying armies. Never been fully attacked by Kairos. Kairos has attempted attacks and failed.

Opaques: They have two legs, four arms, and their bodies are made up of reflective glass. They appear invisible because they are constantly reflecting the world around them. Their shadows can be seen if the light hits at the right time or if you pay close attention.

Toxotes: The planet of dragon beings.

General Planets:

Scorned Planets: The planets that were manipulated by Kairos and fought his authoritarian dictatorship. They still refuse him to this day but are slowly collapsing and trying to rebuild their armies. The only thing keeping them safe are Vakander's armies.

Neutral Planets: Planets with beings that only care to benefit from whoever is currently winning planetary wars. They can side with the Scorned or Templite Loyalists.

Templite Loyalists Planets: Planets under heavy Templite control. These planets are testing grounds for many Templite experiments. Most things done to the citizens on these planets are then later done to the Neutralists and the Scorned. They have been heavily propagandized. The indigenous populations that ones inhabited these planets have since fled or forced to assimilate by the colonizing population of travelers who settled. Most Titus Kronos Templites are scattered to the cosmos waiting for the return of the rightful hair to the Templite Throne.

Pulse: A heartbeat-shaped black-hole that opens up in to Limbo.

Limbo: A desecrated area in space full of dead timelines. Basically, a highway created by Templites with the help of a variant race of Fairies, called the Guerrerros, in order to teleport one self across great distances across the galaxy.

Abilities:

Ethereal controlled abilities: Abilities beings are born with that Ethereals can block access to at any point.

Gravity Rings: A man-made ability uncontrolled by the Ethereals.

Man-made abilities: Abilities created by beings that can't be controlled by the Ethereals.

Natural born abilities: Abilities that Ethereals can't block a user from using. Most of these abilities are evolutionary responses to the control the Ethereal's have had over being's powers.

Pulse: A heart-beat shaped blackhole. The fissure in the universe opens in to Limbo.

Ropes: A natural born ability uncontrolled by the Ethereals.

Secondary Form: a second evolution off of the first form. Usually a power that is overpowered or made for war. A form that allows for the being to gain more powers or adapt to their environment.

Power Source: The ability to unravel ones' Threads that make up their bodies and share it with another being. This leads to the creation of a spherical energy source that both or multiple beings sharing energy can take from. They can use this energy to attack then the energy from the attack returns to the Power Source. The misuse of a Power Source can lead to melding with the other being and could result in a mass creation like the War Birds but once these sources are used up, all beings melded together die from improper use of Power Source.

Weaving: Unraveling the Threads of your existence to create a shadow form or to produce a Power Source with another.

Raven Man-made Abilities:

Fuego – Fire (Cooks, soldiers, and secondary Power Sources.)

Gaia – Ground (City named after this element. All that involves the grounding elements in the universe).

Nieve – Ice (Soldiers, creating a wall of ice blocking tsunamis from hitting the main stone walls.)

Nu – Water (They can move water away from walls and drain any stray waves out of the city. They use water turbines to give power to the city.)

Objects:

Ship: A massive spaceship used to invade planets. In Kronos's times, it was used to transport refugees from the dead timelines across the timeline we see in Spike's Last Life. Can hold up to eight billion beings.

Craft: A smaller version of a Ship. Can usually hold up to three hundred passengers at one time. Usually they are fighter jets or escape jets depending on the use.

Placenta Pod: A placenta attached to a bunch of wires and cables encased in a bean shaped, half-transparent and half-white, pod.

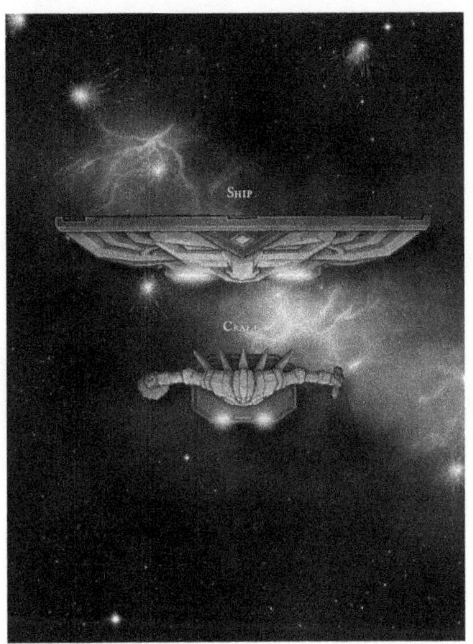

Medications:

Vida Viles: a serum that extends the users life cycle by, more or less, a century. It allows them to stay young as long as the organisms in the serum remain alive.

Lingua Viles: a serum that allows you to understand other beings. It auto translates whatever they say to your language and vice versa.

Imbarasi Viles: Lycan and Barrettan women were given these Viles to repopulate their planets after their mass casualties. These Viles ensured every person who gave birth did so to at least two children, and, sometimes, more would come out.

RACES AND ORIGINS

Races Translated From Former Venus Terms To Present Day:

[Different races evolved through planetary exploration and different climates. Genetics led to new abilities, new accents, and appearances for all races mentioned below. Life began on Venus and branched in to the cosmos. Beings decided to leave Venus as climate change ravaged the planet.]

Asian Descendants – Tanieans (Taniea)
African Descendants – Fongos (Fongo)
Latine Descendents – Melivians (Melivia)
Caucasian Descendents – Oretanians (Oretan)
Middle Eastern Descendents – Ethsans (Ethsan)
Canadian – Nunaques (Nunaque)
Australian – Isakays (Iskay)
European – Lonussians (Lonussia)
Native American – Furuits (Furuit)
Samoan – Samanesians (Samanesia)

———

Current Races and Their Origins:

*Colonized by Oretanian Settlers over centuries.

** Colonized by Tempus

Siren Cannibals – Descendents of Templites and Melivians.

Time Keepers – Descendents of Melivia. *

Vampires – Descendents of Melivia and Furuit.

Seers – Descendents of Samanesians.*

Sea People – Descendents of Furuits and Samanesians.*

Minotaur – Descendents of Ethsans.

Bird – Descendents of Tanieans.

Dragons – Descendents of Nunaques.

Werewolfs – Descendents of Tanieans.**

Witches – Descendents of Fongos and Melivia.

Fairies – Descendents of Samanesia, Fongo, Oretan and Furuit.

Opaques – Descendents of Isakays and Lonussians.

Venus – Descendents of Old Earth. Remaining beings there subjugated to policing and certain living quarters. Races vary depending on survivors.

Gamma- 2 Firestarter's – Descendents of Melivia and Oretan.

Centaurs – Descendents of Oretan.

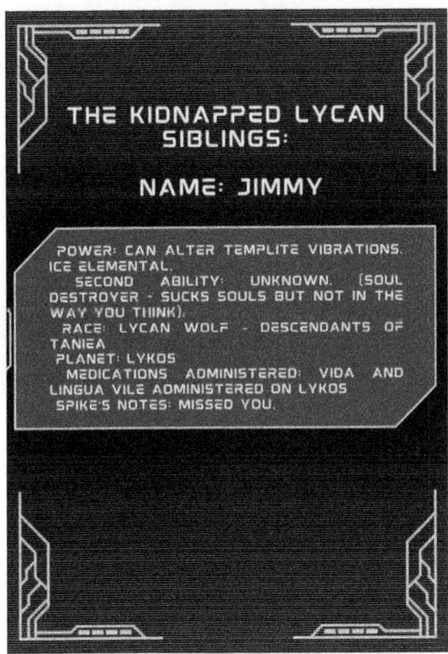

The Kidnapped Lycan Siblings:
   Name: Jimmy
   Power: Can Alter Templite Vibrations. Ice Elemental.

Second Ability: Unknown. (*Soul Destroyer - sucks souls but not in the way you think*).

Race: Lycan Wolf – Descendants of Taniea

Planet: Lykos

Medications Administered: Vida and Lingua Vile Administered on Lykos

Spike's Notes: Missed you.

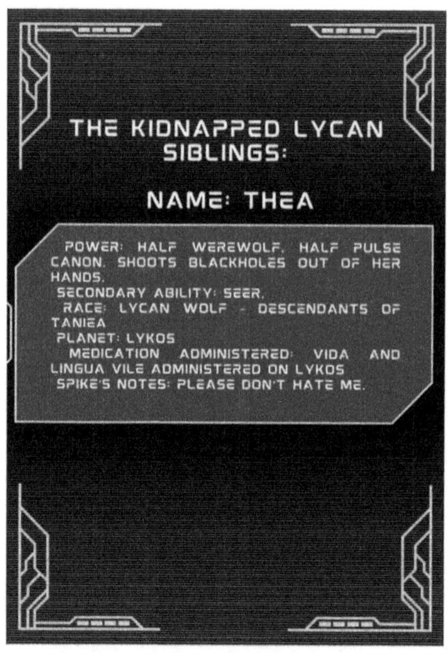

Name: Thea

Power: Half-Werewolf, Half-Pulse Canon. Shoots blackholes out of her hands.

Secondary Ability: Seer.

Race: Lycan Wolf – Descendants of Taniea

Planet: Lykos

Medication Administered: Vida and Lingua Vile Administered on Lykos

Spike's Notes: Please don't hate me.

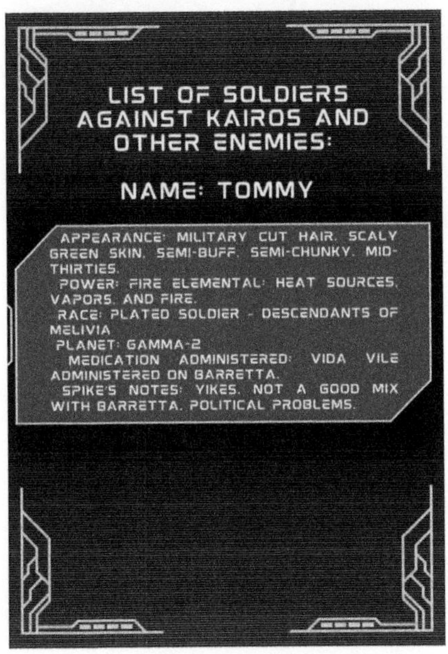

List of Soldiers Against Kairos and Other Enemies:
Name: Tommy

Appearance: Military cut hair. Scaly green skin. Semi-buff, semi-chunky. Mid-thirties.

Power: Fire Elemental: heat sources, vapors, and fire.

Race: Plated Soldier – Descendants of Melivia
Planet: Gamma-2
Medication Administered: Vida Vile Administered on Barretta.

Spike's Notes: Yikes. Not a good mix with Barretta. Political Problems.

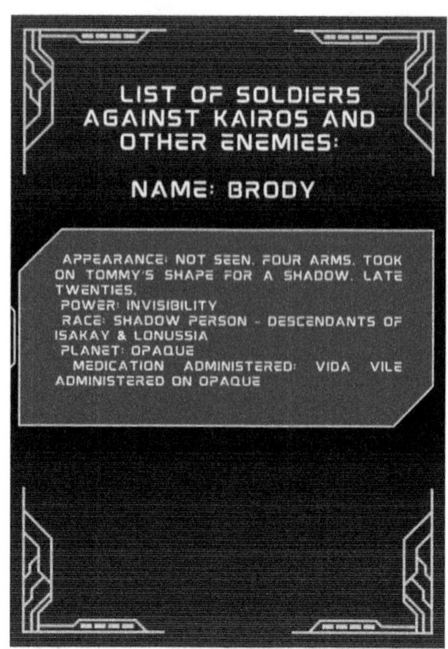

Name: Brody

Appearance: Not seen. Four arms. Took on Tommy's shape for a shadow. Late twenties.

Power: Invisibility

Race: Shadow Person – Descendants of Isakay & Lonussia

Planet: Opaque

Medication Administered: Vida Vile Administered on Opaque

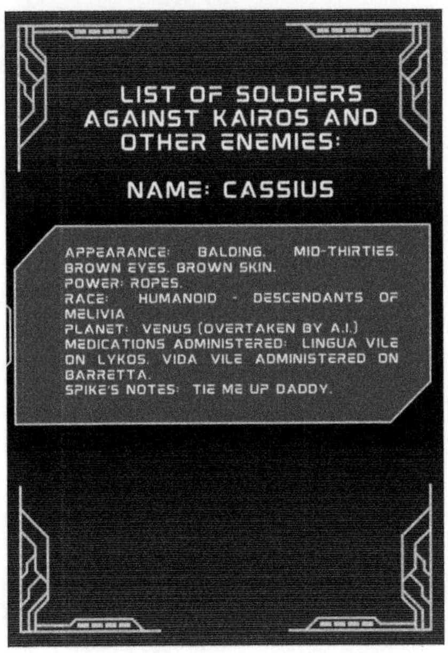

Name: Cassius

Appearance: Balding. Mid-thirties. Brown eyes. Brown skin.

Power: Ropes

Race: Humanoid – Descendants of Melivia

Planet: Venus *(Overtaken by A.I.)*

Medication Administered: Lingua Vile on Lykos. Vida Vile Administered on Barretta.

Spike's Notes: Tie me up daddy.

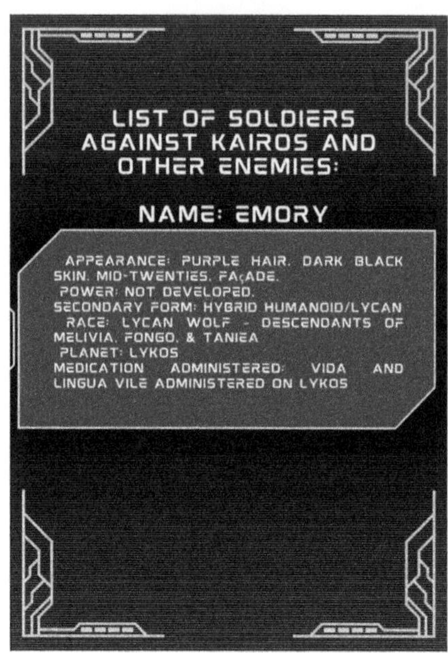

Name: Emory

Appearance: Purple hair. Dark black skin. Mid-twenties. Façade.

Power: Not Developed.

Secondary Form: Hybrid Humanoid/Lycan

Race: Lycan Wolf – Descendants of Melivia, Fongo, & Taniea

Planet: Lykos

Medication Administered: Vida and Lingua Vile Administered on Lykos

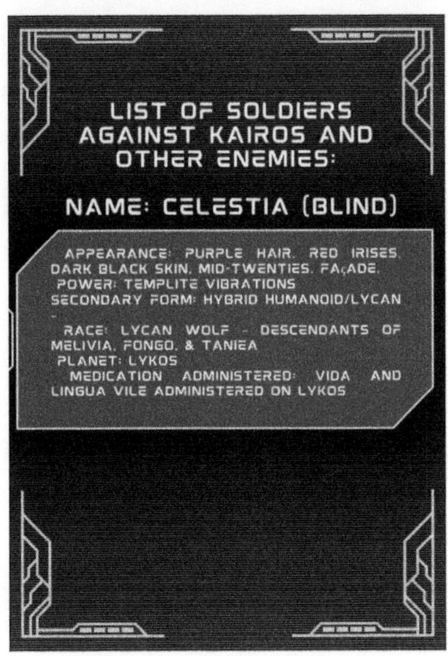

Name: Celestia (Blind)

Appearance: Purple hair. Red irises. Dark black skin. Mid-twenties. Façade.

Power: Templite Vibrations

Secondary Form: Hybrid Humanoid/Lycan

Race: Lycan Wolf – Descendants of Melivia, Fongo, & Taniea

Planet: Lykos

Medication Administered: Vida and Lingua Vile Administered on Lykos

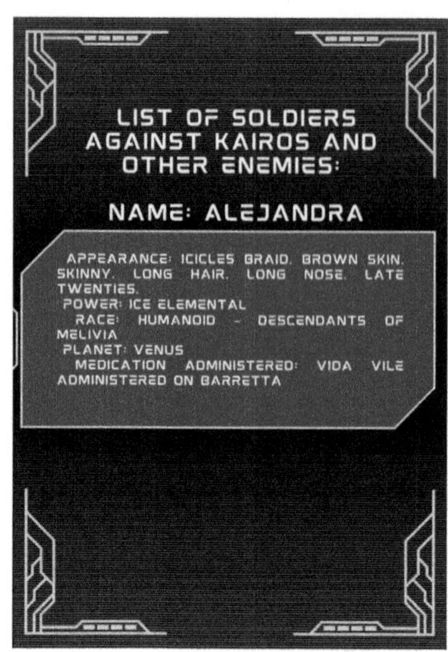

Name: Alejandra

Appearance: Icicles braid. Brown skin. Skinny. Long hair. Long nose. Late twenties.

Power: Ice Elemental

Race: Humanoid – Descendants of Melivia

Planet: Venus

Medication Administered: Vida Vile Administered on Barretta

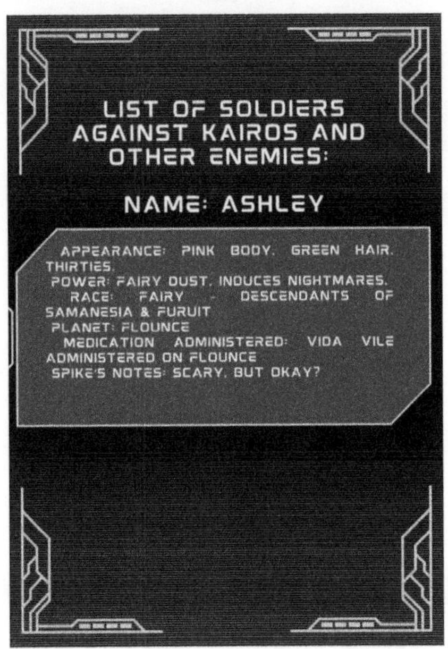

Name: Ashley

Appearance: Pink body. Green Hair. Thirties.

Power: Fairy Dust. Induces Nightmares.

Race: Fairy – Descendants of Samanesia & Furuit

Planet: Flounce

Medication Administered: Vida Vile Administered on Flounce

Spike's Notes: Scary, but okay?

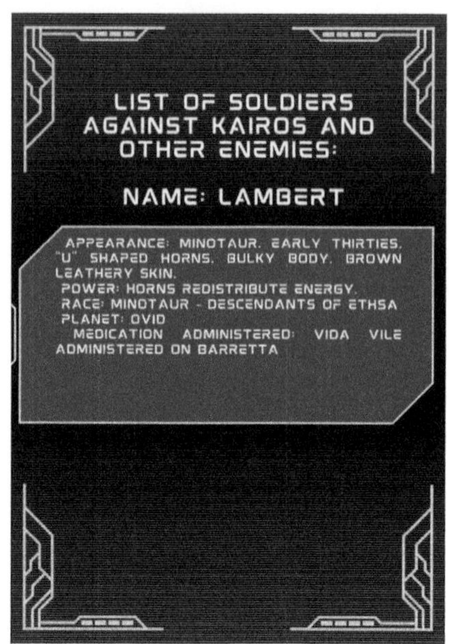

Name: Lambert

Appearance: Minotaur. Early thirties. "U" Shaped Horns. Bulky body. Brown leathery skin.

Power: Horns Redistribute Energy.

Race: Minotaur – Descendants of Ethsa

Planet: Ovid

Medication Administered: Vida Vile Administered on Barretta

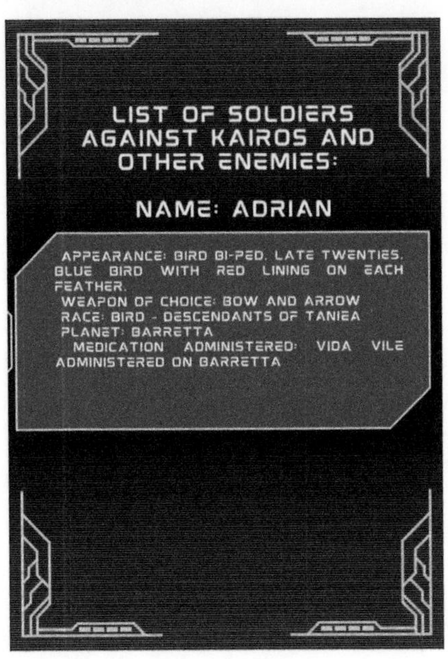

Name: Adrian

Appearance: Bird Bi-ped. Late twenties. Blue Bird with red lining on each feather.

Weapon of Choice: Bow and Arrow

Race: Bird – Descendants of Taniea

Planet: Barretta

Medication Administered: Vida Vile Administered on Barretta

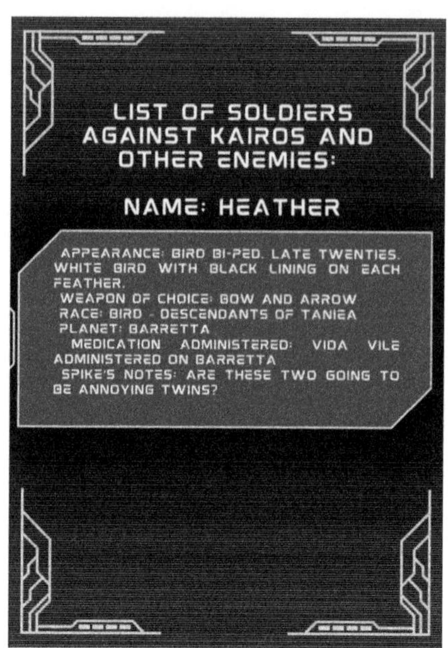

Name: Heather

Appearance: Bird Bi-ped. Late Twenties. White Bird with Black Lining on Each Feather.

Weapon of Choice: Bow and Arrow

Race: Bird – Descendants of Taniea

Planet: Barretta

Medication Administered: Vida Vile Administered on Barretta

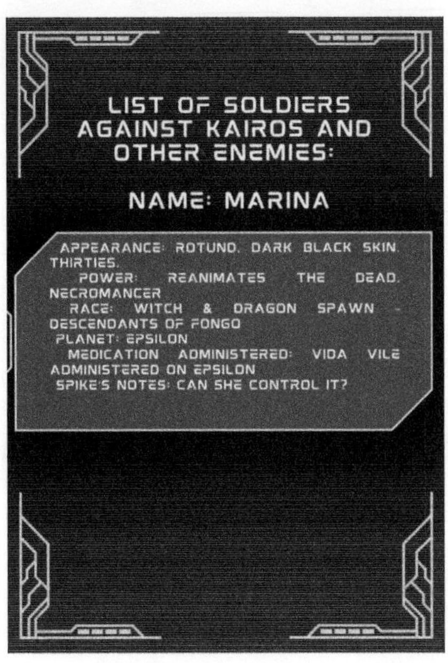

Name: Marina

Appearance: Rotund. Dark black skin. Thirties.

Power: Reanimates the Dead. Necromancer

Race: Witch & Dragon Spawn – Descendants of Fongo

Planet: Epsilon

Medication Administered: Vida Vile Administered on Epsilon

Spike's Notes: Can she control it?

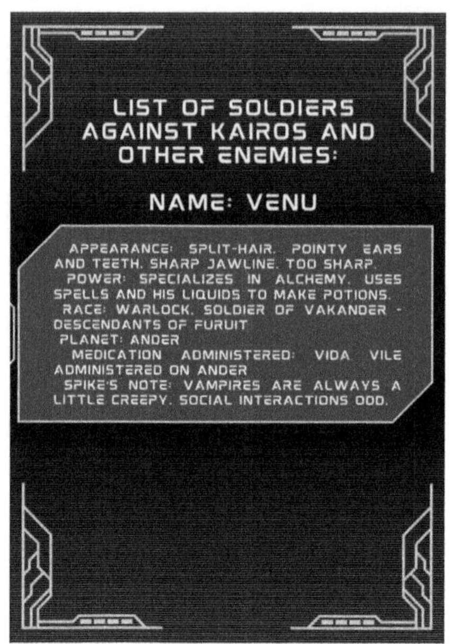

Name: Venu

Appearance: Split-hair. Pointy ears and teeth. Sharp jawline. Too sharp.

Power: Specializes in Alchemy. Uses Spells and His Liquids to Make Potions.

Race: Warlock. Soldier of Vakander - Descendants of Furuit

Planet: Ander

Medication Administered: Vida Vile Administered on Ander

Spike's Note: Vampires are always a little creepy. Social interactions odd.

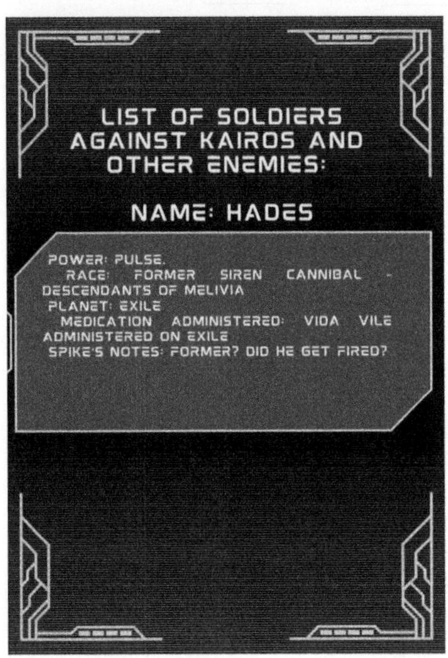

Name: Hades

Power: Pulse.

Race: Former Siren Cannibal – Descendants of Melivia

Planet: Exile

Medication Administered: Vida Vile Administered on Exile

Spike's Notes: Former? Did he get fired?

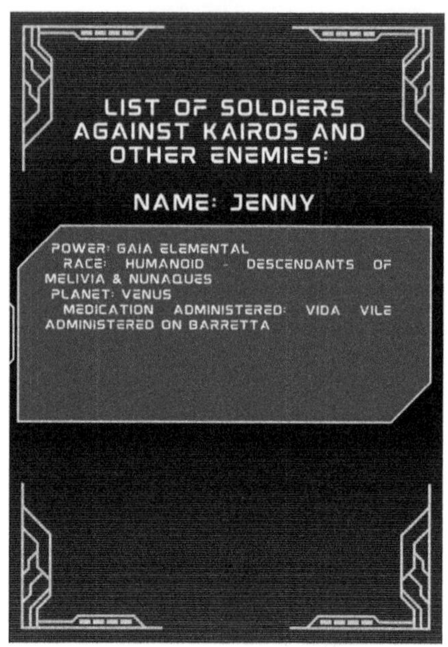

Name: Jenny

Power: Gaia Elemental

Race: Humanoid – Descendants of Melivia & Nunaques

Planet: Venus

Medication Administered: Vida Vile Administered on Barretta

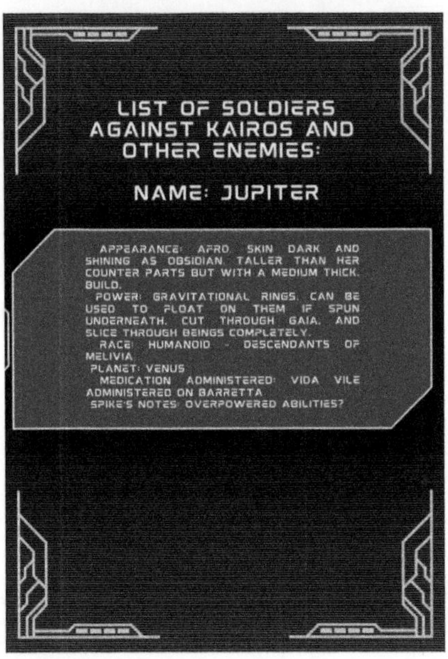

Name: Jupiter

Appearance: Afro. Skin dark and shining as obsidian. Taller than her counter parts but with a medium thick, build.

Power: Gravitational Rings. Can be used to float on them if spun underneath, cut through Gaia, and slice through beings completely.

Race: Humanoid – Descendants of Melivia

Planet: Venus

Medication Administered: Vida Vile Administered on Barretta

Spike's Notes: Overpowered abilities?

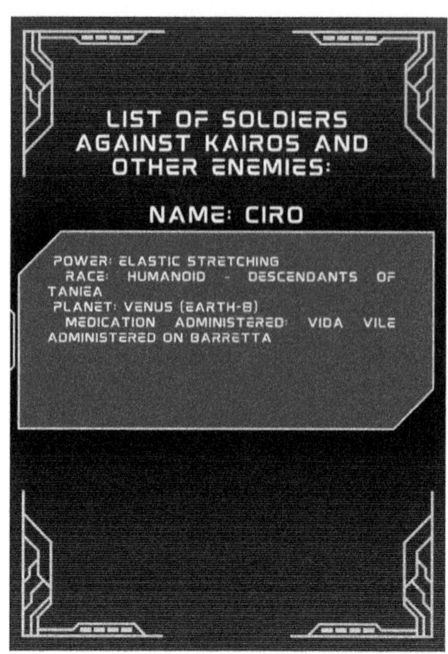

Name: Ciro

Power: Elastic Stretching

Race: Humanoid – Descendants of Taniea

Planet: Venus *(Earth-8)*

Medication Administered: Vida Vile Administered on Barretta

Additional Important Characters:

May: Daughter of Former Time Lord, Titus Kronos.

Numitor: A Member of the Barretta Committee.

Vesta: Leading Queen of the Barretta Committee.

Vakander: Vampire King of Ander.

Mama Reyna: Leading Coven Member of Epsilon.

Mama Amanda: Axel's Mother.

Chaos Salem: Thirteenth Coven Member of Epsilon.

CONTENT WARNINGS

Content Warnings:

It may take a minute to see the whole picture but this book is written in a non-linear format. This story is told out of order. You were meant to be frustrated to simulate losing all your memories and having to regain them all over again.

I care for my audience. I care for your mental health. Please see list below of trigger warnings. Proceed with caution. Please put the book down if it affects you emotionally or mentally.

Talks of mass genocide, racism, mutilation, gore, necromancy, suicide, and sexual assault. Violence inflicted on others. Abusive relationships. Toxic relationships with a stalker as an ex-fiancée. Decapitation and amputated limbs. Descriptions of war and war scenes. Graphic violence. Immigrants fleeing violence and having violence inflicted upon them.

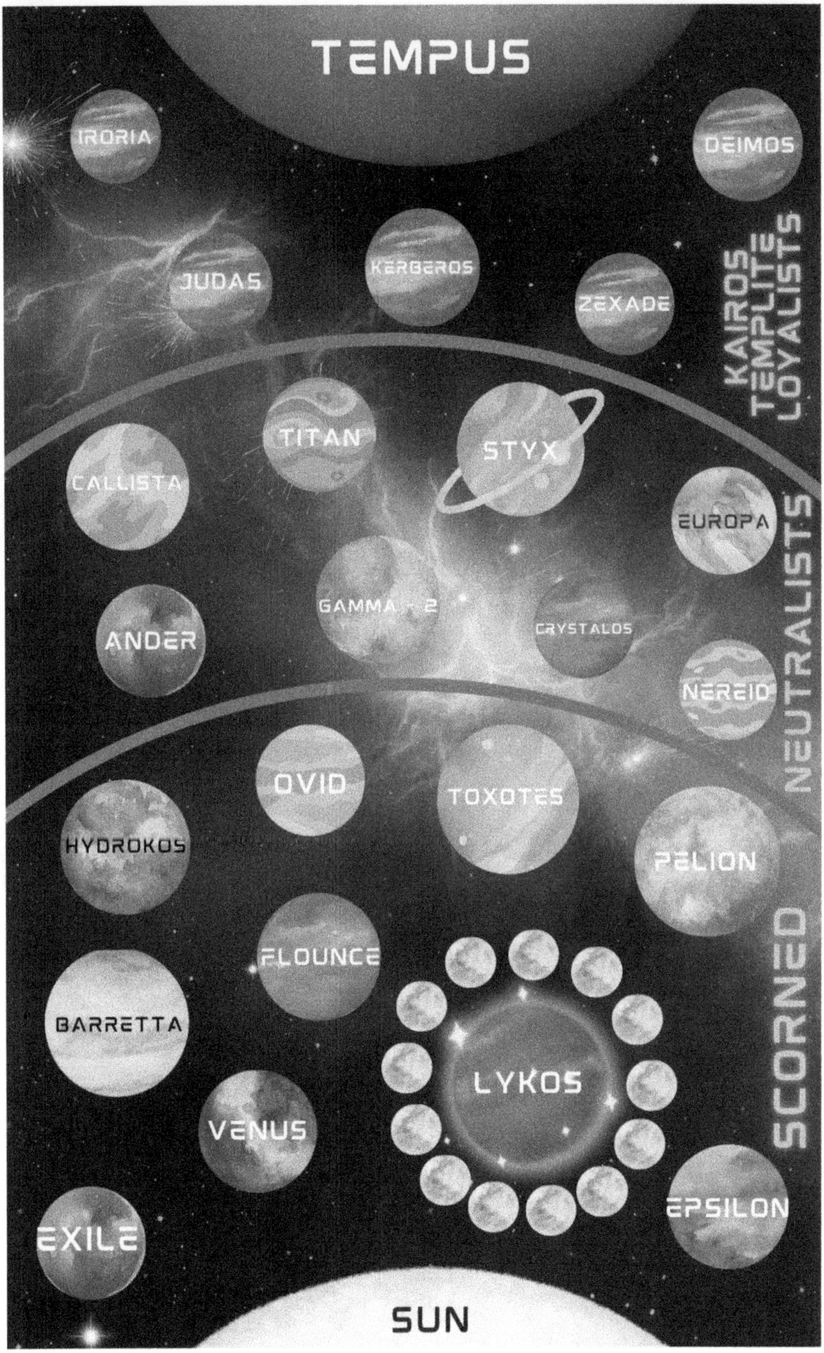

TEMPUS
IRORIA
DEIMOS
JUDAS
KERBEROS
ZEXADE
KAIROS TEMPLITE LOYALISTS
TITAN
STYX
CALLISTA
EUROPA
GAMMA - 2
CRYSTALOS
ANDER
NEREID
NEUTRALISTS
OVID
TOXOTES
HYDROKOS
PELION
FLOUNCE
BARRETTA
LYKOS
SCORNED
VENUS
EPSILON
EXILE
SUN

CHAPTER 1
ACTIVATED

SPIKE DIED today on his twenty-fifth reincarnation.

He knew it in his core before it happened. All his memories rushed back to him like a deep breath after being submerged underwater for too long. His soul started to recognize the flaws in everything around him.

Then, he died alone.

This is story of his last life.

Central Lykos Main
Water Source
Royal Lycan Castle
Landing Pad

THE NIGHT SKY is lit up by the collapsing universe. Bright fissures of green, pink, blue and white hues consume Time Keepers, Lycans, and Lykos.

My blood-soaked half-wolf and half-human hands don't keep a sturdy grip on the slicked blade. I try to use my powers and nothing comes out. Something or someone is tying the Threads of my abilities to prevent me from using them.

The sword plunges in to my rib cage. A mix between a howl and cry chokes my throat. My hybrid form strength momentarily deters the blade from going in deeper, but the damage is done.

Avi smiles above me laughing.

Iridescent pockets of the universe shimmer and open all over Lykos.

My blood. My people. My family.

Time Keepers panic trying to seal the wounds in the universe as they grow exponentially larger.

My death. My powerlessness. My failure.

All this is a sick joke to this callous man.

Fuck.

This is how I die. With my family dispersed fighting their own battles. I die a failure. I can explain to you the pain of the blade cutting through my body. Long winded details of each calculated slice. But I don't feel that pain. I feel the pain of being a failure. A bittersweet melody of the circle of life. To twisted beings, murder is an essential act done to others for the sake of enjoyment. They will find ways to justify their actions with religion or the greater-good. Don't be fooled. All murder is born out of a need to feel better about oneself. I failed my people today by dying. I am their queen and I could not outlast these heartless, murderous men.

Heartless, murderous men always tend to survive longer. Is there any real justice and accountability for these vile men?

Fires consume Lykos.

My beautiful planet.

The battle wages on in front of the castle, inside the castle, and throughout the Central City. Ships hang in the sky above drifting through billowing clouds of black smoke. Our himeji castles wither to ashes. Wolves all over the planet devour Time Keepers pushing back their invasion.

Spike opens Pulses, blackholes, all around Kairos. Kairos stands three stories high in his Alpha Wolf Form clawing at Jimmy, my brother, to his right. Waves of ice magic freeze Kairos's feet. Jimmy's rage only grows deeper. He surges his secondary powers through Kairos. A planet splintering howl quakes the ground. That's when I notice the scythe-shaped ice formation going in through Kairos's stomach and out his upper back. But that isn't what's causing the howling cries of pain. Jimmy is trying to destroy his soul.

Avi stabs his sword deeper in to my rib cage. My weak bleeding hands meld with the sword against the serrated edges. I can't keep going. Kairos is temporarily immobilized.

Jimmy leaves Spike's fight to help me. Time Keepers flood his surroundings blocking him from stopping Avi. His ice powers desperately cuts through Time Keepers. Every ounce of pain clouds his eyes as he is forced to fight for his own survival instead of mine.

My hands tremble. I'm losing the fight. Spike opens a Pulse

through Kairos's chest. Jimmy sends a crown of icicles in to the Time Keepers and Kairos. The icicles decapitate Kairos's wolf head. It rolls beside me. Avi screams above me. His smile turns to bitter rage.

"Just die already." He instructs me.

With all his frustrated force, he stabs the sword through my heart. My vision blurs. And in the blurriness, I see wings surrounding me. An essence flows through me.

———

The following days were filled with picking up the pieces of our shattered kingdom. At some point last night, Spike was taken back to Tempus.

Avi used the last of his energy after he saved Kairos. The Queen's body disappeared. Wolves worked to rebuild their *great* kingdom. My brother joined me in my unscathed bedroom overlooking the half-shattered, half-intact buildings. The eastern portion of our castle burned to the ground. Along with it, the Weaponry, soldier's barracks, and extra food supplies.

"He took Spike." Jimmy holds back angry tears at the bedroom door.

"You'll survive."

"Mother's gone. Father is being healed." Jimmy's frustrated voice erupts, "What are we going to do?"

"Rebuild."

"I know that. But what about Spike and Mom?"

"Love comes and goes. Let us fortify our kingdom and rebuild our armies."

"You are so cold." Jimmy stares at me trembling, "It looked like you died last night."

"'*Nothing kills a wolf. Not even death.*' Isn't that our family motto?"

Jimmy's suspicious eyes flicker from me to our kingdom's destruction.

"I'm going to find mother." I smile, "And we will take them down."

Jimmy leaves me alone slamming the door to the room. Moth wings sprout from my back and I soar among the lingering smoke clouds.

Many homes lay in various states of rubble and destruction. Medics individually haul deal bodies on to fire-proof stretchers to man-made fire pits. They place the stretcher on automatic, small elevators lowering them slowly in to a purple flame. A thin black tray underneath catches the ashes. The ashes are poured in to an urn and distributed to the family members.

Deaths in mass cancel all rituals that a normal death would require. Normally, the bodies would be washed so they can pass cleanly in to the afterlife. A ceremony would proceed the event with families and friends. Priests would gather and chant their prayers until every single member of the family has wafted incense on the urn and the priests are done with their prayers.

Or so I've heard.

Today, no prayers are uttered. A deafening silence interrupted by the crackling of wooden beams and buildings collapsing. Fire fighters battle between helping the remaining wounded and putting out fires.

As I pass the outer edge of the city, I cross in to woodlands. Enormous, thick black trees with purple leaves and waving purple hills lead to the base of a snow peaked mountain. A lake at the base of the mountain supplies the Central Kingdom of Lykos all the fresh water it needs. I land on the shore crunching on the black and brown sand.

My hands dig through the wet sands and summon the Purple Poison Kairos injected in to the planet last night. The clear blue water turns the color of ink. Fishes rise to the surface belly up. The water boils angrily. The poison creeps up the mountain side ensnaring deer and foxes. Their bodies mutate with multiple heads and spilling organs. Their eyes vicious. Intentions deadly.

The mutated animals descend upon the villagers below and cause mayhem.

I unravel the Threads of the universe and cross in to the Fourth Dimension. My wings dodge angry Thread Beasts and lost souls. I open a rip through Tempus' Throne Room and close both holes behind me. An injured Kairos with his head in a cast sits on the throne.

"We are one step closer to destroying the wolves. The Poison has been activated."

"How are you enjoying your new vessel?" Kairos painfully bellows.

"I'm getting used to it. She was easy to push out. The brother seems to have his suspicions."

"Nothing to worry about. We'll have control of Lykos soon. The brother won't matter then."

EMERGENCY TRANSMITTER NETWORK:

The wolf soldiers at the Central Kingdom have been corrupted. -J

Safely evacuate the citizens to the Steps. I will be waiting for you here. What about Thea? -Unknown

She is different. Old motto from Kairos' reign was spouted by her. Dad's acting weird too. -J

Trust no one. -Unknown

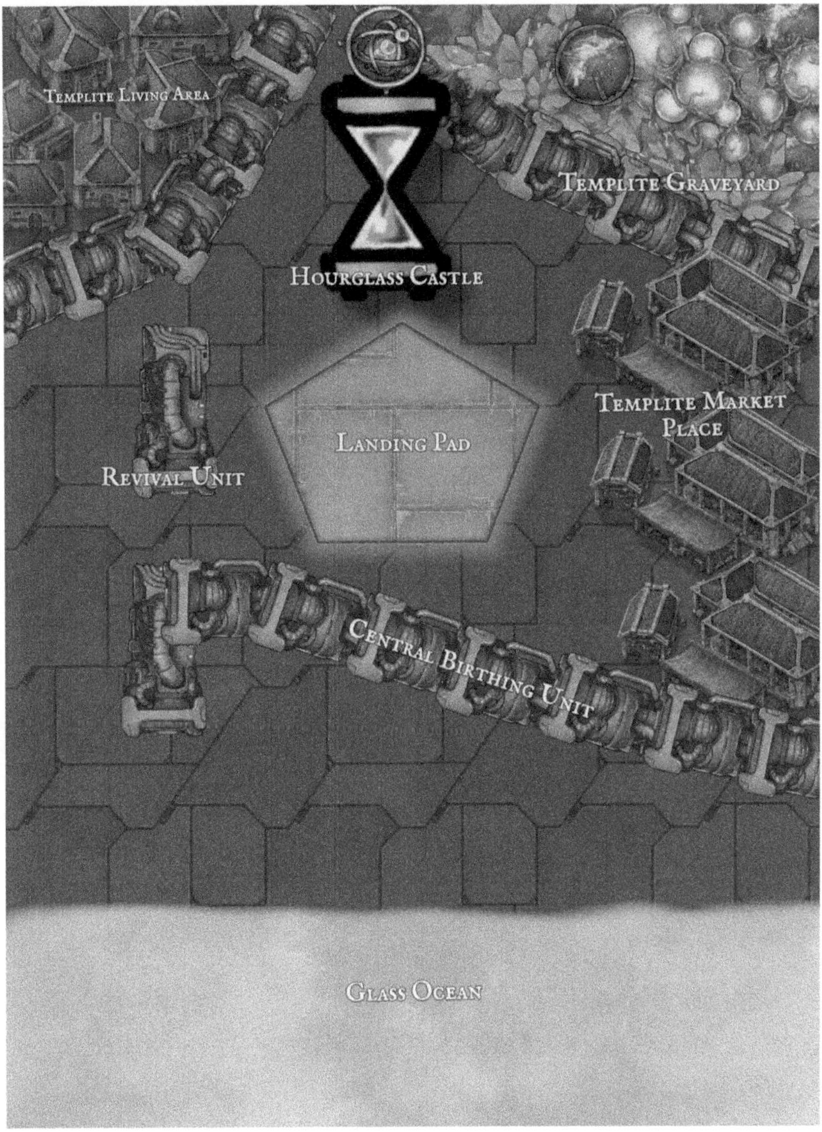

Templite Living Area
Templite Graveyard
Hourglass Castle
Templite Market Place
Landing Pad
Revival Unit
Central Birthing Unit
Glass Ocean

CHAPTER 4
SPIKE:
TWENTY-SIXTH INCARNATION.

THE ELDERLY VOICE speaks to me in my dreams, *Remember to always be a spike in his side. And never forget, I love you, my little Spi.*

Spike Guerrero. My name is Spike Guerrero.

I'm Activated? Already. They would never activate me right away. Activation is like waking up from a nightmare. Before you were Activated as a Time Absorber, a sleeper agent of Tempus, you had no control over your body. You could see out of your eyes before they flipped the switch and you had thoughts, but you were basically a robot. A tool used to spy on others. When the Activation switch was flipped, you started to remember your past life times, you could see who you actually were as a Time Absorber, and you were finally conscious to the world around you. You were no longer trapped in the dreadful subconscious of data-collecting.

I'm in the same Venus, humanoid body I was in for my twenty-fifth incarnation. Flesh and bone, yet still alien underneath. Odd for Kairos, Avi, and the Time Keepers to put me on the same planet and body twice in a row. Every time I have been revived, it has been in a new body from one of the twenty four planets in our galaxy. Something is different this time around.

For starters, alarms are blaring throughout the Revival Building. I want to stab my ears so I don't have to hear them.

Vakander shakes me violently, "C'mon, Spike. Shake it off. We have to run."

His caramel hands slap my face until he realizes I'm fully awake. He wears a black trench coat with a white shirt underneath. His black slacks are wrapped tightly against his skin.

My blurry eyes allow the blank, white room to come into focus. Red flashing emergency lights strobe through the darkness. Operating artificial intelligence and needles full of serums in the ceiling look like octopuses swimming through the air. Templite medics lie dead on the ground. Blue blood coating the tiled floors. My reflection in the blood shows that I've been de-aged. I have to be at least twenty-four. Vakander sighs relieved that I'm awake. He drops to the floor, picks up a Soul Core - a cubic, metallic frame with a circular, iridescent core at the center meant to capture souls before they pass onto the Cataclysmic Realm – and he starts dragging me out of the room.

"We need to get you the fuck out of here." Vakander pulls me into a bright white hallway rushing towards a glass window. I never liked bright lights. Curses to the fuckers who installed them. We run at an awkward speed. My legs are still partially asleep. He continues, "Avi will be here in no time. May kept him distracted."

Templite guards step out of an elevator on the opposite side of the hallway.

Vakander shoots the glass in front of us. Glass shards raining everywhere. How pretty. Sparking fragments twinkle against the grey Tempus skyline.

The guards pull out their Pulse Blasters and fire rapidly. His leathery, burgundy wings sprout through the chaos. Vakander wraps his hands around me and jumps out the window. Immense winds toss us around like being on a first date with the wrong man. Or right man depending on how he performs.

We free fall towards Tempus' cobble stone streets. Vakander opens his wings and we are lurched back up violently.

All of this maneuvering is making me queasy.

Below, May waits in a trapezoid-shaped Craft in front of the Revival Unit. I can see her yelling for us to "fucking move it" from the front windshield. We fly through the rear cargo door and buckle into the seats beside May. Inbetween the seats sits my Placenta Pod.

They got my Placenta Pod? A round, oval-shaped white pod that looks like a bean.

Kairos will no longer be able to track me. A contained elation bursts out as a laugh. Relief would soothe my soul if it weren't for the hordes of Templite soldiers on our backs.

May rapidly takes off into the atmosphere. We leave behind the Hourglass Castle, the Revival Unit, and Tempus. My stomach rolls with unease.

"This is a nice way to wake up from being reincarnated." I state frustrated, "Couldn't have lubricated the experience before you fucked me?"

"Don't say weird shit like that to us. This is the best we could do." Vakander reminds me.

"I just spent the last thirty minutes fighting your fiancé." May yells dodging Templite Crafts cutting us off from the front and sides. She continues while swerving down, around, shoots them out of the sky, and then back up, "Don't give me any shit."

May shifts the Craft into space mode. An oxygen preservation windshield covers the first one. Vakander and May press countless buttons. The Craft breaks through the outer layer of the grey, abysmal atmosphere and crosses into space.

Fifteen Disc-shaped Crafts, with a pilot pod in the middle, shoot lasers at the rear of our Craft. May releases her purple Betrayal Pulse mirroring the attacks back to the attackers. Vakander stares out the window and uses his infiltration powers forcing himself into the minds of every enemy pilot.

"Crash into each other," He orders them. Within seconds, every enemy pilot's eyes cloud with a white substance, and they collide into each other.

May opens multiple Pulses and flies through Limbo. The Craft bypasses Vakander's armada surrounding the Neutralist and Scorned Planets and through random areas of space to avoid Time Keepers.

———

May places the Craft in autopilot the moment we are light years away from Tempus. Vakander infiltrates the Craft's processing software, lulling it, "No one can see you," and it camouflages itself.

"Thank you for helping me." I tell them.

"Anything for you, Spike." Vakander adds in a nonchalant tone.

"Kairos and Avi are going to come after us with an army," I warn them.

"Our armies are keeping his men at bay." Vakander explains, "If we had done nothing, if we had let you be controlled by Kairos, more planets and universes would suffer from the Cleansing. We had to get you away from that life of data collecting and resurrection. Whatever you do, you're caught between two swords."

"Getting caught between two swords doesn't sound too bad." I retort.

"Go get some rest." May tells me, "We have work for you to do already. And this might be the last night you get good sleep."

"I never sleep well anyway," I add. Time Absorbing life is constant data collection. Even when I was sleeping my brain would be programmed to send information to Kairos through my Placenta Pod Data Link. "What happened to my Data Link? I don't feel the connection to him anymore."

"We severed it when we took the Placenta Pod from Tempus." Vakander replies, "Kairos can no longer control you as long as we keep the Placenta Pod hidden." He pauses, "Now, rest. We still have a long way to go before we're safe. You can ask more questions when we get closer."

CHAPTER 5
THEA:
DYING ON LYKOS

THE SWORD GOES *through my heart. My brother stabs Kairos with an ice scythe.*

Moth wings beat clearly above me. But he's a shadow. Pan? The Ethereal who died on Epsilon years ago. What is his soul doing here? If he was at peace it would've gone to the Cataclysm Realm. A hole in the universe seals behind him like flimsy, loose clothes threads getting sewed back together.

Avi discards my body once he sees Pan's soul. Fires burn a quarter of our kingdom to the ground. Let's hope the Step Islands can push them back. Time Keepers swarm Jimmy but he holds them off by skating on the ice. He refuses to shift in to his wolf form. An oversized tendril drops from the sky in the distance near the mountains and digs in to the ground. A purple liquid bubbles until it's buried in the dirt. Red tendrils of power escape Avi sewing Kairos' dismembered head to his body. Life resurges through the massive,dead wolf.

"You still fight?" Pan questions.

"I will not die here." I bite back.

"Oh, but my dear, you are already dead." Pan's voice doused in fake pity, "My life force is the only thing keeping your body alive. Once

my soul has melded with your body, you will transition in to the Cataclysm Realm."

I will not die here. My kingdom needs me.

In the distance, My brother is swarmed by even more Time Keepers flying in on Pegasi. He is desperately trying to help Spike and me.

Avi and Kairos attack Spike from all angles, injuring him further. Jimmy loops and dives. He slashes down hordes of enemies all while screaming, "SPIKE. THEA. I'm coming! Just hold on."

His screams tremble Lykos.

"SPIKE. THEA. I'm coming. Hold on!"

Kairos clamps Spike in his jaw and crushes his body in two. Avi catches both halves and restrains them with the help of other Time Keepers.

"Spike!" Jimmy breaks inside. He stops moving allowing all the Time Keepers to swarm him. Don't give up Jimmy.

I'm not giving up. *Jimmy Mind Links to me.*

Jimmy traps the surrounding Time Keepers in a web of icy wrist restraints and starts Siphoning all of their energy. Avi opens a Pulse and carries Spike in to Limbo. Kairos turns to Jimmy preparing for one last fight. Kairos growls, "You know you can't win."

The portal closes behind Avi. Jimmy consumes the souls of all the Time Keepers for energy. A rare ability amongst wolves passed along generations through a mutated gene. The gene was given to the War Commander of Lykos to protect their home. This child has forever been named Soul Destroyer. The ability bars the soul from passing in to the Cataclysm Realm. It will forever be haunted living in the Fourth Dimension.

"Your brother is brave for going up against Kairos." Pan commends him.

Kairos charges at Jimmy. Triangular blocks of ice spears impale Kairos. Gaping wounds drip pools of blood everywhere. The injured tyrant shoves the ice to the side and gallops towards Jimmy.

Jimmy's fingers curl as he lures strands of blood from Kairos's body. He freezes the strings and leashes Kairos in to one spot.

Blood ice spears blast Time Keepers out of the sky. Spirals upon spirals of blood spears twirl through randomly opening Pulses. The Pulses close as their owners are killed. Pegasi fly off abandoning their riders. Jimmy creates a bridge to Kairos's face. His voice on the verge of being lost, "Don't you ever come back to my fucking planet." Jimmy plucks out both of Kairos's eyes, "I will be reunited with Spike." Jimmy twists Kairos's jaw out of place, "And the next time I see you in the flesh, I will personally obliterate you from existence."

Jimmy places his hand on Kairos and starts to steal his soul. Kairos lashes at his bloody leash.

The gaping fissures in the universe start to close.

Avi returns to Lykos. He uses the corpses sprawled on the floor to tie a separate leash on Kairos. Avi and Jimmy play a game of tug-o-war.

Pan's soul consumes my body. My vision starts to blur...

"Let him go." I yell to Jimmy.

Jimmy turns my way confused as he releases the leash, "Thea?"

"I'm fine. My regeneration powers healed me."

I stare confused. I didn't say that.

Avi retreats with Kairos and all his other Time Keepers. Avi nods in my direction before closing the portal.

The Mind Link between me and Jimmy severs.

PRISONER MOUNTAINS
BARRETTA COMMITTEE CASTLE & TOWERS
NOMAD SANCTUARY

CHAPTER 6
SPIKE:
SPIKE IS BACK - DAY 1

WHITE NOISE from the buzzing engines keeps me awake. I lie in bed cuddling my blanket as the planets and stars zip outside my bedroom window. A rare, peaceful silence that I have been longing for, for a while now. Nothing to worry about. No duties. No tasks. Just quiet. I know I can leave this room whenever I want to. Today is the first day of my life where I'm not expected to do anything everyone asks of me.

One thing is very clear: Kairos and Avi are nowhere nearby.

I ignore the voice messages playing in my room.

Come to the bridge when you wake up. We need to talk. May. Five minutes ago.

The stars sing me to sleep.

———

After eight hundred years of enslavement, it's nice to take a warm shower with no one watching your actions. Before, an invisible tether collared me to Tempus. You can get used to a collar, but it will always slightly tug on the neck. A reminder that you're not free. You are trapped. You can't roam around and be free. You are designed with a purpose in mind. The purpose to serve those that yank on the collar. I cherish the seconds of solitude. I've always felt lonely, but being alone and feeling lonely are two different ways of living life. One allows you to relax and quiet the nasty noises of the world. The other envelopes you with an endless depression in a room surrounded by others. I rub my neck worried that one day the collar will reappear and will once again chain me to Kairos and Avi. Their world isolating and suffocating. My world liberating.

For now, I'm safe. Thanks to my ever-so-gracious parents the collar has been temporarily removed. Time Absorbers and Time Keepers don't show affection the same way those on Venus do. On Venus, kisses, hugs, and showers of affirmations give you the perfect doting parent. On Tempus, children are raised with no connection to their family members. From a very young age, they are given to Kairos to be used as Time Absorbers. They are a reconnaissance tool used to benefit Tempus. Parental affection on Tempus looks like saving your son from a genocide hungry ruler of the universe at their earliest convenience. They only had one chance to come for me and they had to make sure they used it properly. Kairos wouldn't allow Vakander or May to try again if they failed the first time. Eight. Hundred. Years. That is how long it took for them to get me with only one chance.

Now, I'm free.

I smile as tears rush down my face now that the collar is gone.

———

There is a sudden change in speed. Our Craft is cruising slowly. I'm cradled by my bed peering out the circular, dome window. Four planets – Barretta, Exile, Flounce, and Venus – hang in a misplaced formation. Three moons hover in between Barretta and Exile. I've been to them before. They lie nine billion miles away from my home planet of Tempus. They are apart of the Scorned Planets that Templites don't bother to visit unless they are searching for valuable

Time Absorbers or fleeing war generals. Tempus is far behind us now.

When I finally jump out of bed, I walk over to the door. It *swooshes* open when I press a metallic square to my right. I walk down a rectangular corridor full of rooms before passing through another door and entering the round bridge. May and Vakander stand in front of a circular table with a holographic grid of Exile. They pause their conversation and look at me as I get closer to the table.

"What are we doing all the way out here?" I ask.

"Helping you escape came at a cost," May smiles, "It's nice to see you smelling fresh."

Vakander walks over to me with a purple vile in his hand and uncaps it, "Here drink this," I've seen them before, but I've forgotten the name. He continues seeing my hesitation, "It's a Vida Vile. It will stop your aging process for the next hundred years. Any illnesses will go away instantly. The only thing it can't cure is death. So, don't die."

Oh yes, the forever-living-potion-thingy-that-makes-you-live-for-a-really-long-time.

"What happened to the one Kairos injected me with?" I ask holding the vile in my hand.

"Apparently, Avi and Kairos extract it from your body every time they revive you... as a precaution. In case, we came to save you."

I drink the contents of the vile. My face twists and my throat burns. Tiny organisms crawl underneath my skin and work on my body. I've never had a Vida Vile while conscious before, but I have seen it administered to many a Time Keeper. The Time Keeper remained partly moody for days because of the microscopic bacteria pulling at the aging strings inside of their bodies to bring them to a halt.

"I felt a stop earlier, but I was too tired to get up. Did you hide the Placenta Pod somewhere obvious?" I ask, trying to distract myself from the awful initial experience of a Vida Vile.

"It is safe." Vakander comments annoyed by my question, "We

wouldn't go through an ordeal to save you just to lose you again, or the Placenta Pod."

"So, where are we going?" I spin the map of Exile and explore a temple on the opposite side. A small, light-blue dot blinks. I hid an Artifact there in one of my past lives. In every life time, I gained these mega abilities that make me super overpowered. Usually, after I acquired them I would *magically* be Activated and Kairos needed me back on Tempus. The Artifacts were trinkets my grandfather gave me to hide away my powers from Kairos. So. I said fuck him. And I separated the powers from my body and hid them across the universe out of my uncle's tiny overlord hands.

"The Barretta Committee offered us refuge from Kairos and Avi," May explains, "They're willing to give us their armies and protect us in the event that *they* come after us, and they will come after us, but Vesta gave us a few tasks."

We just escaped and there is *already* some shit we have to do. Typical.

"What are the tasks? Bootlicking the leaders of the Barretta Committee."

"We have to clear all the Siren Cannibals from the next-door planet, Exile. They have been kidnapping and murdering children to sustain their life force." Vakander says as if he doesn't believe it himself.

"Hmmm." I retort in disbelief.

Odd...

Siren Cannibals were Time Absorbers at one point with the same powers as me, Pulses, to open blackholes in time by traveling through Limbo. They were specialized super soldiers used in the Templite Armies when Tempus was first founded. A blue fourth skin pigment that has since been exterminated from Tempus. Citizens looked up to and wanted to be them. Statues and buildings were built for them. They were praised by the masses. In the end, these soldiers turned on Kairos, my twisted uncle, when he killed the original Time Lord, Titus Kronos, my grandfather. Kairos banished them to Exile when he became Time Lord where he expected them to die after poisoning the planet. The poison was meant to kill all Siren Cannibals, the planet they were on, and their food source. Back then, they were known as just Sirens. As the natural resources of Exile started to die off with the poison, they gained the secondary label once they started feeding off deserter Time Absorbers. The deserters skyrocketed in groves when the Old Templites soldiers were forced to assimilate or join Kairos's army. The deserters weren't opposed to mass killing innocent people, they were just scared they'd become a target at some point. They saw how the civilian citizens of Old Tempus were subjugated and forced to accept the new regime without being able to fight back. When civilians did fight back, they disappeared. A divided Tempus didn't matter when Kairos's militia kept people in line. Those few civilians that could flee found ways to infiltrate the government, steal their Placenta Pods, and escape with nothing to their names. Though, very few, millions of Old Templites wait across the galaxy for it to be safe to return home. And, many have accepted that they will never return. They've made peace with never seeing the home they were driven out of. Tempus as we know it today, like Lykos before it, became colonized with the indigenous population scattered to the cosmos. We knew the Siren Cannibals were doing this for decades and turned a blind eye unless they kidnapped an important Time Keeper.

They are still formidable foes to the Time Keepers. Siren Cannibals are only supposed to feed on Templite soldiers. Anything else is Time Keeper propaganda... unless...

Their story is bullshit.

And Barretta has their own twisted propaganda against Siren Cannibals, or they're hiding something. I decide not to push.

"We?" I ask out of all the genius questions I could ask.

"The Barretta Committee has a group of soldiers that we were assigned to train," May turns the hologram into the Barretta training field: a clearing on the side of the castle, "You will be training them on Pulses. They will teach you about their abilities."

This is all too good to be true.

Surely, Kairos and Avi have to be after us.

May hears the thought bubble in my head and says, "He can't reach you this far. The further Kairos is from Tempus, the less powerful he is. The former Lycan ancestral souls are the only thing keeping him alive after the damage Jimmy did to him on Lykos."

"What about that bastard Avi? He will eventually come and try to kill me." A legitimate concern. Avi, my forced lover and cousin, has never stopped searching for me. He constantly tries to come back for me, hitting harder and harder each time. And each time I resist him. Or I should say, try to resist him. No doubt, he will retaliate against those around us.

May bites her lip, "And we shall expect his visit," her eyes fall on the Soul Core beside her, "We have other plans for him. From now on, you should be worried about the beings Kairos inflicted pain on."

"Why?"

"They will sense the energy radiating from you. Beings from around here are resentful survivors of war. When they find out who you are, they will want to kill you. In their eyes, you are the *other*. Time Keepers destroyed everything they know. They are the plague of the universe. It's been eight hundred years since Titus passed away."

"Murdered." I correct her. "My grandfather was murdered."

"It has been eight hundred years since your grandfather was murdered. Your grandfather's legacy of Tempus has been colonized by my hateful brother. And they have never met Templites from before the fall of the Old Time Lord. You just have to show them that you are on their side."

Their side? I scoff at the statement. Beings make war conflicts about friend versus foes. There will always be a face of the enemy. Unity eroded by the division of us versus them. Except their vision of us versus them is always oppressed versus oppressed. It is never the oppressed versus *our* collective oppressor. The ones on top always know how to divide. A trivial issue can be exploited to pit us against each other. Low class workers versus low class workers. Prejudices expanded upon and hate amplified to distract from the rich paying poor people unlivable wages.

Their side, their side, their side. Propaganda fills the streets painting one peaceful group as the aggressors while the opposing side stomps on their throats to control the narrative. Silence obtained by force. From the eight hundred years that I've lived, Kairos has painted the Scorned as the aggressors. I'm on the side that wants to stop Kairos. But I know the Scorned have had their fair share of blood on their hands. They are not saints either. I will never submit to another tyrannical force that assumes they are doing good. Even if they appear as the good guy.

I rotate the map back to Exile and point to the temple, "You started looking for the Artifacts without me?"

"You were busy, Spike." Vakander informs me, "We waited for quite some time for this Activation. But it seems Kairos was holding you hostage. He must have known we were after you once we started our Artifacts search. The day you were Activated on Venus, we took our positions on Tempus to extract you."

"How many have you found?"

"Twenty out of twenty-five," May nervously picks at her nails, "Did you have to make the last five so difficult to find?"

"Yes," It was a death sentence otherwise. I explain, "If Kairos finds them, we might as well hand ourselves over to him." My eyes instinctively look for the twenty artifacts.

"They are not here," May reassures, "They are somewhere safe on Barretta waiting for your return."

"What about this body?" I ask missing my Templite form, "When will I be returned to the form I was born in?"

"It would be wise, that until we have defeated Kairos, you remain in this form," Vakander explains, "Not only do we not have access to the Revival Unit but giving you the body of a Templite will only have everyone hate you more. As we said before, once the universe knows who you are, they will direct their anger and hatred at you."

————

Vakander and May leave me with fucking homework.

Memorize the files on all the trainees. They told me to study everyone and form a training plan based off their abilities. While I enjoy a good strategy building session, it feels weird doing it for real people. I sprawl the notes across the main galley floor. I write notes on my electronic tablet sheet as I go through every name.

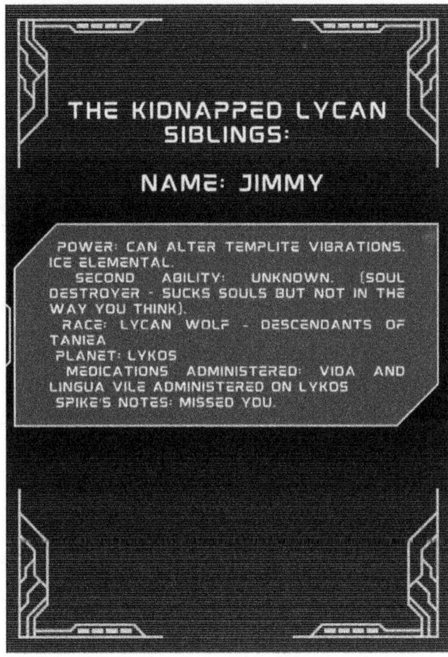

The Kidnapped Lycan Siblings:
Name: Jimmy
Power: Can Alter Templite Vibrations. Ice Elemental.
Second Ability: Unknown. (*Soul Destroyer - sucks souls but not in the way you think*).
Race: Lycan Wolf – Descendants of Taniea
Planet: Lykos

Medications Administered: Vida and Lingua Vile Administered on Lykos

Spike's Notes: Missed you.

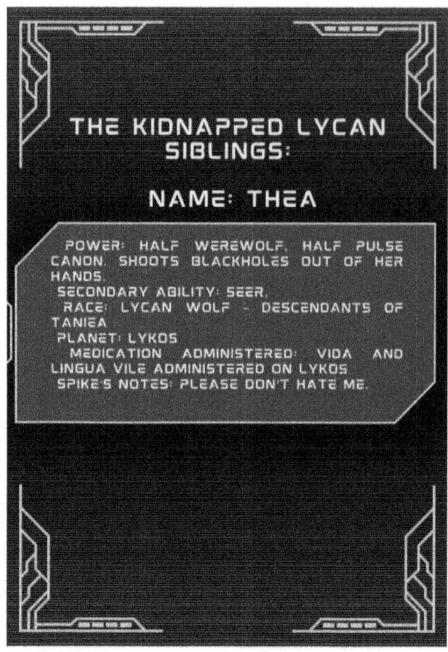

Name: Thea

Power: Half-Werewolf, Half-Pulse Canon. Shoots blackholes out of her hands.

Secondary Ability: Seer.

Race: Lycan Wolf – Descendants of Taniea

Planet: Lykos

Medication Administered: Vida and Lingua Vile Administered on Lykos

Spike's Notes: Please don't hate me.

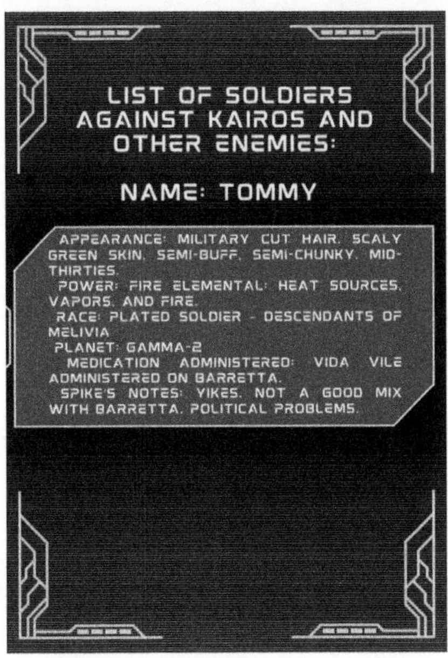

List of Soldiers Against Kairos and Other Enemies:
Name: Tommy

Appearance: Military cut hair. Scaly green skin. Semi-buff, semi-chunky. Mid-thirties.

Power: Fire Elemental: heat sources, vapors, and fire.

Race: Plated Soldier – Descendants of Melivia
Planet: Gamma-2
Medication Administered: Vida Vile Administered on Barretta.

Spike's Notes: Yikes. Not a good mix with Barretta. Political Problems.

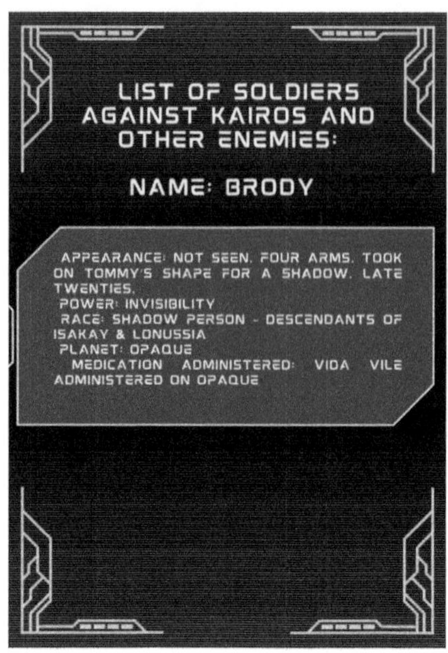

Name: Brody

Appearance: Not seen. Four arms. Took on Tommy's shape for a shadow. Late twenties.

Power: Invisibility

Race: Shadow Person – Descendants of Isakay & Lonussia

Planet: Opaque

Medication Administered: Vida Vile Administered on Opaque

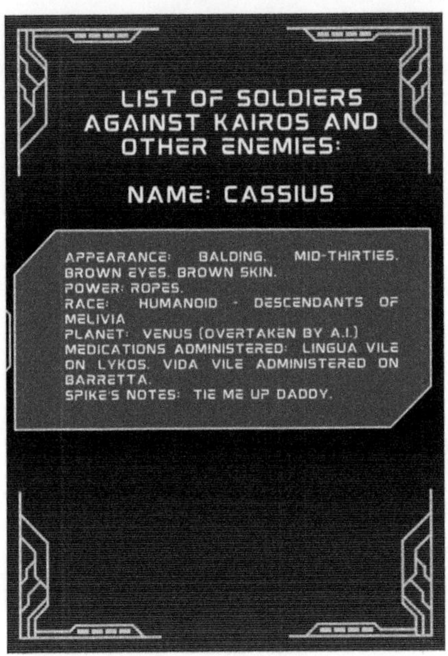

Name: Cassius

Appearance: Balding. Mid-thirties. Brown eyes. Brown skin.

Power: Ropes

Race: Humanoid – Descendants of Melivia

Planet: Venus (*Overtaken by A.I.*)

Medication Administered: Lingua Vile on Lykos. Vida Vile Administered on Barretta.

Spike's Notes: Tie me up daddy.

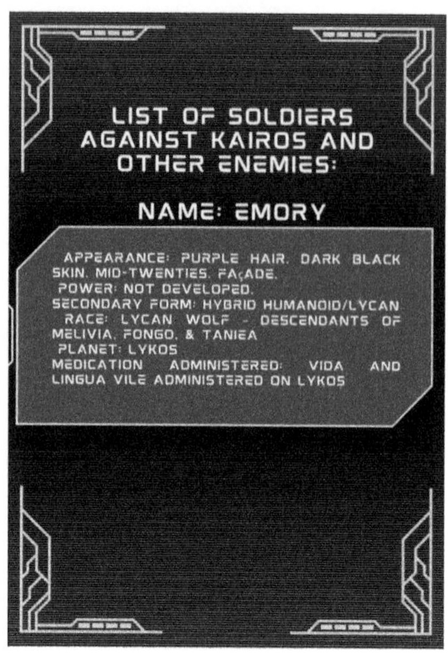

Name: Emory

Appearance: Purple hair. Dark black skin. Mid-twenties. Façade.

Power: Not Developed.

Secondary Form: Hybrid Humanoid/Lycan

Race: Lycan Wolf – Descendants of Melivia, Fongo, & Taniea

Planet: Lykos

Medication Administered: Vida and Lingua Vile Administered on Lykos

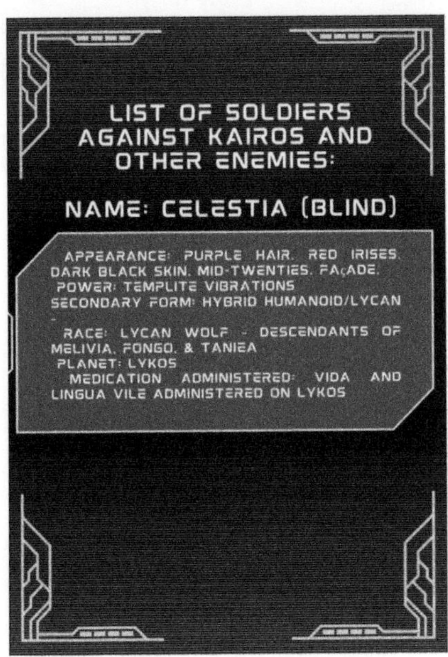

Name: Celestia (Blind)

Appearance: Purple hair. Red irises. Dark black skin. Mid-twenties. Façade.

Power: Templite Vibrations

Secondary Form: Hybrid Humanoid/Lycan

Race: Lycan Wolf – Descendants of Melivia, Fongo, & Taniea

Planet: Lykos

Medication Administered: Vida and Lingua Vile Administered on Lykos

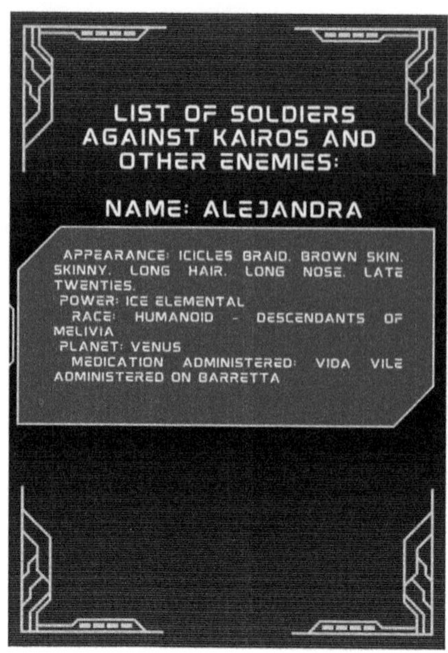

Name: Alejandra

Appearance: Icicles braid. Brown skin. Skinny. Long hair. Long nose. Late twenties.

Power: Ice Elemental

Race: Humanoid – Descendants of Melivia

Planet: Venus

Medication Administered: Vida Vile Administered on Barretta

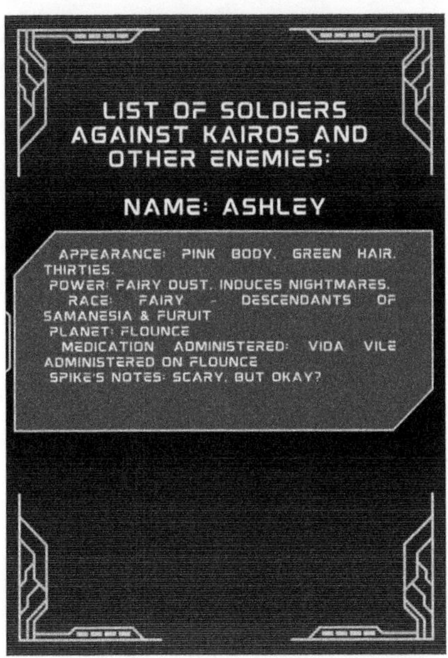

Name: Ashley

Appearance: Pink body. Green Hair. Thirties.

Power: Fairy Dust. Induces Nightmares.

Race: Fairy – Descendants of Samanesia & Furuit

Planet: Flounce

Medication Administered: Vida Vile Administered on Flounce

Spike's Notes: Scary, but okay?

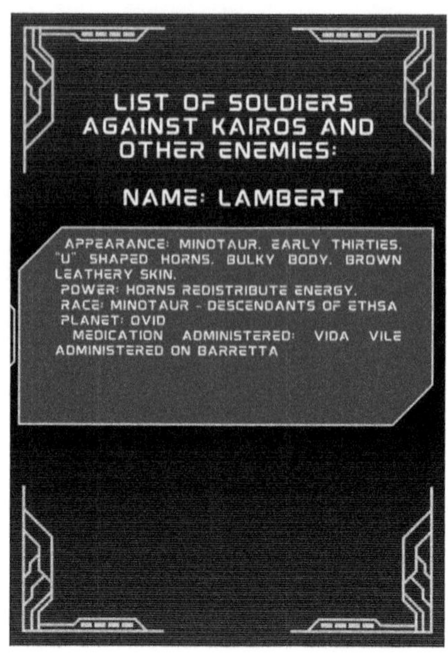

Name: Lambert

Appearance: Minotaur. Early thirties. "U" Shaped Horns. Bulky body. Brown leathery skin.

Power: Horns Redistribute Energy.

Race: Minotaur – Descendants of Ethsa

Planet: Ovid

Medication Administered: Vida Vile Administered on Barretta

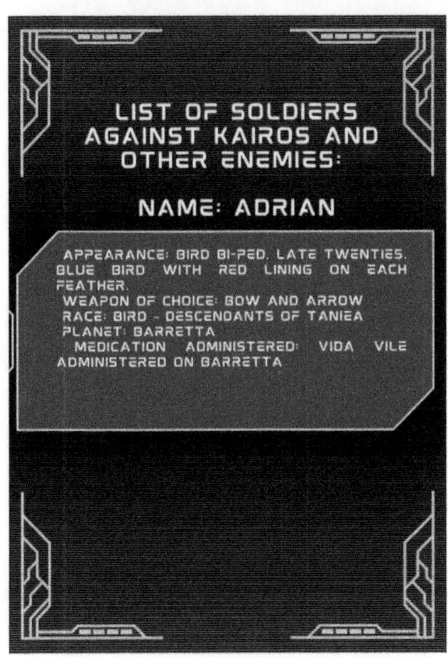

Name: Adrian

Appearance: Bird Bi-ped. Late twenties. Blue Bird with red lining on each feather.

Weapon of Choice: Bow and Arrow

Race: Bird – Descendants of Taniea

Planet: Barretta

Medication Administered: Vida Vile Administered on Barretta

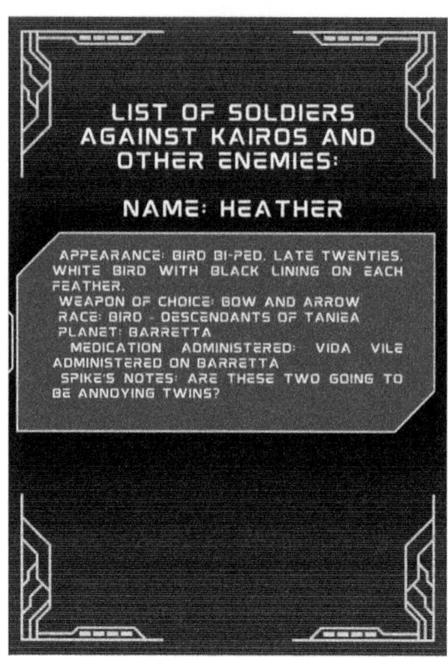

Name: Heather

Appearance: Bird Bi-ped. Late Twenties. White Bird with Black Lining on Each Feather.

Weapon of Choice: Bow and Arrow

Race: Bird – Descendants of Taniea

Planet: Barretta

Medication Administered: Vida Vile Administered on Barretta

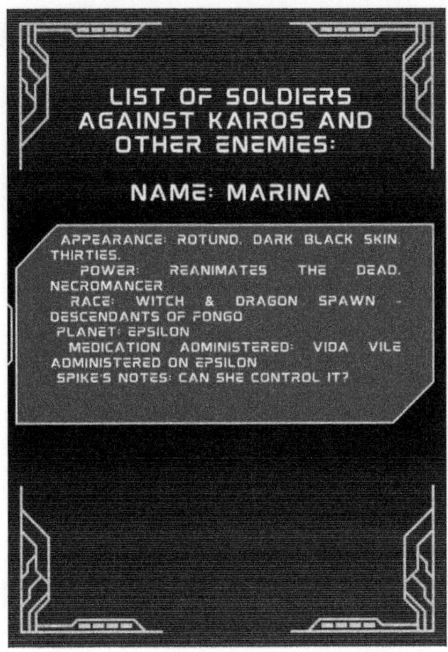

Name: Marina

Appearance: Rotund. Dark black skin. Thirties.

Power: Reanimates the Dead. Necromancer

Race: Witch & Dragon Spawn – Descendants of Fongo

Planet: Epsilon

Medication Administered: Vida Vile Administered on Epsilon

Spike's Notes: Can she control it?

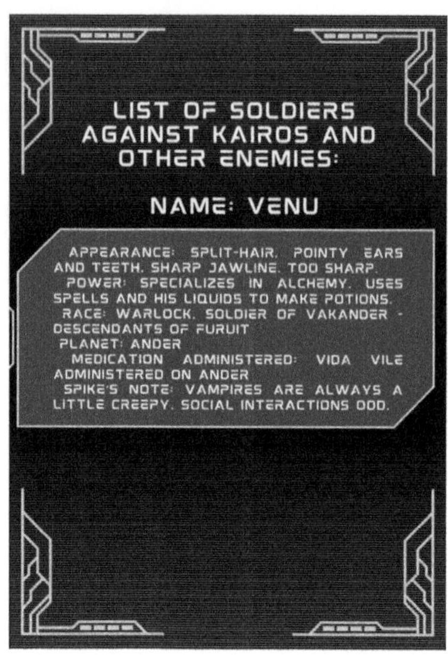

Name: Venu

Appearance: Split-hair. Pointy ears and teeth. Sharp jawline. Too sharp.

Power: Specializes in Alchemy. Uses Spells and His Liquids to Make Potions.

Race: Warlock. Soldier of Vakander - Descendants of Furuit

Planet: Ander

Medication Administered: Vida Vile Administered on Ander

Spike's Note: Vampires are always a little creepy. Social interactions odd.

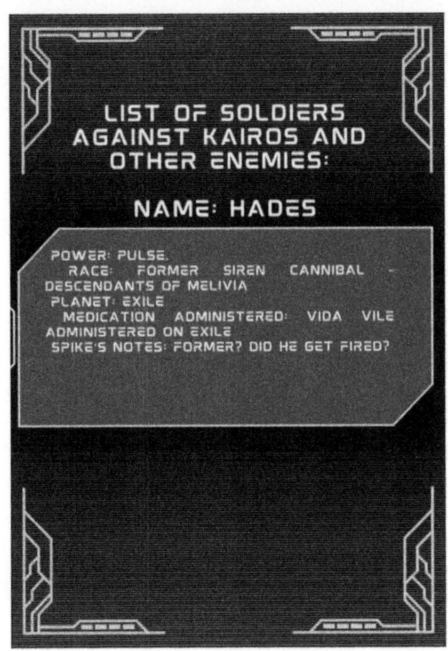

Name: Hades

Power: Pulse.

Race: Former Siren Cannibal – Descendants of Melivia

Planet: Exile

Medication Administered: Vida Vile Administered on Exile

Spike's Notes: Former? Did he get fired?

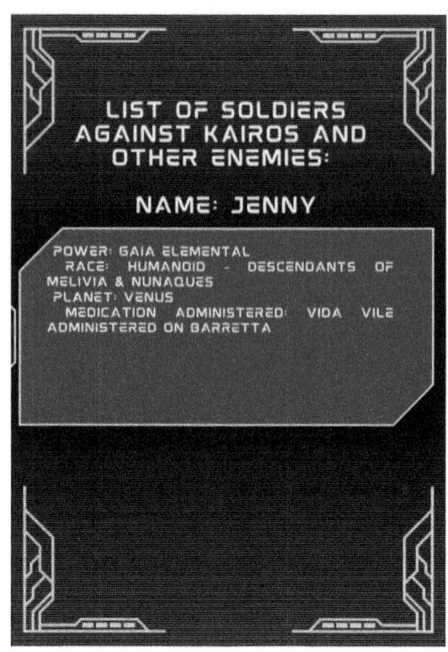

Name: Jenny

Power: Gaia Elemental

Race: Humanoid – Descendants of Melivia & Nunaques

Planet: Venus

Medication Administered: Vida Vile Administered on Barretta

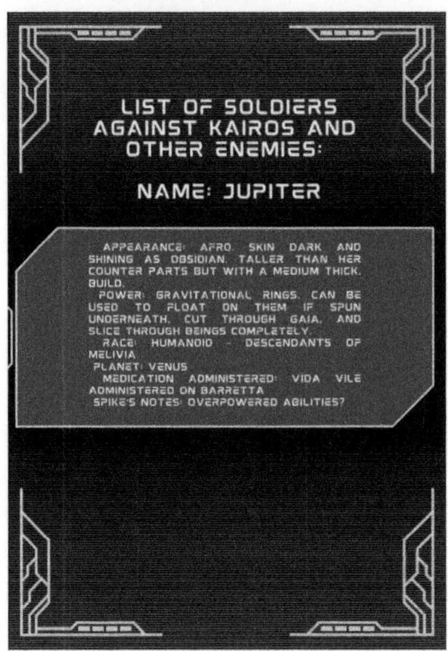

Name: Jupiter

Appearance: Afro. Skin dark and shining as obsidian. Taller than her counter parts but with a medium thick, build.

Power: Gravitational Rings. Can be used to float on them if spun underneath, cut through Gaia, and slice through beings completely.

Race: Humanoid – Descendants of Melivia

Planet: Venus

Medication Administered: Vida Vile Administered on Barretta

Spike's Notes: Overpowered abilities?

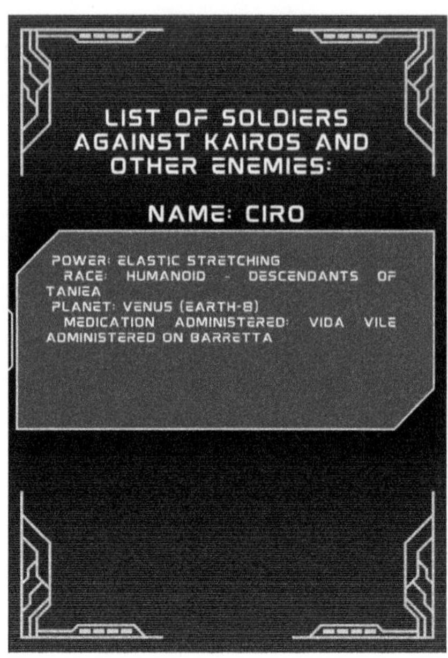

Name: Ciro

    Power: Elastic Stretching

    Race: Humanoid – Descendants of Taniea

    Planet: Venus *(Earth-8)*

    Medication Administered: Vida Vile Administered on Barretta

Spike Notes:

Humanoids may struggle with Limbo for the first time. Elementals are great additions to the team if all of them survive. They can be used on different environmental planets. Lykos, Gamma-2, and Barretta soldiers have me worried. Specifically Gamma-2 and Barretta. Why are the siblings separated from the...

Vakander interrupts me.

"Forty minutes until arrival," Vakander dismisses himself to his

First Officer's jumpseat, "Everyone needs to be buckled in ten minutes."

I haven't experienced a Craft's landing in a while. If I really wanted to, I could just Pulse us onto the surface of Barretta. Not that I would want to. I love when I get to be normal. Pulses are great but they speed up the process of everything mundane. The little mundane stuff like road tripping and sightseeing rare hidden attractions of a vast galaxy. Hovering high above a planet weightless and admiring the beauty from afar. Barretta is one of my favorite planets. Of course, that is what I say about any planet that is willing to save me from Kairos.

After I have collected my files, I buckle in a seat between both of them. We stare out the giant windows arching up behind me. May captains the Craft dipping us through thick clouds for about five minutes. The swirls of turbulence making my stomach tumble. Once we come out the other end, steep white mountains covered in patches of trees and snow fill the ever-lasting landscape. Birds, the size of humanoids in grey clad battle armor, swoop next to our Craft escorting us to The Barretta Committee. In the distance, families of birds nosedive from their multi-story nests to gather water and fish at the base of the mountains. The vast rivers full of fresh spring water never run dry as the weather remains muggy for most of the year. They return to their nests intrigued and disgusted by a Templite Craft. If it weren't for the birds flying us to where we needed to go, we would have been shot down by now. On sight.

Barretta doesn't just have one king and queen. They are watched over by five large family powers that descend from the inception of their planet. This becomes evident as we come upon the center of the planet. The faded pink Barretta Committee Castle spans over various mountains. The main castle can be confused for a mountain itself. The castle sits on an island coated with vegetation and massive rock formations. A landing pad takes up a chunk of the front exterior. As we circle around it, we catch a glimpse of the decently sized training field that tappers off in to a cliff I saw in May's hologram.

Smaller, yet space-consuming, turrets house the five families around the main castle on their five separate islands. Bridges connect the five separate towers together, appearing new and with little use. Probably since everyone here can fly to where they need to go. But what do I know.

May sets our craft down gently on a landing pad adjacent to the main courtyard filled with trimmed, decorative hedges. The Barretta Committee, five kings and queens, mournfully wait for us. Surrounding them are armed soldiers with their metallic bows and arrows at the ready. Draped blue and purple kimonos coated in geometric designs differentiate royalty from soldiers. Soldiers stand wearing armor blankets weighing down their vibrant billowing feathers. At the press of a button, the blankets meld with the bird's bodies and it turns into battle armor.

"I wonder if they greet other foreign dignitaries with bows and arrows?" I rhetorically ask, "Do any of them smile? I remember Barretta being a lovely planet with welcoming bird people."

"Yeah, well," May keeps her eyes forward, "The last time you were here you were incarnated in a bird body. Barrettans tend to trust only their people."

"Great." I bemoan unbuckling my four-point harness in unison with Vakander and May.

Vakander presses a button and releases the rear ramp, "It was nice seeing you two again. Have fun on Barretta and Exile, Spike."

May walks ahead of me. I'm taken aback and stare at him confused.

"You aren't coming with us?" Trust me. Vakander isn't the most interesting soul to hang around. But he's useful to have around when you need to make an escape from a hostile planet.

"Nope. I have my own part in this war to tend to."

"You're not going to tell me?"

"Look, you're on a need-to-know basis. Survive Exile. You'll see me once that's over. We'll catch up then. For now, worry about what's in front of you. You'll have enough time to worry about what I'm dealing with." Vakander grabs my hands in his, "Be careful out there, buddy. Hopefully, the next time I see you, you're not left jaded by this clunky part of the universe."

"Too late to not be jaded." I sarcastically drawl out my self-deprecating commentary, "I've just been rescued from eight centuries worth of enslavement. And everyone is pointing weapons at me already. Can't tell where I'm safer, here or Tempus?"

You start to feel numb to your own suffering when seen through hindsight. You diminish it because others have been through worse experiences. It never seems like it will live up to the stories of beings having their homes and families ripped away from them.

"All I'm saying is find it in you to remember the end goal of this life."

"And what is that?" There's never been an end goal. My thoughts are in constant escape mode. Escape is the endless thought when you are fleeing from a captor. How does one think of a life after they were told they were destined to die young in an endless loop?

"For you to live, here, present and in the moment." Vakander buries his good-luck necklace in my hand. A pendant with the seven symbols of the Ethereals dangles off a leather strand. The seven Ethereals were a symbol of unity through community in our galaxy. One could not live as a whole while the community suffered or went missing. Vakander continues, "Us adults made a mess, now we're trying to clean it up with our children." He smiles, "Go. Don't keep your May waiting. See you in the near future."

I put on the necklace and give him a hug. Vakander awkwardly and stiffly holds me unsure of how to handle the affection. Affection was not normal between Templite family members.

I pull away and run towards the cargo door.

"Don't die, Vakander," I yell behind me clanking my feet against the metal of the Craft. I run down the ramp and catch up to May. May stands bowing in front of the Barretta Committee and I follow her lead. Behind us, the Craft slowly rises into the air far above the height of the mountains. Then, it makes a hasty exit.

The soldiers fix their weapons on me.

Honestly, I did nothing directly to these people. I don't understand why they have to greet me in such a disrespectful manner. The last time I was here I was royalty. Now I've been demoted to war criminal. I recognize all these people except some of the soldiers.

Vesta, the queen in the middle of the two other couples, speaks in an accent that sways like a song, "Welcome Spike. May your addition to our team deem valuable," Sheesh, that's a harsh way of saying hi, "We have work to do. We will monitor and evaluate your work. I will be the voice of my fellow colleagues in deciding if we allow you to remain among us."

May pats my back and pinches it. That's my cue.

"And may I prove my worthiness to everyone here," I smile in the professional way of saying screw-you-yet-thank-you. The good ole corporate smile.

The Barretta Committee, except Vesta, fear smiling more than frowning. Each one taking relentless turns glaring at me like I killed their children. They aren't seeing me right now. They are seeing past me. They are seeing other Time Keepers destroying their Barretta from the inside. See, as a Time Absorber I would be planted on different planets as a member of their race at any age to gather intelligence. The intelligence would be recorded with our eyes and ears and then sent off through our Placenta Pod Data Links to the Central Birthing Unit. From there, the information would be sorted through different channels and secretaries. Domestic affairs and war issues went straight to Kairos. Threats and civil unrest between the planets were Avi's division. And the soldiers were given intel on armies and weak spots in the government. The sharing of information then leads to an attack on a planet or the Cleansing. The Cleansing was Kairos using his Pulse ability Shadow Poison to infect an entire planet with a toxic poison that fed off the natural resources. If a planet required iron or water for hydration, the Shadow Poison would taint the supply leaving no visible trace. And anyone who drank the water would slowly become a pawn for Kairos. The Pulse would attack the brain until the person could no longer control themselves. From there, Kairos could utilize the newly corrupted citizens to turn on their own people. They were to take the planet by any means necessary. Kairos would then send his own soldiers to finish the job. One Time Absorber in the correct position of government or as the child of a government official could take the whole planet down. Exile citizens being the only beings in the universe to be able to counter the poison's control.

As a Time Absorber, they would extract me, change my form, send me to a different planets to act as a sleeper agent, and repeat the never-ending cycle of spying. Since I was last here, Kairos invaded in his mission to Cleanse the universe. Obviously, he didn't win because their society still stands strong, but he was successful enough to earn me resting-bird-faces from every single being on this planet.

"Good," Vesta twirls robotically, "Follow me."

———

Vesta guides us through a dark hallway underneath the castle lit by neon glowing flowers.

"Dallies make good for light in the dark but are poison to the touch. Be careful if you come upon them through your journeys. Dallies are also good indicators of allies and friends," She says as she turns right to a fifty-foot archway. Beyond the archway are spiral stone staircases going up, down, and diagonally leading to countless chambers. The endless domed ceilings etched with black and gold paintings of old war victories and galactic battles run down like bleeding ink to where we stand. Royal guards perch on stone branches scattered and camouflaged all over the building.

"Welcome to our Orphanage," Vesta smiles proud of herself.

"This is an Orphanage?" I ask astonished.

"We believe everyone should be given the same opportunities no matter where you come from or your circumstances. We house refugees here as well. You will be staying here while you train our soldiers. Your roommate will help you train your comrades."

"Why do I have to have a roommate?" This place seems nice enough to have enough rooms to house people individually.

King Numitor bites at me, "We grant you protection. You put our people in danger by being here and this is how you thank us by complaining about sharing a room."

Vesta holds her hand up for him to stop, "He is our guest."

"He is no guest of mine." Numitor stares at me as if he recognizes me. I stare back at him silently.

"Yes, he is. He is a powerful ally to have," Vesta adds, "But an even greater foe if it were to come to that. Which side would you rather him be on, ours or theirs?"

Theirs. There it is.

Numitor and his wife turn away from me in disgust and anguish. My guilt pushes my eyes to Vesta.

"We've given each of our soldiers a roommate because trust is a fickle concept," Vesta explains as she holds her hands together, "We want you to be protected while you are here for you have more enemies in this fortress than friends, but we also want to make sure you are not a rhino-boar in a feather-cleep's clothing. Do you understand?"

Her understanding of Venus animals is skewed slightly.

Say no more.

I have trust issues too, girl. I have no point in double crossing them even if I really wanted to.

I nod.

"Great," Vesta cheers, "I'll take you to your chambers. My colleagues have other, more important matters to attend to."

May grabs my arm, "I'll see you in the morning."

"You're not coming with us?" I ask slightly worried.

"No, I have my own tasks to get ready. I'll call for you in the morning before breakfast."

May follows the Committee Members down another corridor leaving me alone once again.

CHAPTER 7

THEA:
THE FOURTH DIMENSION

MY LIFE PLAYS *before my eyes. I am no longer in control of my body. A back seat driver to my own story. My soul floats in the air as a loose, purple flame formation. Trapped as an observer.*

"Souls don't always fight so hard after they pass." A detached voice explains to me, "They usually cross over in to the Cataclysm Realm and live their happy little lives in ignorance."

Am I stuck here?

"No, you can leave whenever you want." Pan. He's using my body as a vessel.

You poisoned my kingdom.

"That is no longer any of your concern. Death frees you from all ties to the physical world."

Then why did you fight so hard to steal my body.

"You were already dead. You didn't need it anymore."

Pan deflects the question.

I will find a way to destroy you.

"Will you, my dear? What power does a soul have?"

To avenge an entire kingdom.

"Well, your voice has become rather bothersome and repetitive?" Pan sighs, "You have two choices: sit back and enjoy the show, or, you can garner resentment and unresolved dreams in the Fourth Dimension."

Pan slices the air with my fingernail. Threads of the universe open to the Fourth Dimension.

"Find peace. You do not need to see your people suffer. Or, remain trapped in the pit of darkness I crawled out from. Your choice."

What did my people do to you?

"Your people did nothing to me personally. But when one of the biggest armies in the universe threatens our chances of taking over the galaxy. We have no choice but to take them out."

The darkness calls to me. It sings a melody of reassurance. I'm tugged in two directions. My people or the unknown.

Take the leap, Thea. *An unknown voice tells me.*

I look out of my eyes to the kingdom I lost. I promise that I will come back to restore you.

"I thought you were going to destroy me."

I wasn't talking to you. I roam in to the darkness and accept the tragic song. My soul tears open as the uncertain Threads close behind me. Yet, the darkness feels like home.

CHAPTER 8
SPIKE:
CASSIUS & THE ROPES – DAY 1

VESTA LEADS me up the diagonal spiral staircases with two soldiers on our heels. I try to ignore the perched birds aiming their weapons at me ready to strike. They hungrily wait for me to take a breath in the wrong direction.

"Is this your first time on Barretta?" Vesta tries to make some sort of conversation as we walk up what seems like ten stories.

"I was reincarnated here once. It was before Barretta attacked Gamma-2."

"Ah, yes. I remember those years. They were so calm like a morning wind. A breeze that led to a storm we were not completely prepared for."

"I never visited the Orphanage before. This is nice."

"It is quite something else."

There's an awkward pause.

"What's wrong with Numitor?"

"He is afraid of you. Fear makes men angry. You're a foreign concept to him."

"You're not afraid of me."

"Should I be?" Vesta smirks like if she could snap my neck with one of her feathers.

"No."

"Well, I won't be. If you create a reason to be feared, then I will have to take care of you another way. Besides, how can I be afraid of someone wanting to stop Kairos? We have a similar goal. Stop the Cleansing. What Numitor doesn't understand is that a war can't be won with just your own people. If you start thinking like the enemy, you unwittingly become them. We have to unite as partners to accomplish this feat. Even if we are the most unlikely of partners."

To be honest, I have never wanted anything to do with the war. I just really want to dethrone and murder Kairos. A vicious cat and mouse game that I never win. But doing that requires war.

"Do you think it can be done? Do you think Kairos can finally be beaten?"

"There are multiple possible outcomes. If we play it right, then we could win, otherwise we will lose. But if we don't try to overthrow him, then we've lost already. We can't stand around and allow him to continue his awful actions. I saw a world before this war. War is not my normal. I want to return to my normal, but we cannot do that if we don't fight. If not for me or you, then for future generations of beings that will exist."

"That's the thing. Let's say we defeat him. Won't there just be another being like Kairos who will want to rule the universe?"

"Of course. And when that time comes, future generations will have to decide if they're going to allow it to happen. But those are worries for the future. One dictator at a time." Vesta reaches a landing and cocks her head towards a dark hallway, "C'mon, let's show you to your room."

Vesta opens the door to my room. A stoic balding man in his late thirties stares through me with his dark brown eyes. Black glasses give him a sense of maturity. He wears a black dress shirt and black cargo jeans tucked in black boots. The dark grey room made of rock is barren except for two beds.

"What took you so long?" He barks at me.

"Excuse me?" I respond.

"Spike," Vesta interrupts the weirdness of this situation, "This is Cassius. I'll leave you two so you can get to know each other. Others call for my attention."

Vesta runs out of the hallway and jumps off the platform releasing her wings. She slowly glides out of sight.

"You were supposed to be here a week ago." He stands up two inches taller than me.

"I didn't exactly plan my escape in a certain time frame. I didn't plan it at all really. I was kinda taken hostage. And how did you know I was supposed to be here a week ago?"

"Thea told me."

I stare at him wide eyed. The last time I saw Thea she had a blade in her chest. She was dying on Lykos under Avi's hand. Jimmy and I fought off Kairos until we were overwhelmed.

"Am I supposed to know who that is?" I feign ignorance. My memories are slowly trickling back so it's not entirely a lie.

"She said you two have met in another lifetime." Cassius sees through my bullshit.

"Look, I've met thousands of people," I continue the nasty façade, "You really have to narrow it down with a picture or a really good drawing of the person. Is she somewhere around here? Or..."

Cassius stares at me confused, "They haven't told you what we're doing here, huh?"

"Training soldiers? Searching for the remaining Artifacts once I get back most of the memories from the Artifacts they do have? Deal with some Siren Cannibals?" I say the bare bones version.

Cassius touches his chest and closes his eyes. A faded teal translucent string appears from Cassius's chest and trails out the door. He plucks the string, and it expands into a giant image. He zooms out on the stringed image. The more he zooms out the further you can see the string trailing out of the castle and off Baretta. The string extends onto Exile. From Exile, he zooms in on Exile to where the string is leading to a vast wilderness area full of ruins. As he completely zooms in on the end of the string, it disappears into a circular zone of clouded nothingness.

"What am I looking at?"

"This is where we're going. We have to follow this string to this place. Thea is hidden behind where my powers are being blocked out. Siren Cannibals have this kind of effect on my powers. Their Siren Song unravels my Ropes. We are going there to rescue the Royal Lycan Wolves."

The "missing" labels beside Jimmy and Thea in the documents May gave me make more sense. Vesta is lying to both of us. I don't know how yet but everything isn't adding up. My knowledge of Siren Cannibals. The wolves being taken hostage by a harmless race of beings painted as evil. Vesta's plan to train the Orphans. She is moving pieces without Cassius knowing. I feel for the guy. His unwavering faith, in a deceptive leader leading him blindfolded in to the darkness, is impressive.

"They told me we were going to Exile to get rid of the Siren Cannibals?"

"That's their main mission. Mine is different. I'm going there to help get Thea away from the Siren Cannibals."

"What makes you so sure she's still alive? Sorry to say this but Siren Cannibals usually don't let their prey survive the night." I tease. "They even eat the bones of their victims. You get the best vitamins from bones, you know."

"Our hearts are still tethered by these Ropes. If she had died..." Cassius pauses at the though, he is trying to ignore the thought, "Or if anything bad happened to her, the Ropes would be frayed. That's how I know she's safe."

"So, your Ropes show love connections?" I prod.

"They show all sorts of relationships and special bonds."

"But no boy travels to a hellhole to save any girl unless..."

He interrupts me, "She's a good friend."

My eyes go wide, "Look, I'm a complete stranger. You don't have to prove anything to me. If you want to cherish a random stranger with your love tool, that's none of my business."

"You may not remember her, but you will speak about her with respect." Cassius commands while towering over me. He doesn't scare me. I respect a moody man in love. He isn't bad looking either. Not too fit, more of a dad bod but a good time for a nice girl.

I drop the taunting.

"Can I be candid with you lover boy?"

"Please enlighten me."

"I was told we were going to Exile to save children from Siren Cannibals. Something about their life forces being drained."

"We still have to do that. But we have another mission on top of it. Save Thea and Jimmy."

"You don't need to trust me, but please listen to what I have to say next. Vesta is lying to you."

"How can you say that? She is sheltering you here. You're the liar. You've been here five seconds, and you act like you don't know Thea."

"I do know her. I can tell you about the last time I saw her. She had a sword in her heart."

"That's not possible."

"The last time you saw her. Was she acting odd?"

"She's been off ever since her kingdom was attacked by Templites like *you*. Her mother went missing too."

"Templites like me?" I scoff, "Well, I was fighting by her side against the Templites. Thea might not be on our side anymore."

"Then, why would she be helping Vesta find your Artifacts?"

"Was she always helping find the Artifacts or did she start the day after the Templite attack?"

Cassius remains in thought. His mind not wanting to respond.

"The day after the Templite attack." He responds.

"Do you know what I hid on Exile?"

"An Artifact."

I raise my eyebrows.

"What are you getting at?" He asks.

"Souls of beings with unresolved trauma end up in the Fourth Dimension. When a being dies in the universe, if their death creates a tear in the universe, a fourth dimensional soul can jump in to their body and take over."

"You're saying Thea died?"

"Yes."

"So, who is in her body?"

"Who benefits from finding my Artifacts?"

"An advisor for Kairos."

I nod.

"I know this is a lot to process. Leaders like Vesta have to lie to us. Right? If they tell us too much, we run the danger of telling others. And not everyone is trustworthy. You're one of two people, maybe three, if you include that Vesta bird lady, that I know on this planet that doesn't instantly want to kill me. *Your* anger stems from a severe case of blue balls. Yes, I just met you but besides this whole angsty lover-boy act, you seem like you'd be a cool person. I'm willing to help you if you cut the "you-were-supposed-to-save-my-fake-girlfriend" act."

"You have no choice. You have to help me."

"That's where you're wrong. I don't need to be here, but they offered an army to protect me, in turn I train their best soldiers. They give me food to eat, and a place to sleep. I'm as selfish as you are..."

"I'm not selfish."

"But you are. I'm here to stay alive. You're going to Exile to save your damsel in distress. I'm here to do the bare minimum and appease my landlords, the Barretta Committee. You'll allow many men to die before you allow her to die. We're the same person. Now relax. If she's safe, then she's safe. But I'm here to do whatever needs to be done to survive and to kill Kairos."

"But how do you know she's safe?"

I know that's not what Cassius wants to hear. I know he wants to hear that I'm a valiant hero willing to give up my life for the universe.

The sad truth is that I'm still trying to follow my destiny with survival in mind. Everyone in this dreadful galaxy is just trying to survive, aren't we? A cast full of ensemble characters told they mean the world, but they're just dots in the background. Somewhere, in another universe, I've lost this war or won it. I don't know. All I know is I'm alive now awaiting my trials ahead.

"So... you'll help me?" Cassius questions me.

"Yes. Every knight needs a reason to run into battle."

I lie on the bed with my hands behind my head and Cassius squints his eyes at me angrily.

"Why are you so heartless? Why don't you care about anything or anyone?"

His question is loaded and has many answers to it.

How do you explain to someone that you want to go home? That you want to go home, and no one will let you. That home was where you were raised and all your good memories except the newest terrors lie. That the bad men took over and now you can't go home. Home is not always a place. It is sometimes the feeling of elsewhere. It can just be a concept. Not always a regional area. Home was my grandfather. My castle. My past lovers. The minute experiences in between that really mattered.

It's not that I don't care. It's that I am numb. Everything was taken away from me. All anyone can ever care about is who I am because of Kairos and his Cleansing of the universe. They see me and I am the enemy. They know no better because their leaders have pointed fingers and said that I am the enemy. They do not see that my planet was colonized. That good people were taken over by external forces full of selfish and evil beings. Templites were not always evil. They did not have a negative connotation to their name when my grandpa ruled. But, in this day and age, the people who look like me and act like me are now the face of evil. To them, I am evil incarnate waiting to murder their loved ones. My grandfather, Titus Kronos, was never that person. He was not the face of evil. He loved all and he cared for all beings. I am not him. But he is the person I look up to when everyone stares at me with contention. I look to the very few memories of him when unrelenting daggered eyes judge me for breathing. I am not a burden for existing. People like my grandfather will exist in the future. People like my grandfather are my people. I believe that somewhere on Tempus and the remaining planets surrounding Tempus, his people are still there too. They wait for us. They wait for our people to unite as one and overcome the mess Kairos has made. That's why I decide to help this helpless puppy leashed to their possessed owner.

There are no words that you can explain to a person who is not in your skin, not in your shoes, that can ever explain your experience. I long for the day where my people are not categorized by the actions of a corrupting entity. I long for the day that I am home, and my people have had their homes restored.

"I care about humanity when it cares about me. I care about friends when they're mine. I know no one here except a few people. I could cut six fingers off my hands and still have to cut a few more in order to count the people I care about."

I have no one. Sure, May and Vakander saved me but after how long.

Why should I care about Thea? Why should I care what Vesta wants? They are using me the same way I am using them.

"Such a sad shameful life to live. Not caring about anyone."

I bite my cheek and frown, "I didn't choose this life. It was given to me. So, I must do as much as I can with it. When it starts giving me meaning, I promise you I'll start caring."

"That's an ugly way of thinking."

"Have you seen a being die right in front of your eyes?"

"Of course, I have."

"What if everyone you always cared about always died? And you were reborn each time to watch them die again in your memories? Reborn to love anew and watch new lovers die as well. Never remembering them completely because you erased your own memories so Kairos wouldn't find your loved ones? But still remember a whisper of who they were. What they meant to you. All those feelings coming back while struggling to unlock full memories that can only be unlocked by Artifacts. Would you care about anyone then? Or would you love numbly and desensitized by the gruesome reality of your existence?"

Silence.

I smile, "A grim thought I know. That's where I'm at. I've lived too long and am too tired of this existence."

"No," he pauses, "I would still care about people. I would want the galaxies to change my fate and design a new storyline."

"If only it were that simple to want something and get it." A foolish thought from a boy who has lived only one life. Tragedy. Jealously. Misery. Ignorance. Death. Post cards sent to the back of my eye lids as I sleep every night. Every life I lived felt real until I was onto the next. Every new body acquired new skills. Every partner lost to the cosmos ripped from my warm hands until they turned to ice.

There are days I feel agony for a long-lost love I don't remember. Because my most precious memories are locked in the Artifacts. Glimpses of incoherent befores and afters. Memories that might as well be fever dreams with no rhyme or reason. I remember Thea and Jimmy because I hid my power in the Artifact and not my actual memories of my life with them. I let Avi and Kairos see my happy existence with them. Almost all of my Artifacts contain unlocked memories I stored to detach myself from feeling all those emotions all the time. So, to put it plain and simple, I have memories of very little from my past lives. I made sure to retain specific knowledge in case I ever needed it.

I do remember Jimmy's touch. His embrace. Every affectionate touch. Our fairytale romance that made me feel immortal and invincible.

I remember Thea and her love for her people. Her love for me. The day she found out I was a Templite, she was ready to fight for me tooth and nail when she realized I was trying to escape Avi and

Kairos. I had told her of the gruesome and sadistic torture they dragged me through with each lifetime and she was ready for blood.

I do want to help Thea. But just as much as I want to help her and will help her, I want to forget. It's easier to forget. To ignore pain and hope it doesn't fester like an open infected wound.

I'm helping him because of Thea and her love for me. She should not have showed me the love and welcoming she did. She should not have shown me that she cared. She had every right to see me as the enemy and she didn't. But I don't want to remember her. Selfish as it might be. I hate Cassius in this moment for opening old wounds. I hate him for reminding me that I failed to save her. That she lost her life that day trying to protect me, and I still didn't have enough power within me to stop Kairos from taking me back to Tempus.

And now, we have been thrown again in to political games with too many moving pieces for me to form a completed picture.

I turn to my side facing away from him. I draw imaginary objects with my finger on the grey stone walls.

"How do you get over losing someone?" He asks me. I hear the springs jump up and down as he plops on the bed.

"Find it in yourself to pull through."

"How do I do that?"

"Trust in your power. Trust that it's telling you the truth. Intuition seems like an old Epsilon's tale but if your power is telling you she's unharmed, believe it. Confidence in one's self is important in a selfish world."

He asks me one last question after a pause, "How can I trust you?"

"By allowing me to show you who I am. If I betray you, you'll learn the hard way. If I don't, maybe we could be friends after that."

I'm pretty sure he asks me a million more questions, but I'm knocked out before I can answer anymore.

I SNEAK through the sewer grates and air vents.

Air vents are usually easier to work with since I can manipulate the hot air to shoot me up through them faster. The carved wooden jester mask doesn't help the crippling claustrophobia.

Numitor is next on my list. I've killed enough "innocent" birds. Each one helped her. They helped her carry out their plan against my people. I know it would be easier to collapse their whole society but I don't want that. Barretta is still an important planet to stand against Kairos. He is the true enemy.

Killing each remaining surviving general and soldier that helped her will bring me some peace. Vengeance is satisfying. Those who say vengeance is never the answer have never felt it. I want everyone with blood on their hands dead so that they can't do it again to anyone else.

I stand at the ceiling vent above Numitor's room with a katana at the ready. He dies today.

The voices stop me from rushing in to the room.

"You intel is important to me."

"Destroy her, Kairos."

"Easy. We get to finish what we started centuries ago. With Barretta gone, we only have a few planets standing in our way."

Numitor, you fucking slimy ass bastard. It never fucking ends does it.

They continue their conversation pointing out weak spots in the Barretta Castle and Orphanage. The portal closes and Numitor lays down to rest in a separate bed from his wife. She cries in another room saying a familiar name over and over again.

The name echoes in my brain lingering on my tongue.

I wait until the sobbing stops before moving through the vents to Numitor's other bed. I quietly pop open the vent and use the hot air to float on top of Numitor. I straddle his sides locking my legs under his body as I hold the katana to his throat.

"You've come for me." Numitor quakes.

"Of course." I press the Katana to his neck.

"I waited years for this moment. What a bad time. No matter. End it. Kairos will end all of us."

"Oh, I heard. Small mercies."

"That information dies with me."

"I'm not killing you. Not yet." I jump off of him and grab a book off his dresser. I throw it at him. The book groans as it hits his chest. With my other hand, I grab an ink well and place it in his hand. I pluck one of his feathers and hold it out for him. He grabs it shaking.

"What do you want me to do with this?"

"Write down every weak spots in the castle you told him, where we lack soldiers, and the quantity of soldiers he would need to destroy Barretta."

"I'd rather die right now."

"Gladly," I throttle the loose skin at the back of his neck and start dragging him out of the room.

"Wait. Where are you taking me?"

"Vesta."

"No. I'd rather die a quick death."

I throw him on the ground, "Write the plan down."

"Why are you doing this?"

"You will die when the time comes. But I will protect mine."

CHAPTER 10
ASHLEY:
ALLIES AND FOES – DAY 1

THE BEAUTIFUL, curvy Epsilon girl motions for me to join her. I would do anything this goddess incarnate told me to do. Her hand closes in a claw and goes to her mouth. She wants us to have breakfast together. We had breakfast together every morning since I arrived on Barretta. I assume they placed me in the same room as Marina the moment I went crazy on the bird soldiers. They were doing nothing to save my people. They sent no Crafts that I know of to Flounce. No plans were being made to send aid to save my planet.

It has been approximately ten Flounce days since I barely escaped the invasion of my planet. For some odd reason, no one, not even Vesta, has given me a Lingua Vile. Lingua Viles allow our tongues to vibrate at different frequencies while directed at different beings. The new frequencies allow language barriers to be removed.

For ten days, I have drawn detailed pictures of Flounce, of my family, and the fairy warriors that visit my dreams. This was our best form of complex communications. Marina picked through them when I was done and smiled. She always wants another drawing. She gets excited to know more about who the fairies were, but I can only explain so much before we descend into mumbles of incoherent frustration.

The other day, she sounded out her name to me in a strange Epsilon accent. What I assume must be Marina. But it could be anything. She trained me for two hours on saying her name correctly.

Marina and the drawings have kept me sane in an insane world. What do you do when all you want to do is lash out on everyone but you have to remain calm because you're on foreign land? How do you keep your anger bottled up when the enemy is out there destroying your home? And you can't do one thing about it. What do you do when you feel helpless? So full of power yet nowhere for it to go. How do you not lash out at everyone around you?

Ten days and no Lingua Vile administered. Ten days of living on a planet where no one speaks my language. They don't look like me. They aren't the people I loved and left behind to stay safe from death. And they do the bare minimum to help.

Marina grabs my face and rubs my cheeks. She places her forehead on mine. She does this every time I lose myself in a trance. I tend to get lost lately and quiet easily. Every time she sees me lose my mind to the rage, she reels me back in. I nod.

I start to cry and rock back and forth. Marina stays with me until I'm ready to go. She plays with my messy, bright green hair and massages my pink hand. We stay there for another ten minutes before we leave.

———

Bird soldiers grab their lunches from a gaping hole in the side of a chamber where a missile must have burst the wall open. We wake up earlier than the other Orphans. Not that it matters since we don't interact with them. It's already hard enough trying to understand Marina. I don't need more people to try and figure out. I don't want to give the wrong impression to someone who I just met.

The dining chamber is a vast, open chamber with vaulted ceilings. Round ajar windows relieve the cafeteria of all scents and heat coming from the kitchen. One hundred tables that hold a hundred soldiers. Each table spans for what feels like miles. Chatter is constantly filling the empty spaces between their festered conversations.

The birds eat seeds and gigantic worms sliced in to cubic pieces. Marina devours any meat and cheese she can find. My vegan diet is accommodated as best as possible with soggy fruits and lukewarm synthetic eggs and potatoes. There is no real dairy in the eggs. As far I'm concerned, they haven't gotten me too sick so I keep eating them. Marina stares at my food in disgust and I laugh. I emote as best as I can to show that the food is bad but edible. I doubt Marina knows Flounce sign language. She shakes her head startled. *Never* is what she replies, or so I assume.

The ugly split-haired warlock bumps Marina's shoulder forcing her to cough out her food. He sneers something in Epsilon. She jumps up to face him slinging insults back. They have some sort of beef going on. Ander and Epsilon share the same language because they used to be a unified nation thousands of years ago. They had a partial break up over land feuds that resulted in a vicious war. When too many innocent people died, both groups ironically decided peace was the best course of action. And since the vampires and dark warlocks threw the first stone, they self exiled themselves to the planet of Ander which already had vampires ruled over by Vakander. They were welcomed probably just as much as I was because vampire tensions between the Vakander Vampires and Old Epsilon Vampires soured. For a thousand years, they have remained stable through Vakander and dark warlocks keeping the peace. Even after Vakander fucked up and fucked the whole universe. Then, he turned his back on Kairos. The vampires remained loyal to Vakander. Thank you royal history lessons.

Fuck, a Lingua Vile would be so nice right now so I could join in on cussing him out.

Her voice gets louder and everyone in the dining room turns. The Warlock and Marina bicker until two birds separate them. The Warlock backs away from Marina laughing manically.

The moment the Warlock has food in his hand, Marina whispers an incantation. It seems like nothing happens until the Warlock spits out his food. He points at Marina and screams. He bites his thumb at Marina. She whispers again and the food smacks him in the face.

The purple haired, dark skinned werewolf twins, Celestia and Emory, sit at our table across from us. They've already had Lingua Viles administered on their home planet of Lykos. They are the only ones that can help Marina and I speak to each other properly.

Marina says something.

"She says that she wants to kill him." Celestia translates for me.

"I figured," I tell Celestia, "He's a pain in the ass."

"A pain in the ass that will be training with us." Emory adds.

Marina scoffs and tells them something.

Celestia stops eating, "A Templite is in the castle?"

Marina nods and continues.

"Why didn't Vesta tell us about him?" Emory asks.

Marina shrugs.

"She said that a Templite arrived not too long ago and that she saw him with Vesta on the way to the showers before breakfast." Celestia explains to me.

"Why would a Templite be in the castle? I thought they were the bad guys."

"I did too," Celestia sighs, "I'm not worried. Emory and I have been dying to taste Templite blood."

Celestia loses focus. Jupiter, Jenny, and Alejandra sit two tables down.

Jupiter throws glances at Celestia and waves.

"She knows your blind, right?" Emory sneers.

"I heard her, so I sent Vibrations out to see her," Celestia adds. From the little time I spent with Celestia, Vibrations are sonic waves she emits in to the world, like echolocation, in order for her to navigate it a little better.

"Then, wave back." Emory says.

Celestia waves awkwardly. Jupiter sits down and doesn't look back.

"She wants you to chase her." I add.

Marina says something.

"She is very pretty." Celestia responds, "But I don't know what to say or talk about."

"We're all adults," Emory pokes her, "We don't just need to talk, you know. I don't use Tommy for talking. His mouth works for other things."

"It doesn't feel right to just use someone for sex either." Celestia sighs, "One day. I'll shoot my shot."

"Have you asked Vesta about our Lingua Viles?" I change the subject.

"Yes," Celestia groans, "She said to wait again. During training, they will administer a vile to every trainee. It's ridiculous. She has her reasons for everything. Everything is a lesson for us to learn on our own. Vesta seems more on edge than usual."

"It's probably the Templite's fault." Emory adds.

"No," Celestia shakes her head, "Her and Cassie have both been acting suspicious lately. Their heart rates are off. Besides the Flounce invasion, there is something going on they aren't telling us about yet."

Marina is about to say something when the twin birds show up. Adrian and Heather fly through the breakfast room singing, dancing, and shooting arrows. They do everything in their power for attention.

"Not these fuckers." Emory rolls his eyes, "They always get feathers in my kibble."

"Yeah," Celestia gets up with her food and walks out of the dining room, "I've had enough fun for today, I'm taking my food to go."

She extends her walking cane and leaves.

WE ZIP through the dining room doing our performance. Our feathers fly all over. Some feathers aimed at pre-placed targets on the walls and others can't find direction. I force myself to try and control them. Adrian shoots four arrows as a signal to enter into our third act. The four arrows release four stages hovering in the air. We fly around the stages full of fire hoops, water spouts, and spinning landscapes.

After a few minutes, our feathers are aimed at the final targets left on the stages. They whistle striking the targets. Adrian and I fling our arrows in the shape of a War Bird onto the ceiling. The crowd cheers and applauds our show. A few birds cry. They love to see us honoring the bravest sacrifice a bird soldier can make by sacrificing their lives for their community. A last resort attempt at protecting the planet, the honorable War Bird.

The first time I ever saw a War Bird high in the sky – a bunch of bird bodies fused together to create an aerial strike – was the day Gamma-2 attacked Barretta. Three War Birds hovered in the air taking out the last of the Gamma-2 armies. Our parents were soldiers in the war. Both willingly ready to give up their lives for us. That was the last day I saw our parents.

Adrian shouted at the sky cursing our parents as Gamma-2

soldiers fled for the mountains behind the castle. To this day, there is a forest we are not allowed to enter because lingering Gamma-2 soldiers are heard to be living there. They live in underground catacombs and caves. Every once and awhile you see a fire come up from the mountains and know it's them.

Endless tears streamed down everyone's faces. But mother always said to smile. Smile on the bad days. Smile on the good days. Never let them see how they break you. Never let them prove that their actions negatively affected you. The night we lost our parents, I patted Adrian on the back and whispered to him, "We're going to be fine, Adrian. Mother and father's souls will always be with us and they will always protect us. Smile. One day, we will have our chance at revenge."

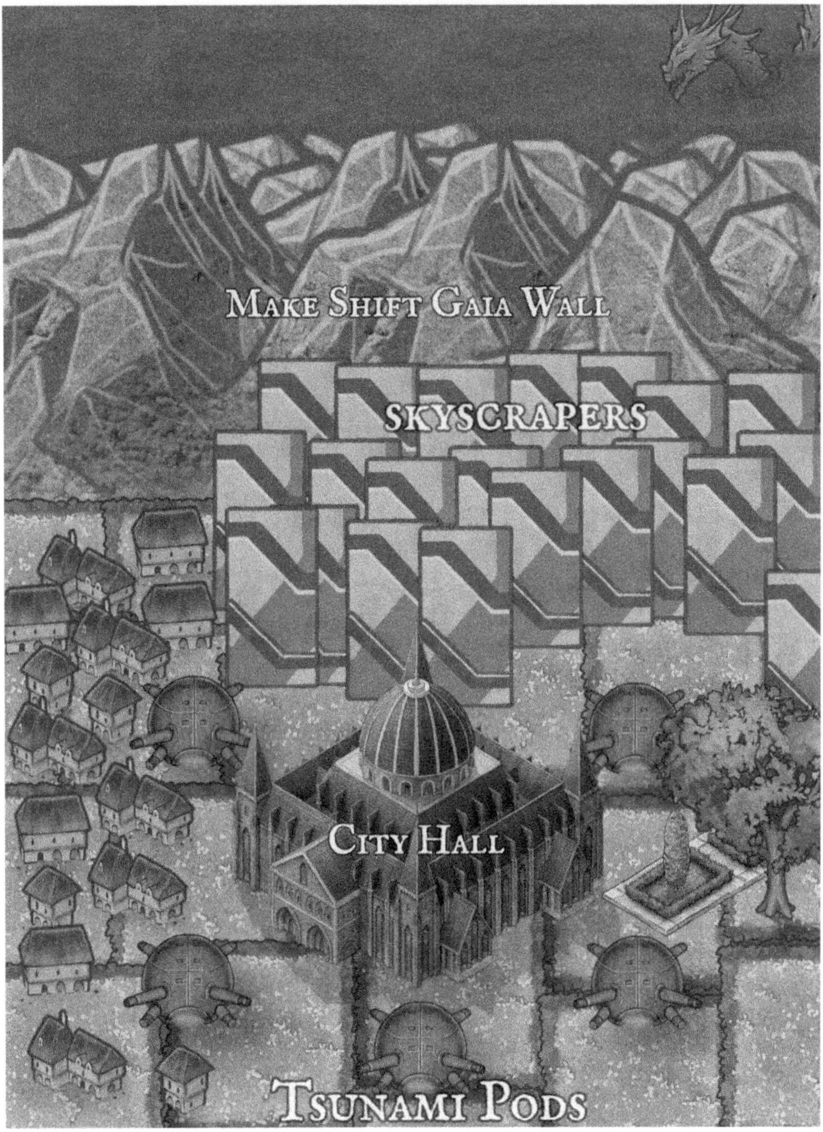

Make Shift Gaia Wall
Skyscrapers
City Hall
Tsunami Pods

ALEJANDRA AND JUPITER,

Vesta wants me to record an account of what happened on Venus. She says it is important to keep accurate historical records in case Venus ever becomes fully habitable again. Our records can help override the Templite propaganda that filters out our voices. She says people must learn from their elders. I never thought I would make it this far. When you're in the middle of an invasion, all you can think about is surviving. When you've been burned alive and left for dead, you don't expect to come back. When the scientist pokes and prods at you with her experimental hands, you picture a future where misery is not your everyday, but you never assume that you will survive.

I miss my home. I miss my books. I miss my family.

———

Mom used to make tamales on the seventh day of every month because she said it was lucky. I don't think there was any Melivian lore behind that. I think she just made them for me. I love the tamales de res, tamales verdes, tamales de rajas, and tamales de freza (without the weird raisins). She would come over on the seventh of every month to drop them off to our apartment. We lived in that three-bedroom apartment in a high rise in the middle of the city. My mom and I would take the tamales out on to the balcony, eat them, and talk about everything. We had a crude sense of humor that Alejandra could never get out of her. After all, Alejandra gravitated more towards dad and was a papi's girl. I had my tamales and these conversations with my mom. They meant the world to me.

———

I miss Gaia City. The skyscrapers. The ocean that cradled the perimeter of the city sending salt mists over the edge. Our city held one billion citizens. The children of Nu, water elementals, who liked to cause mayhem by splashing entire waves against buildings whenever they were feeling bored. The smoky smell of Fuegos, fire born, playing fiery hacky-sack filled the carless streets. Me and my Gaia abilities and Alejandra with her nieve powers.

The forced proximity of everything cancelled out the need for cars. Entire Venus cities live under water now. Sea creatures that were found inside of melted icebergs were reanimated and reintroduced in to the wild, uninhabitable parts of our world. Science and technology created humanities greatest feats. And the misuse of it became our downfall. Our families and us three died in wild fires that ravaged our city. Wild fires brought about by technology's mass deterioration of our ecosystem. Our bodies were charred close to ash. Preserved by Raven.

The Elementals were a positive side effect of deceased human reanimation that resulted in the Hybrid Robots - half-human and half-robots that never aged once they were created - and Rogue Robots – bots controlled by major corporations and malicious government entities. Our creator, Raven, formulated us, Hybrid and Rogue Robots, in to a perfect image to benefit human kind. But it was humans who corrupted that image.

I'm still traumatized by everything we went through in the revival process. Luckily, she created us with minimal need for maintenance and upkeep.

Rogue Robots and fascist groups took over all major cities. Regular people were cut off from the internet as a whole. Everything that connected the world through communication was destroyed. Only the New World Order, the singular government made up of all combined governments across the globe, was allowed to have access to the global networks. The subjugation of the human race caused many Hybrid Robots, like ourselves and our families, to flee all over the world to various safe havens. These havens gave us peace for a few years and allowed us to live normal lives until they were raided and we'd find new ones. All of us always lived a life on the run. It didn't help that when ocean levels started rising, they pushed people inland and closer together. Oceans devoured the little land people had to run to that wasn't controlled by the New World Order. Hundreds of years ago, our people flocked to Gaia, our circular city, helping regular humans and other uncorrupted robots live freely without being subjugated to slavery or death.

Hackers worked day and night to prevent the Rogue Robots and Hybrids Robots from finding us on our little self-sufficient island of Gaia. On their maps, our home looked like a sunken city in the ocean. A completely decimated wasteland with no future advancements in sight. Drones flew in the air every hour of the day masking our home from New World Order military planes. Venus as a planet no longer existed a long time ago.

Gaia was our final safe haven. Our last hidden city of this destroyed world.

And we were safe... until Kairos attacked.

———

Four Primary Elementals Created By Raven And Their Jobs In Our City:

(Other types of powers created through torture. The four primary elementals were integral to the functionality of the city and all protections against enemy forces.)

Gaia – Ground (City named after this element. All that involves the grounding elements in the universe).

Nu – Water (They can move water away from walls and drain any stray waves out of the city. They use water turbines to give power to the city.)

Fuego – Fire (Cooks, soldiers, and secondary Power Sources.)

Nieve – Ice (Soldiers, creating a wall of ice blocking tsunamis from hitting the main stone walls.)

(From what we learned from traveling outside of Venus is that Elementals are a natural occurrence in most societies besides Venus. Which begs the question: did Raven know that our society had not evolved to have those types of powers? And did she force evolution's hand by creating us?)

———

Most Gaia Elementals like me worked in reinforcing walls around the city eroded by waves and molded to withstand a tsunami. We worked in shifts of ten each staggering rotations. Tsunamis came randomly and our alert systems always gave us enough time to construct various levels of walls to withstand a blow to the whole city. Nieve borns were tasked with freezing a wall of water before it hits our walls of stone.

Since the founding of our city, we have stopped ninety-six tsunamis from collapsing the city. There were ten close calls where the waves were too large and flooded the first three stories of each building. Evacuations procedures included how residents in the first three stories would move upward in case of flooding. An emergency evacuation system in each building would be set to trigger on separate floors. The system worked off sensors, cameras, and artificial intelligence. Ideally, it was created to help in any scenario for any evacuation. In a tsunami's case, the alarms were meant to warn the next four floors that three stories below had been completely flooded. Prompting them to start grabbing their necessary belongings and moving upwards.

Tsunami Pods, scattered at every major intersection, would activate. All artificial intelligence in the city was powered by the remaining friendly A.I. software left on Venus, Wvyern. Wvyern's programming used the Tsunami Pods to scoop up registered citizens and civilians drowned by any stray currents.

———

"Your turn for wall duty." Alejandra woke me up in the middle of the night.

"Ugh, can you pull a double shift?" I told her still hungover from earlier tonight. Jupiter and I hosted a party for both of our families to celebrate my aunt's engagement.

"Next time don't drink so much before work."

A thunderous crack erupted from dam walls surrounding the city. Alejandra and I ran to the window and saw a missile had taken out the north wall of the damn. Water flowed in rapidly activating Tsunami pods across the city and setting them to work.

"Have the Rogue Robots found us?" I asked Alejandra as we rushed to the closet and jumped in to our battle wet-suits. These suits were designed primarily for underwater skirmishes but worked moderately well above ground as well. A waterproof watch imbedded in the wet suit held a hologram calling system that could be used to contact different soldiers.

A Templite Ship glimmered slightly camouflaged by the night sky. Templites on Pegasi swooped down above rescue pods and started blasting holes in them.

Jupiter crashed in to our room yelling, "Let's fucking get going."

Jupiter shot a Gravitational Ring at the window to break it. Her Gravitational Rings were gold and spun so fast they looked like neon vinyl records. They redistributed gravity and could be directed at beings and objects to slice through them. She grabbed us and sent a

Gravitational Ring underneath all of us. It spun and sent us flying towards the Pegasi. Alejandra used her Nieve powers to blast icicle tridents at the Tsunami Pod attackers.

"Get me close to the wall so I can repair it." I commanded Jupiter.

Alejandra hopped off the Gravitational Ring and ice skated on sky bridges she created from the water. Pulses opened all around her. She reflexively sent waves of solid ice on top of the Templites. They wailed as they were swallowed by the unrelenting solid waves. The Tsunami Pods went to pick up the Templites out of the water, but their navigation systems blurted out, "Unauthorized Rescue. Unknown Individual."

Jupiter and I left Alejandra behind. She angled me towards the wall and I strained to patch the enormous hole. The rubble rose blackened and mismatched. I reshaped it and melded the remaining useable fragments.

The was was newly sealed. Water stopped flowing through the walls, but the damage was already done. All Tsunami Pods were activated. The city lay under six stories of water. Nu Elementals activated drainage systems in the remaining walls pushing the water back to sea.

Another missile appeared in the air above us pointed at the eastern wall. Jupiter launched herself at the missile. Her rings spun around the projectile until it was facing the Ship. She released it. The explosive struck the haul of the Ship. Fiery Pegasi and Templites rained from the sky. Not enough to send the Ship crashing in to the sea. Just enough to take a chunk of their soldiers out.

Two missiles, aimed at the east and west walls, appeared. Jupiter immediately sent the missiles back at the Ship. The entire Ship was on fire.

The invasion temporarily stopped.

———

In the break from fighting, Alejandra killed the remaining Pegasi and Templites. Jupiter collected Alejandra and flew us to the roof of the city hall building. The Tsunami Pods collected the rest of the civilians from the surrounding buildings.

Darius, a dark skinned Fuego and overseer of the city, met us on the stone roof of the City Hall building.

Jupiter landed beside him exhausted. She collapsed on the ground heaving.

"That's a Templite Ship." Darius started, "We have to evacuate to the sea."

"Split the Elementals," Alejandra suggested, "Take half of them with you in the Tsunami Pods and the rest leave to defend the city."

"What about all of you?" He grabbed Alejandra's hand and stared at her longingly.

"I'll... We'll be fine. Go. Save all of them."

"Have you figured out what they're after?" Jupiter asked through heavy breaths.

"My best guess is we had a Time Absorber among us at some point and they revealed our location." He shook his head. "But to have a Templite army after us is off."

"What could they be looking for?" I asked.

"No guesses here." Darius grabbed Alejandra by the waist and pulled her in for a kiss. Once they stopped, he laughed, "If we're going to die, I want you to know I love you."

"I love you too." Alejandra replied to him.

Darius started running downstairs, "I'll see you in the next life."

"Or in this one hopefully." Alejandra's eyes drooped as he left.

The Tsunami Pods continued evacuating the city. Prehistoric sea creatures collided with Pods while others remained impaled on skyscrapers. The Pods entered buildings and scooped people from their homes. People brought supplies to last the Pods a week's worth of food. As the Pods reached capacity, they grew legs and started crawling over the walls, dead sea creatures, and jumped in to the sea. One by one, the Pods slowly combined in to a larger undersea vessel.

Nu Elementals returned the sea over the wall draining the streets. Shells, coral, and sea weeds filled the streets.

Thirty thousand Fuego, Nu, Nieve, and Gaia Elementals filled the city streets ready to push back the next wave of attacks.

A red, dark figure floated down from the sky at the end of the empty street. He floated in front of the building we're on like an impeding tsunami. Power radiating off of him. His fingers flicked. Corpses of Templites rose again. Their eyes blaring red. Undead bodies, full of puncture wounds Alejandra inflicted, contorting in a dance.

Fires turned corpses to ashes. Ice tridents and bridges took out hordes of the dead. Nu soldiers used the moisture from the shells and seaweed to drown their attackers. Spherical, stone enclosures crushed bodies.

"He's bringing them back." Jupiter stared baffled.

"He's headed this way." Alejandra offered up, "What the fuck does he want with us?"

"You did kill a lot of his soldiers." I said.

"But for him to head our way. There are Elementals all around him taking out the corpses and he's ignoring them." Alejandra pointed out.

She was right. Elementals battled reanimated corpses all over the city. Every time the dead were taken out, they would spring back up good as new.

"We need to get out of here." Alejandra warned, "I don't want to leave the other Elementals but there's a reason he's coming this way, and I don't want to find out why. And we can't fight him."

"We need a plan." Jupiter stood spinning a Gravitational Ring underneath us. We floated in the air. "Let's pull him away from the Tsunami Pods for now."

A Pulse opened behind us with the red figure coming out of it.

Jupiter sliced the man in half with a Gravitational Ring. We flew towards the Northern Wall.

"He's healing." Alejandra's panicked voice warned us, "Fly faster."

Jupiter pushed her rings to work at full speed. Pulses opened up, down, left, and right. Corpses fell from the sky and bounced off the Gravitational Rings. A few hands made it through and clawed at our flesh. Nails ripped off and were left in our skin. A red electricity bolt struck Jupiter. Fire and pain seized every atom in our bodies. Jupiter screamed sputtering her Gravitational Rings with all her might. Her flimsy maneuvering crashed us in to the top story of a sky scrapper. Our bodies broke the glass and struck the floor. All the air left my lungs. Glass shards imbedded in my skin beside the reanimated Templite nails.

All of us gasped for air.

Debris fogged the air. No red being remained in sight. I was the first to crawl towards the window. As the dust settled, a modern styled apartment revealed itself around us. I stared at the city searching for the red figure.

A missile rushed past our building and struck the Northern Wall. All the Tsunami Pods were gone. Elementals ran from their current fights as tidal waves consumed the city.

"No!" I screamed.

Nieve and Gaia Elementals use their ice and stone bridges to evacuate as many Fuego Elementals as possible from the water. Nu Elementals redirect the tidal waves to the armies of reanimated Templites. Whirlpools form all around the city drowning the corpses that can't seem to stay down.

Another missile struck the Eastern Wall. More waves rushed in to the city sweeping away the Nu Elementals with their backs to the Eastern Wall. A few large bubbles with air in them were created by the Nu elementals. The corpses in the water swam in to multiple bubbles. The dead bit in to and clawed at the Nu beings until their bubbles were overridden with Templites and blood.

A large purple tendril like an octopus arm stabbed Venus and started pumping a purple liquid in to the planet.

"What is that?" Alejandra asked with a bloody lip and closed, bruised eye.

The sounds of glass shattering filled the air. We leaned over the *edge of the window. Templite corpses scaled the building we were in. Alejandra used her Nieve powers to throw ice tridents at the dead. I ran over to an unconscious Jupiter and shook her violently. She groaned, "Everything fucking hurts."*

"We have to move. The corpses are coming for us." I informed her.

"Can't they give us a break?" Jupiter groaned.

"Go," Alejandra started running towards us. A corpse leapt on to her. Their fists pummeled her on to the floor. Jupiter sliced the dead in four with two Gravitational Rings. The two rings also knocked out a group of corpses that were climbing over the window.

I grabbed Alejandra off the floor and pushed her through the apartment. Jupiter held them back as we rushed past the living room and out the front door. We ran down the hallway only to find it blocked. Corpses burst from the other apartments obscuring our path to the elevators.

We scurried back bumping in to Jupiter and pushing her to the emergency stairwell on the opposite end. Jupiter pushed the door open and we all filed in.

We took the steps two at a time.

Sirens went off. The beige stairwell lights turned dark red.

"The emergency stairwell has been opened. Stand by for emergency exit instructions."

The automated speakers blasted over and over.

"Scanning building for emergencies. Stand by."

Our feet frantically stumbled down four flights of stairs.

Corpses wailed behind us throwing themselves haphazardly down various flights. An unorganized cluster fuck of attacks. The chaos was the only thing keeping them from getting to us immediately.

"Reanimated corpses breached the building. All uninfected floors will be closed off for your protection."

Jupiter flung an emergency exit open and yanked us onto the sixteenth floor. We all pressed our body weights against the door waiting for the inevitable impact. On cue, screeching and vigorous pounding erupted against the opposite side of the emergency exit. A metal door started closing on the other side of the exit. The corpses struggled to try to push it back open. Jupiter released a Gravitational Ring through the door slicing the dead in half. Bodies bunched up and blocked the exit. A crunching sound pulverized the corpses.

The metal barrier thudded. Screeches ceased to exist.

We all collapsed on the floor.

"What now?" Jupiter heaved, "he can just Pulse in here. Nowhere is safe. We have to keep moving but where?"

My work watch chimed. A hologram of Darius popped up, "Ohh thank the universes you three are alive."

"We need out of this building." Alejandra told him.

"Did the Templites follow the Tsunami Pods?"

"Luckily, they were too focused on you three to even throw a sideways glance at us. We initiated a distress beacon to Barretta. They are currently on their way to save us but you have limited time. Once they get here, they're taking a risk to save us all, so they're not waiting. You have about two hours until they're here."

All of our watches synced up.

The timer started ticking: **01:59:59**.

"There's one problem, we're locked in. The buildings emergency systems worked a little too well." I said mournfully.

"Can you get to the stairwell? I can try to override it."

"It's blocked with corpses."

"Give me a second to see the lay out of the building."

There was a long pause.

"None of you are going to like this."

"What?"

"There is a main trash chute on that floor that drops down to the basement's housekeeper quarters. You take one stairwell down and the maintenance service tunnels for the underground subways are right there."

"But..." Alejandra asked.

"Corpses are waiting outside the housekeeper quarters."

"That's okay, I can work Gaia the closer we are to the ground level and hit them with some concrete." I explained to Darius.

"And I can get us down the trash chute with my Gravitational Rings." Jupiter said.

"You can't all go together. There's only room for two of you max." Darius knew I hated enclosed spaces.

Alejandra looked to Jupiter before they turned to me. Jupiter cleared her throat.

"So, I'll lower Jenny and Alejandra first, then take myself down."

CHAPTER 13

THEA:

WELCOME TO THE FOURTH DIMENSION

DARKNESS.

Endless nothing.

I roam the darkness for what feels like centuries. Red, green, and white Thread strands float aimlessly while others are held taut. All concept of time is lost. For the first time in my life, the air is odorless. I'm a singular flame in a sea of endless Threads.

Nothing.

Nothing for miles but Threads.

Nothing here or there.

I'm nothing.

Nothing in my aching soul left to project on to this miserable landscape. Tears are trapped. How does one cry in soul form?

I'm a purple flame in a dark room.

A heavy breath practically blows me out. I turn around and find a giant outline of a creature. A triangular face with a pincher-like jaw turns its green and red Threads to observe me. His eyes completely filled with white strands. It prowls around me on all fours sniffing my flame. Growls communicate to another creature in the darkness. Normally, fear would course through my whole body. Luckily, I don't have one of those. I have plenty of nothing though. If they were to snuff me out, it would be the last tendril of misery they could take. A peaceful act of mercy.

The two creatures howl in to the bleak nothingness.

"You found her." A femme presenting voice announces.

Her voice crackles like a warm fire in the middle of summer.

A tall curvy woman made of Threads reveals herself. She says, "I have some revenge I want to inflict upon others myself. Let me help you find your way home."

———

Stationery Thread Beasts play around a moat. A multi-tiered castle made of red and green Threads rises in to the darkness. A vast sky made up of tiny strands imitates the opposite colors of a sunrise. Winged beasts fly over the castle in a constant loop. Thread imitation iron gates open up and swallow us.

"Welcome to Paradise." The mystery woman pets the Thread Beasts at the gates to calm them as I pass, "I am the queen of Purgatory, Beelzebub. We are in one realm of the invisible Fourth Dimension."

"What happened to you to end up here?"

"Kairos came for me personally. All of our stories start sounding very similar when we have all gone through the same experience."

Beelzebub rotates her hand bringing the castle towards us without us moving closer to it.

"Were you someone important?"

"We were all important. That's why Kairos felt the need to take us out. Our voices are made of gold. Our fury and fight forced their need to vanquish us."

"Why'd you come for me?"

"I already told you. I lost my kingdom once too. I have an affinity for lost beings... and revenge."

———

Inside the gothic castle, Thread Souls stroll the halls as if they're still living. The Thread Souls take different red and green forms. Dragons, bi-pedal reptiles, humanoids, and demonic entities with horns and long sharp finger nails.

"How do I get a form like you or them?"

Beelzebub stops at the foot of two spiral staircases. Her fingers grab a Thread from the staircase. "Reality is a series of Threads sewed together to make a beautiful tapestry. Our existences and meeting intertwined with our deaths," She sewed two Threads together while taking two more and weaving them in between. Her hands move in circular motions as she speaks forming legs, arms, brains, and eyes for a creature, "As much as we hate Kairos, his decisions have caused this event in this realm. Our meeting could only happen because of him. A meeting he has no knowledge of. An outcome he did not expect." She holds a baby Thread Beast out and it licks my flames. It burps a plume of smoke and wags its tail. "I extended a hand to bring you here. To help your cause. We are only as strong as our deepest desire. The Fourth Dimension is very similar. It is an endless opportunity to reach all planes of existence. We can reach all our wants and needs here. While the physical world limits us in a body, here you need only have the desire to create, heal, and push the limits of the Threads and it will respond. All you have to do is manipulate the confines you were boxed in to with your physical form to gain a form like mine."

CHAPTER 14
JENNY:
DIARY ENTRY

THE TRASH CHUTE *wasn't big enough for two of us.*

It was barely big enough for one of us.

"Change of plans. One of you two has to go down first." Jupiter ordered.

I started to hyperventilate. I was never good in small spaces, and it became worse after Raven and her henchmen experimented on me for years. I wasn't supposed to feel anything. I was dead. But I was brought back to life and the pain of being poked and prodded never seemed to cease. Days dragged on to weeks which dragged on to months. The same happened to Alejandra and Jupiter but I was the weak one. I was the one who had ended up fucked up in the head.

Alejandra stared at me and grabbed my hand, "I'll go first. Then you can go, and Jupiter will be right above you."

I nodded breathing in and out.

Needles prodded me.

Raven cut me open and placed large pieces of cement and rock in to my arms. She did it until I was numb. Until I no longer cried, and I was used to the pain. Eyes blood shot and tears dried.

"Jenny, I don't want to rush you." Jupiter massaged my back, "But that maniac is on our tail, and we have to keep moving to lose him."

I shook my head and took a breath, "I got this."

Jupiter placed a spinning disc on the floor. Alejandra stepped on top of it and crouched in order to fit in to the tight opening. Once inside, she stood at full length with her hands on her sides. Within a few minutes, she touched the ground safely.

The disc returned. I stepped on it and repeated the crouching motion.

"You'll be okay, I promise" Jupiter reassured. The darkness slowly devoured me whole.

The disc took forever to reach the bottom. The hologram lights up with Darius on the screen.

"Hurry up. A vent on a floor below you has been breached."

Corpse hands punched through the vent. I narrowly missed its nails. Jupiter sped the disc down but it still was not fast enough. More hands punctured the trash chute scratching at my neck, eyes, arms, and legs. I started to scream. My breaths firing in and out of my lungs before they could be processed. A trash chute door opened up and a pile of corpses attacked me. My screams reached their pinnacle. Blood clouded my eyes. Corpses bit in to my neck. They tore flesh. And scratched at my body.

Excruciating pain.

It felt like I was a paper being shredded in to a million pieces.

I finally reached the ground floor and we all collapsed on to the ground.

I reach for the sliver of powers I had left. Alejandra shoved the corpses off stabbing them with ice tridents. I sent a concrete slab up the trash chute crushing everything inside. When the slab returned, bloodied limbs, decapitated heads, and hands still holding chunks of my flesh rolled out of the chute. Jupiter came down the chute slicing the next wave of corpses.

Alejandra burst a water pipe and blocked the exit with an ice block.

I was fading in and out of consciousness.

Darius popped up again. But he was muffled. Or am I not hearing right?

"There's enough water pipes to fight our way..."

"I'll put her on a ring and float her o..."

"She needs severe medical..."

"...help you once... on the underground vessel."

Screeches rung in my ears. Water pipes burst and, finally, silence.

CHAPTER 15
THEA:

———

CELESTIA, *Emory, Jimmy, and I run through the mountains under
five of thirteen visible Lykos Moons. Their various yellow, grey, and
blue colors light up the dark forest. We explore caves and venture as
far as we can before we are too scared to continue. We settle in an open
meadow with purple grass and bioluminescent flowers. The meadow
sits perched on the side of the mountain. A perfect place to watch the
stars fly past. And our kingdom lit up by lanterns and life.*

A relaxing breeze brushes my fur and traps me in this moment.

*"You have to let these memories go. They bind you
here."*

Beelzebub stands next to my purple flames in the grass.

"Although, Lykos was always my favorite planet to visit."

————

I'm dressed in a black ball gown. Atop my head elegantly sits an ivory white crown bejeweled with amethyst gems. Lace arm sleeves reach past my elbows. The throne room is triangular with the main throne at the peak. High vaulted ceilings with archers, wolves in their hybrid form, perched above to protect me from any assassination attempts.

"As Thea's father, and in coordination with the royal decree, I'm glad to announce the next heir on, this, their sixteenth birthday. I hereby announce Thea as the five hundredth queen of Lykos. Jimmy has conceded his throne to Thea and her future children."

Citizens all around cheer. The kingdom bows at my feet. Celestia and Emory toss faces at me saying, "Don't let this go to your head."

A funny looking middle-aged man with a balding head stares at me like I'm the most beautiful girl in the world.

"You were very beautiful." Beelzebub adds.

————

"You are very beautiful." Cassius massages my face as we both lean in *for a kiss. His warm lips reach mine. We don't break apart until he is unraveling my black gown. He kisses my neck and works his way down my chest. He uses his teal Threads to string me up...*

————

Cassius and I lie naked cuddling each other. The fire place sears my back. I want to remain here in his arms forever. I'm not leaving this place...

———

"Gamma-2 attacked Barretta." My father announces, "They have asked for our fiercest representatives to defend the planet while they regroup their armies."

"How long will they be gone for?" I ask.

"Until they can rebuild their armies. Which can be years, possibly decades, or centuries."

———

"Are you going to Barretta?" I ask Cassius.

Cassius nods.

"We are too," Celestia adds, "We will take care of him for you."

"Can I come visit you?" I eagerly plead.

"Yes. But you have a kingdom to run here. Take care of your people first."

———

Our launch pad lies at the edge of lake behind the castle surrounded by a forest. The Ship taking Cassius, Emory, and Celestia leaves to Barretta. Jimmy and I stay behind crying.

"They'll be back." Jimmy holds my hand reassuring me.

CHAPTER 16

CELESTIA:

SCALING THE BARRETTA CASTLE- DAY 2

EMORY, Brody and I climb the castle spires to see five of the thirteen Lykos moons tonight. They are usually hidden by the constant blanket of Barretta clouds and nightly rainstorms. Tonight is the clearest it has been in awhile. This has been the driest week on Barretta since coming here all those years ago.

The night air cools our overheating bodies in our secondary hybrid forms. We jump from protruding jagged stone to jagged stone, meant for soldier birds to guard the perimeter of the castle, until we are all perched diagonally on the roof of the largest turret. I've memo-rized the amount of space needed to climb the castle. When we first moved here, I used our Mind Link to see out of Emory's eyes and observe the landscape. Anything I couldn't observe with the Mind Link I would use my Vibrations to send out an echolocation. The echolocation would transmit back perfect dimensions of my perime-ter. The migraines are the only problem with the Vibrations. I have what the Lycan Wolves like to call keratoconus. A frustrating condi-tion where my dome-shaped corneas over time turn cone-shaped. My field of vision is an inch in front of my eye. Everything else in the world looks like blurred phantoms moving around. It's terrifying actually especially in the dark. Normal colors are distorted. Thick glasses didn't work so they moved on to the next best thing. They tried to create hard plastic contacts that could go over my eyes and they worked in my normal form. They weren't perfect, of course. They hurt my eyes if I kept them in too long or if my eyes were dry. Mucus would develop if my eyes were irritated. I had to put them in a solution to clean for six hours before bed each night. So, I was essentially blind for six hours each day. Ethereals forbid I had to see in the middle of the night because of an emergency. The problem arose when I would shift from my first form in to my secondary half-wolf and half-human form. Since I grew in my hybrid form, the contacts would break when I would transition from my first form to my secondary form. I tried three times with malleable contacts that the eyes doctors experimented on and it always led to broken glass in my eyes. When Thea and her mother found out what the eye doctors had been doing to me, they were fuming. They forced the doctors to no longer work on live subjects and gave them life-like wolf mannequins that could change from first form to secondary form to third form, full on raging wolf. I didn't stick around Lykos long enough to know if those doctors ever created a perfect tool for me to use. I just resigned myself to believing that hopefully they would figure their shit out for the next warrior wolf with my condition. That way they wouldn't be forced to quit. I would have been forced to quit too if it weren't for for my Vibrations.

We avoid leaving evidence by not clawing our way up the turret. Vesta hates it when we mess with the infrastructure of the castle. I hear Brody inch closer to Emory trying to seem slick. Emory humors him until Tommy flies through the air on his Nomad, Pudge, who in the form of a large bird. A Nomad is a fleshy creature with no eyes, no nose, and no mouth. It eats mush through its pores. They read the minds of the people around them, and when they find a compatible being, they take on the form of their most treasured animal or being companion. They are creatures made up of stardust, supernova explosions, and the cosmic garbage of the galaxy. All creatures start off as Nomads and eventually branch off in to different species as they take on different forms.

"I didn't want to miss anything." He lands in-between Brody and Emory. Tommy scoops up Emory and kisses him, "I missed my little pup."

Emory laughs. His body vibrates as if blushing from head to toe. Brody's heart rate rises in anger and jealously. I don't understand why Brody is so jealous. Emory just uses Tommy for the "brick" between his legs.

You shush. Emory Mind Links me, *If Brody wanted me, he would make a move.*

I think he was trying. Then, Tommy interrupted.

Male Opaques tended to be voyeurs until they found a mate they thought would be suitable in a monogamous relationship. Brody floats to sit by me. His angry heartbeat closer than before.

Are you mad? I ask Emory. *Or can I use the Mind Link to see through your eyes?*

Go ahead.

I focus my attention on guiding myself to his corneas. The image is not entirely clear. It is slightly blurry from having a forced filter over it. Areas are foggy and others are pixelated and incomplete. The five moons are different colors. Two are yellow, one is blue, one is pink, and the other is orange. The visible stars are illuminating the sky in oceans of beauty. I could send out Vibrations to see but I do not want to deal with a searing migraine tonight. I just want to enjoy their company and the soothing breeze.

The breeze reminds me of Thea. Of when we were younger and we galloped across the Lycan Forest. How she has been trapped on Exile while we just sit here waiting for someone to save her. If I had the tools to save her I would do so in a heartbeat.

I let go of the Mind Link and lay my head on Brody's shoulder. Tommy and Emory have forgotten we are here and kiss almost non-stop. I put my fuzzy hand in-between their faces to make them stop.

"I did not come up here just to listen to you two conceive a child." I inform them.

"We would make cute fiery furry babies." Tommy pulls out a bottle of alcohol from one of Pudge's traveling sacks and pops it open.

"A fire wielding werewolf?" Emory questions, "Who is going to calm it down if it has temper tantrums?"

"I can," Tommy smiles.

I cringe and take a sip out of the bottle. The burn sliding down my throat slightly distracts me from the erratic movements of the cuddle session. Brody takes a huge gulp and tries to take another one. I hear the liquid in the bottle and grab it from him whispering, "Drinking is for fun. If you're doing it to forget, it becomes a problem."

Brody yanks on the bottle but I rip Emory away from Tommy.

"Your turn little brother." I loop my arm around Emory keeping him at my side.

We all take turns until four bottles are gone. Drunk-flying-Brody challenges Tommy and Pudge to a race around the mountains and castle. I'm on team Brody. Emory is team Tommy. Emory narrates the action for me. We lose focus on the race when it extends itself past the fun.

"This dick twirling contest has gotten boring quick," I shake my head burping.

Emory and I laugh at the burp, and I do not know why. None of it makes sense. Nothing ever does. Does it?

Nothing matters so I should be like Emory. Having two boys fight over him and not caring how long it takes for them to squabble.

Fuck. Me. I want her. I do not know if it is the alcohol… or if I am just… I want her. Everything about her body.

Her beautiful, round, glowing dark face clouds my mind. Her bouncy hair floats in my daydreams. Night dreams? Whatever. The sacrifices I would make to have my hands clinging to the back of her neck like her own living necklace.

"Someone has a girl on the brain." Emory taunts. He yells to all of Barretta, "Celestia has Jupiter on the Brain!"

I shove his shoulder slightly.

"Ow," Emory fakes pain, "What was that for?"

"For being a dick."

"It's not my fault you don't act on what you want."

I wish I could be mad at him but he is not wrong. I just do not know what to say it. What to talk about with her. How to say anything other than fucking mush.

"Just tell her she is cute. That is what I did for Tommy. You are so blunt about everything else. You can easily go up to her and just say 'You are the sexiest person I've ever seen. Let me eat you out or whatever girls say.'"

"That sounds like possibly the worst advice I have ever heard."

"But it is advice." Emory starts singing a pop song the Royal Wolves would always play for us. "This is my song." He starts dancing to his own singing.

Emory is right. I cannot have something I want by wishing.

I want to share my life with her. Who is her? The idea or the woman. I do not know. I do not care. But I want to be buried every morning in her beautiful curls. My arms wrapped around her brown curvy waist. And when she wakes with night terrors, I can be there to nuzzle her neck to sleep.

I want to share my life with Jupiter.

That is freeing to share. Freeing and embarrassing.

"It is only embarrassing because you are afraid of rejection." Emory sings to me, "If I can get two boys to fall for me, you can get fifty woman to worship you."

"I just want one."

DRYAD CASTLE
ANCESTRAL FOREST

TRAINING ARENA
CRYSTAL PALACE

I'M FALLING AGAIN. The last time I fell like this, Salem was dropping me on to Barretta. My body tumbles through red, green, and black Threads of the universe. Every night since I arrived here my dreams have gotten worse.

———

I already did this before. I've been here before.

The Mothers of Artemis stand around the Ancestral Forest Crystal in a circle holding dripping multi-colored candles. The six women wear black lace dresses and black veils over their faces. Their prayers are cast upon me and the iridescent purple crystal. Blue and red radiating crystals surround the forest. The crystals intermingle with beautiful, ancient trees. Pink fireflies light up the purple crystal. Moon rays peek through dancing and rustling leaves.

I walk up to the crystal and place a pink hand on it. The voices of my ancestors speak to me.

Protect the innocent.
Carry on our legacy.

Dismantle evil.
We give you the power of all our lives.
We give you the power of our souls.
We give you the solution of the Guerreros and the
     Threads of the universe.
Our births.
Our deaths.
Our memories good and bad.
Our decisions that have led us here. All yours.
We grant you our strength. But, we cannot grant you
     the right to become an Ethereal.
Carry our Fairy Dust with you and vanquish all evil.
Love deeply.
And die a worthy death.

My hand slowly dissolves the purple crystal in to Fairy Dust. Neon glittery airborne particles dissolve against my skin and enter through my nostrils and mouth. My irises turn purple. Invisible Threads yank me in to the air. My green hair floating around gracefully. The fabric of the universe around me ripples in waves.

———

"The ancestors choose you to carry on the Fairy Dust?" My mother questions while pacing the room. Her arms and neck are covered in floral tattoos. Her pink pointy ears twitching nervously. Her long billowing white dress drags behind her. Her white hair braided in a crown around her head with two strands draped out the front and the rest falling out the back. We stand in her cluttered study. Open books filled with pictures of previous Ethereal Ascensions coat the brown weathered pages. Diagrams of Crystals hang from the walls labelled with their different components.

"Yes."

"And Artemis did not greet you?" She quickly asks.

"No."

She stares at all the books and starts flipping through every diary entry. She massages her forehead whispering to herself until she has forgotten I'm here.

"Can I go?"

My mother jumps startled by my words. She sighs, "None of this makes any sense. Artemis picks her Ethereal Successors by the voices of the Ancestors. If the Ancestors picked you, then why didn't she pick you? You are the obvious pick."

Ethereal Successors took on the mantle for Ethereals. Ethereals controlled different pipelines of magic. Artemis controlled all magic pertaining to Crystals, Threading of the universe, and Fairy Dust. The Successors were chosen as a back up in case an Ethereal died. The last Successor died a few days ago. Usually when a Successor dies, the Ethereal Artemis sends a beacon to their Ritual Crystal in order for a replacement to be sent to the forest. This time around nothing was sent. No signal came in. Ancestors sent nightmares calling us to the forest. They always sent nightmares when they needed us to urgently listen. In times of great need, they made sure their voices overcame any physical barriers. The nightmares were always their memories, our memories, or stolen Seer visions.

"Maybe I'm not ready yet mom."

"Kairos is getting closer to Flounce. You have to be ready or else I don't think we will stand a chance against him."

"Our armies are formidable. We can handle Kairos."

"Artemis has always found it in herself to protect us. Why has she left us?"

"Ethereals can be just as flawed as we are. We hold them to a higher standard than we should. Maybe she is tired of us."

"No. There is something wrong with her. Our powerful protector has left us."

She's probably just paranoid. That's what I will keep telling myself because her words unsettle me. Because when the all powerful beings that are meant to protect disappear, what then?

———

Our crystal castle was built upside down and suspended between three hundred story trees. The Trinity of gigantic trees were grown by the founders of Flounce. The day they landed on Flounce they committed to growing these saplings in to a safe haven for all beings throughout the galaxy. Parts of their roots twisted together and buried beneath the ground to grow as one solid unit. The branches were braided in to each other to create landings that housed villages and bridges that connected each community. As beings evolved and the universe gave birth to us fairies, we formed the Crystal Palace from Fairy Dust. Since then, other trees have sprouted around the Trinity reinforcing and expanding upon their endless roots.

Artemis placed the Ancestral Forest Crystal in the forest behind the Trinity. The Ancestors would pass on the Fairy Dust ability to one person they deemed the most powerful. It was usually an heir of the king or queen of our mainland section of Flounce. Ideally, it could go to anyone as long as they were deemed strong enough by the Ancestors. The power usually went to someone who didn't want it and didn't desire to use it for wrong doing. In this case me. The Fairy Dust wielder would then continue to teach their powers to their kingdom's citizens so they can all protect themselves. As a precaution, Artemis would pick the next Ethereal Successor to be the protector of Flounce and the fairies.

Artemis has lived for a very long time and is never expected to die. The point of the Ethereal Successor is, in the event she does die, someone will always be there to take on the mantle. Artemis will Siphon a fraction of her powers in to her heir at the time of their Ethereal Ascension. They will use that connection to Siphon the rest of her powers in the event of her death. Though, Ethereals can only pass on powers to their Successors before they pass and not after. At the Ethereal Successor's death, the Crystal would leave their bodies and be guided back to the woods by the Ancestors. The Ancestors built a protective film around the Ancestral Forest until the ritual was completed.

So, why was I worthy to the Ancestors but not Artemis? Is mom right?

My father and I walk through the various communities greeting our citizens and stopping to hear their requests. Clouds of Fairy Dust fill the air as children play catch the leaf ball, a big wad of leaves stuck together by powers, before it hits the ground. We are on the seventieth story admiring an aquamarine blue pool of water that rests between the Trinity.

I sit on the edge of a sky bridge swinging my feet over the ledge. A tense band of stress compresses the area between my neck and forehead.

"Something bothers you, my dear." My father, a tan skinned older man with white, long hair like mothers, says.

"Why is mom hyper focused on having Artemis bless me when we have armies at our disposal?"

"Armies are good to have. We need our armies to protect our people. But the Artemis Successor has always carried the burden of a target on their back. The Artemis Ethereal abilities grant you control over the Threads, crystals, and the Fairy Dust of the universe. Yet, it also grants you the ability to block certain users from using the powers for evil. Essentially, we want you as the Artemis Successor to block Kairos from any abilities that he or his soldiers could access with Artemis gone."

"But she isn't gone. She's missing."

"Her voice has been quiet for long time. The ancestors call us every night. They warn of an invasion. They warn of a loss."

"What kind of loss?"

"The language of the Ancestors is versatile. It can have many meanings. The nightmares have been of children crying, your mother alone, and fire. I assume they mean loss of life, power, citizens, and family."

"You and mother make it sound like Kairos will make a move on Flounce."

"I have no doubt that he will. We have a vacuum of power. We are not missing a king or queen but we are missing our protector. Flounce has heavily relied on Artemis and their Ethereal Successor to protect our people. Kairos will destroy everything he can."

"And you have just accepted our destruction?"

"No. Your mother hoped you would become the Successor which puts a lot of pressure on you for a decision you have no control over. Our armies are ready for him to show up at any point. There's not much else we can do. We've asked Epsilon for assistance."

Lykos and Venus are the closest planets but can't help. Venus is at war with itself. Robots versus humans and hybrids. And Lykos is still recovering from Kairos attacking.

"What have the witches said?"

"They are sending reinforcements."

"Will it be enough?"

"I hope so."

———

The reinforcements arrive a week later. Dad communicates with them as he knows their native tongue. I just smile at them when I'm told to. The witches sent a hundred soldiers. Their leather outfits fitted tightly around their bodies. Spell books, miniature crystals, and herbs take up their pockets. Red cloaks keep them visible around the Trinity at all times. Fifty work through the day and fifty work the graveyard shift. They roam around the Trinity scowling at their boredom. Every warlock, witch, and warwick sticks to their native tongue so I don't bother speaking to any of them. Or so, this was the case, until, a warwick with dark skin and long braids startled me on my favorite high-up perch overlooking the Trinity pool. Their muscles bulging from their tight uniform. I nearly jumped off the perch with the jolt that ran through my body.

"You are the heir to the Flounce throne." The warwick has a femme voice but masc appearance.

"You speak our language."

"All the soldiers here do. They recruited us based off our abilities and knowledge of your culture. My comrades just decide not to speak to you." Although they spoke Flock, they still had a slight accent. Not Epsilonese accent. It is familiar. I've heard it before in an old video during history.

"Not very friendly of them."

"They are speaking their comfort language. Do you blame them? War is not friendly to any of us."

"You consider us to be at war?"

"Peace does not require soldiers to prepare for an attack at any moment."

"I assumed war was the state of another planet attacking another."

"War is when aggressors decide they do not want anyone to live with ease. Peace is the post-war period where many have died to silence the aggressor before another war is imminent."

"Hm." I smile, "What made you decide to talk to me?"

"I would like to know who I will die for."

"You're prepared to die for us?"

"I'm prepared to protect *you* against Kairos." The way they says 'you' throws me off.

"I don't understand the value he sees with our planet."

"Understanding a mad man will drive you mad."

They smirk and swing their feet off the ledge. Their hand sticks out to reach mine, "I'm Salem."

"I'm Ashley."

"Enjoy this moment, Ashley. This may be my last."

———

"You will marry her." My mother demands.

"As much as I love trees, I don't want to marry one I just met."

"She is not a tree. She is a nymph. And we are doing this in hopes that Artemis sees your willingness to stand with people who do not necessarily look like you. Maybe she will finally pick you if she sees you have fallen in love with nature."

"So, your way of trying to get me an Ethereal's approval... is to fuck a tree?"

"Come on. Be fair. She is a pretty nymph. I picked her based off your dating chart you gave me."

"Yes. She's perfect. But perfect enough to get married tomorrow?"

"Your father was not my first choice."

"That's rude of you to say right in front of him."

My dad shrugged his shoulders, "She still ended up with me and she was my first choice. So, I don't care."

"She has a pretty name. Calliope." I add with a positive tone.

"That's a step in the right direction. Calliope is Queen of all classes of Nymphs. Her armies would protect all fairy regions on Flounce. They control all the forests, oceans, and deserts on Flounce that fairies have yet to explore or cannot explore due to their treacherous terrain."

"She is already Queen? Don't you need to get married to become royalty?"

"Not Nymphs. They pass power to the next healthy heir when the older royal starts to decline in health or notices that they are no longer making significant change to their communities."

"Why don't we do that?"

"Different cultures have different traditions. The fairies are tasked by our former Time Lord, Titus, to protect our Fairy Dust and crystals. The power we wield could be weaponized in the wrong hands. The ancestors help secure the correct heir."

"So if they didn't pick me..."

"We would have looked for another fairy to be the heir to the Flounce Throne and Fairy Dust."

"But I'm your daughter."

"Picking someone else as our heir was a secondary option. We would not have to resort to picking someone else. You are too powerful my babe. The Ancestors picked you at birth. We still had to perform the ritual to double check. The only thing missing now is your Ethereal Ascension. Your reign as Flounce Queen has been set in stone."

"What happens when I fall in love with someone else?"

"That is an option we have considered."

"And?"

"Calliope is married to one member from each Nymph class. She has six wives. You would be her seventh."

My eyes go wide. Seventh? Why so many?

I'm the seven pick for everything apparently. Seventh Queen of Flounce. Seventh wife. Seventh wielder of the Fairy Dust. And I was supposed to be the seventh Ethereal Successor.

My mother breaks the silence, "All beings can access different abilities through connections. There is a form of magic called Siphoning that allows the exchange of energy to power an individual. But there is a stronger form of magic that Kairos has tried to erase from existence. We call it Weaving. Weaving is the process of Threading strands of the universe among two or more beings in order to become more powerful. Barretta has used this power when creating their War Birds. When used haphazardly, it destroys all users involved and combines their powers in to a different form. Done correctly, Weaving can power all users. Calliope practices Weaving with all of her wives."

My mom's reason for me getting married becomes abundantly clear. There is always a reason for everything she does. Always scheming.

"This marriage isn't just about Artemis. You want me to learn Siphoning and Weaving."

"Siphoning is easy. Weaving is a beast that can erase you from existence if done incorrectly. We need you to learn how to properly do it. Kairos is a looming threat that you need to be ready for."

———

"Are you ready for this wedding?" Salem asks from the door way of my bedroom. Fairies spin lace around my body with their Fairy Dust until they complete a flowing, shimmering black dress. They place flowers in my green hair and braid two strands of my hair in to a flower crown.

"No. But I have to do it for my kingdom." I resent the idea of an arranged marriage. I always assumed I would be allowed to fall in love and find my queen as I grew up. Not this. Not like this.

The fairies leave the room by adding, one final touch, a glowing golden aura around me.

"Would you get married to protect your kingdom?" I ask Salem.

"I would." They sigh, "I've done many awful things to protect innocent people. If you knew, you'd try to kill me. I would leave home in order to protect a home that isn't mine anymore."

"Anymore?"

"Flounce was once home." They leave their explanation there. I don't prod. People who feel like sharing can. It's not fair to pry information from people who aren't ready to give it.

"I just hate I can't make decisions for myself."

"In War, the self is less important than the whole."

"But I want to live. I want to have a normal life."

"Out in the universe, there is a child that lost their family. A mother who lost their child. A grandfather who will never hear the voice of their grandchildren again. They wish to the Ethereals that they too can live normal lives. Sacrifices must be made to protect your people. Our duty as soldiers is to protect the innocent so they never have to wish they could live normal lives. You could not pick the circumstances in which you were born in to, but you have power. You have a power that others do not. And you can use that power to fuck off or you can use it to defend others. There will come a day when you will get to be happy. But right now, you have a privilege that you must do something with."

"How can you be sure?"

Salem grabs my hand and puts it to my chest, "Because you were meant to live a long and beautiful life."

Salem escorts me out my room and down a hallway of three-story high windows and vaulted ceilings. Stone columns make up the interior foundation of the crystal castle. We stop in front of oval stone doors carved with geometric designs. Salem and another warwick soldier open the doors to the throne room.

The throne room is filled with the six classes of Nypmhs: oceanids, naiads, nereids, oreads, alseid, and napaeae. A red luxurious carpet runs up to the alter parting the crowds in to two. Light filtering in through the five peach colored, stained-glass windows basks everyone in a orangey glow. My golden glow separates me from everyone else. The middle-stained glass window reaches to the heavens. On top of it, a round window with sunlight shining through points a spotlight on Calliope.

Calliope, a dryad, is dressed in a bright neon green dress made of moss. Her six wives stand adjacent to her all dressed in their various different classes. The oceanid is in a seashell dress, the naiad wears a moving stream mixed with lily pads and water plants, the nereid has voluminous waves frozen in time peaking past her ears, the oread sports rock like structures coating her plump body, the alseid has the body of a centaur with gold plated sun beams covering her private regions, and napaeae sports a dress made of tree roots.

Lilies fall from the ceiling as I start my walk down the aisle. People slowly bow row by row until I'm face to face with Calliope. Her wooden skin is beautiful. Her features round. She smiles at me and I smile back. My mother recites the opening introductions and opening rites.

Time passes quickly. I hardly have any time to think about where I am. My face sore from smiling so much. I eventually drop the happy smile and settle for a slight dimple lift. Sounds from the crowds fill my ears.

"She is our queen and savior,"
"May she bring us safety against Kairos."
"The Ancestors have picked our protector."

But what if I'm not? What if I'm just some kid chosen by the lottery of birth and nepotism to gain the throne? What if I can't save anyone?

My mother startles me. She grabs my arm and starts wrapping it in a knot with Calliope's. The wedding is over. The tying of the knot officiates arranged marriages. Kissing a loved one during weddings is reserved solely for natural connections made when two souls who found each other again.

Musicians play music on their string instruments and the throne room turns in to a dance floor. My mother guides me and Calliope to a side hallway leading into my new bedroom. The past week they moved my things to my new royal quarters. The room has a built-in trap door for any evacuations. A four poster bed with closing patterned curtains sits against two arched windows. Near the back of the room, a blue wardrobe and make-up station are positioned next to the washroom.

"As your mother, it feels weird to say this, but you and Calliope will use this time to..."

"Mom. Stop."

"You understand?"

"Yes."

"Well." My mother speeds out of the room and towards the throne room to join the festivities.

Calliope is silent and smiling.

"I'm Ashley."

Calliope motions in sign language, *Calliope. It's very nice to meet you.*

I sign back, "*I'm sorry. No one told me you signed.*"

"*It's okay. I'm used to it.*"

"No one should be used to the lack of accommodation for their needs."

She continues, "*We do not need to fully have sex. I know we just met.*"

"*Thank you. You are very pretty. Can I say that?*"

Calliope laughs, "*You don't get six wives by being ugly.*"

I sneer, "*Why agree to my mother's request to marry me? You have your hands full.*"

She rolls her eyes, "*The fairies have the Ancestors that they consult with. We have the Tree Root Echo Ecosystem. T.R.E.E. for short. Trees from different planets can communicate with each other by connecting their roots through the fourth dimension. The T.R.E.E. gave us an order to combine our forces. Seers among us said you would need my knowledge of the Weaving.*"

"*And you just agreed.*" I ask.

"*Of course. I cannot have a life without my people. I cannot live a normal day if I don't prepare for an attack against an aggressor. My life means nothing without my friends and family. If teaching you a new magic system will help us both, then we should share magic. Different communities thrive better when they combine their strengths. When we bar the sharing of knowledge or steal inventions for innovation from a different culture, it harbors resentment amongst communities. I'd rather voluntarily give you the knowledge than have you search it out somewhere or try to force it from us through war.*"

"*You're just going to trust me?*"

"*The Ancestors and the T.R.E.E. may be two different systems of communication but they speak to one another. I know they have picked you.*"

"*Do you have any knowledge of Artemis's disappearance?*"

Calliope stares at me confused.

"*What's wrong?*", I ask.

"*Artemis is dead.*"

———

I wake up to golden Fairy Dust surrounding my bed. Marina sits up wanting to touch it but I shake my head. Marina backs up and shrugs twice pointing at the Fairy Dust. *"What is it?"*

Or at least that's what I assume she's asking. I funnel the Fairy Dust back into my body until it is all gone. Marina nods in understanding.

Marina floats in the air then settles back down. She points at me. *"Your power?"*

I nod.

Marina smiles and goes back to bed.

"Ashley."

A voice echoes through the room. Marina doesn't seem to hear it. Her body still as a board.

"Ashley..."

Green, red, and black Threads unravel opening up to the Fourth Dimension. Unlike Limbo which is in between the universe, the Fourth Dimension is all around us carrying hidden pockets of the universe. Time Keepers navigate Limbo for their abilities. And Fairies navigate the Fourth Dimension. It is a green, black, and red land of unravelling Thread Beasts and Thread Souls with unresolved issues from this dimension. They are trapped there until they work through their trauma.

I reach my hand through the Fourth Dimension. Threads unravel at my finger tips. Green, black, and red strands fall everywhere around my hands. I pass through the unraveling hole and into darkness. Screeches and bellows erupt from all over. I use my Fairy Dust to heal the Threads in our room closing the hole. I light the darkness with my Fairy Dust. Static everywhere. Small windows of light showing veiled glimpses to the real world. These windows are the weak points in the fabric of reality.

Creatures with sharp teeth breathe down my neck. A triangular face with diamond eyes observes me. Bodies muscular and orangutan-like. Their elongated claws click around me. Their eyes and bellies showing no signs that I'll be there next meal. More so, confusion as to why I'm here. These creatures don't have any allegiance to anyone, or so fairies are taught. They attack when souls command them to.

A neon red pair of eyes stares at me then cocks its head. Their presence changes the body chemistry of all the other creatures.

The green, red, and black creatures surround me. They start to growl and block me from leaving.

"What's going on?" I ask the red eyes.

A deep female voice cuts through the darkness, "I've come to make a deal."

"Who are you?"

"I died years ago. Killed by men so unworthy of power they decided they wanted to steal mine. Fools the lot of them." The entity doesn't reveal itself. "If you have to put a name to a face, you can call me Beelzebub. I've been known by many aliases in my past life."

"Is that your real name?"

"Maybe."

"You're Artemis."

The woman laughs, "So clever my darling."

"Why are you here?"

"A woman of many questions. Just how I like them. I've come to strike a deal."

"No, I meant how did you die?"

"Avi and Pan decided to team up and kill me. They found me hunting in the woods and ambushed me. I'm sorry I wasn't there to grant you your powers. You would have been my Successor if I was still alive." She smiles, "Now, for the deal."

"Which is?"

"Find me a vessel to enter and I will grant you your wishes."

"What wishes?"

"Your heart desires a change. All I want to do is get revenge and move on. I promise you that I will not overstay my welcome."

"A vessel? Like a dead body."

"Preferably."

"That sounds tempting but I'd rather die than put my friends in danger."

"Oh, my silly little child. I'm not just talking to you."

"Then who are you talking to."

"Someone with the same need for revenge as me. A lost boy roaming through the universe. He will see this soon. You are merely a messenger."

"So, it doesn't matter what I say."

"Not unless you agree to offer a vessel." The eyes move around me bringing the creatures back to their resting places. She continues, "You may continue on your way. But Ash, this will not be the last time we will meet."

"My name is Ashley."

"Oh, is it?" The woman taunts. "Thank you for visiting me so often. Me and my creatures get so lonely."

"What made you finally talk to me?"

"He will access his Seer abilities again soon. You will teach him how to fly through the Fourth Dimension. You two are cut from the same Threads. Not siblings. But distant relatives. You could bring the message to him that I could not. Farewell."

The hole to my bedroom opens up again. Beelzebub disappears.

I cross into the bedroom and seal the Threads.

What the fuck was that about? Can't I just have one normal day of fucking sleep in peace?

NUMITOR'S HANDS tremble as he hands me everything he told to Kairos. Fifteen pages worth of schematics of the castle, soldier weaknesses, and terrain advantages.

I laugh. Angry tears fall down my cheeks pissed the fuck off that I can't kill this man anytime soon. He will run back to Kairos soon. I need him to strike the fear of Barretta's force in to Kairos. I want Numitor and Kairos to be so worried their plan will fail that they both trip and stumble.

"What's so funny?"

"You. A commonality in all living beings is death. But to play the mastermind of their souls. The mastermind that decides when innocent lives get to be cut short is diabolical. What makes you and Vesta different?"

"My son."

"Oh Numitor. You had your chance to stop her."

I cover his mouth with my hand and carve his chest with my katana. Numitor screams, bites, and cries. When I'm done, COWARD is written on him from breast to breast.

I stand above him smiling.

"You're not going to kill me?" He asks with tears and snot pouring down his face.

"Not yet. I already told you. Anything he tells you. You tell me. Deal?"

"Or what? You can't take much else from me."

"You're right. But there is a sadist satisfaction to seeing your awful work coming to fruition. You act brave but if I were to kill you now, you'd be disappointed you didn't see her and her people suffer. People like you make plans just to watch those plans destroy lives. Every. Last. Word. Oh, and, I get to kill her."

Numitor's beak trembles in anger. "Deal."

———

I use the hot air to fly through the air vents. It takes me about thirty minutes to travel from Numitor's Turret, down underground, and below the main castle to where the war commanders sleep when they're home. They take turns flying off in to space. They have a rotation of twenty-four in space and twenty-four on the ground. Every few months the ones in space are grounded to recover from any injuries and to detox from space radiation.

I look for Germanium's quarters. He is the Head War Commander of his twenty-four. He moves all his soldiers across the galaxy like chess pieces. Ruby red feathers and green highlights make him pop through the air vents.

I drop down and sit in an arm chair by his bed. Germanium jumps out of bed with a knife in my direction.

"You."

"Me."

"I'm going to kill you. You killed some of my trainers." His voice and hands quake.

"You can. Or you can let me kill you for being ready to defend murderers. Or..." I sigh and hold up the papers, "I could just give you these."

"What are they?"

"You have a mole in your midst."

"Are you working with Kairos?"

"Don't be so daft, Germ."

"We're not on a nickname basis."

"Germanium. We both have a lot to lose if you allow this to happen. I'm leaving here unscathed whether you like it or not." I hold out the papers to him.

Germanium stands watching me. I send my katana flying away from my side and in to the air vents.

"Frankly, I don't need weapons to kill any of you."

He puts the knife down slowly. His fingers hesitate reaching for the papers. His eyes rush through the contents.

Our eyes meet when he is done reading the papers.

"Intel for an attack."

"Who?"

"Would you do anything to them if I told you?"

"Of course."

"I made a deal. He tells me everything. I keep him alive."

Germanium hums in frustration, "Who?"

"Numitor. Keep him alive. And I will give you everything Kairos gives him."

"You couldn't just give me this last win?" Numitor asks as he hands me more information.

It's been years since I first caught him. Apparently, Kairos is dealing with Opaques and Vakander's armies destroying his Ships before they could make their way to Barretta. It has bought Barretta and Vesta enough time to prepare the castle for battle.

"There is no winning in the killing of innocents. You could've stopped her from making her decision. I already told you this."

"How could I?"

"Are you not a leader of Barretta yourself?"

"We both know she is the true leader. She pulled all the strings then and now. I lost someone too. We lost someone." Numitor stares at me intently. He knows who I am.

I don't say anything.

"I knew it was you this whole time. Vesta and I have been waiting for years now. Since the first generals and soldiers started dying and disappearing we knew it was only a matter of time. We knew you'd come for us. *I* am on *your* side."

In a fit of rage, I shove Numitor against the wall and slam him multiple times. At the first sign of blood, I dig my fingers in to the opening while keeping him down, "Don't you ever compare me to you. I don't want any of this."

"But you're a killer just the same seeking vengeance." Numitor laughs through the pain.

"For a crime that deserves to be avenged. You will not bring me shame for what I have done to all those loyal to Vesta for her and their crimes. I am not to blame that there were no repercussions for those involved."

"What about your people? They came for us first. They destroyed our lives. There are still people who live today who lost loved ones because of your people. Do their lives mean nothing?"

"If you cared about your people so much, you wouldn't be plotting the same attack on Barretta as my people did to yours. You're asking a question that paints you as a sympathetic bystander. I'm removing the poison. I'm putting a stop to it all. My people were in the wrong and so were yours. I'm trying to burn all loose ends. I already took care of my own people. I killed every last general involved with killing innocent Barrettans. I came here to finish off the poison in your leadership."

A TUGGING sensation pulls me from my deep slumber. What the fuck is this motherfucker doing? Is he performing open heart surgery? Why does my chest look like that?

Cassius is standing ominously over me with his eyes closed. I'm looking at him with one eye opened and steady breaths as to not startle him. I'm a bit fucking creeped out though. Thousands of rope strands leave my body. Seventy-five percent of them frayed or cut. The other twenty-five percent are left unscathed. I wouldn't know who they were going to unless I saw the person.

He hasn't stabbed me yet so that's a good thing.

From the looks of it, Cassius has gone through every rope. There are four specific ropes his focus stays on. He traces them back to their origins with his teal translucent threads. They span from old home planets to Tempus. I don't want to startle him because I'm interested by what he sees too. Yet, he continues to stare at one particular Thread that follows his Thea-Thread going to the unknown territory. Except, my Thread goes beyond the unknown territory and reveals a whole map of where the siblings are being kept. There's a mountain range with a mansion on a lake at the center of the map.

I pretend to wake up.

"You suck at pretending. You're a terrible actor."

I'm taken aback. I'm known for being very over dramatic. How am I a terrible actor?

"It's *weird* to look at someone's heart strings."

"Call them what you may but they're Ropes."

"So, what exactly do they show?" I ask.

He pauses double checking the Ropes.

"They are versatile."

"I am too."

"Not like that. I can read family histories to tell the history of the universe. They tell me all the connections a soul has made in their life time. They can unravel and repair the Threads of the universe much like a Fairy can to enter the Fourth Dimension. Or they can be used to tie people up." That probably comes in handy when Thea is here. Well. The nerd is a freak. Cassius squints his eyes, "This doesn't make sense."

"What?"

"Mansion on a Lake. It's a well-known area on Exile. Anyone could tell you this map is wrong."

"What's changed?"

"Everything is in ruins. Exile was a well thriving planet full of refugees and wildlife. This isn't the Exile many of us have known."

"What are you talking about?"

"There are way more Siren Cannibals than we expected. You can call it an infestation. Wildlife has become extinct, and refugees seem to have fled. This makes more sense."

He highlights thousands of red dots on the map, "These are how many Siren Cannibals surround the Mansion on the Lake. They're all over the place. In the water, in the woods, in abandoned building and temples. It's as if they're guarding something or some-one. We have to go to the Barretta Committee with this information."

The green maps are beautifully made from a smoke-like material. Detailed landscapes of Exile. Eeriness escapes off the images in front of me. But I'm confused, "How were you able to find this place? Isn't it blocked with your Ropes?"

"Yes. But this Rope," he highlights a strand that goes directly to the misty second underground level of the basement, "is connected to you and one of the other siblings."

Jimmy. His musky scent of pine and cardamon. Moments in the woods of Lykos spent making love. Galloping through the forest at nighttime side by side past the hundreds of moons. He was my home. He was where I felt like I belonged. Kairos never let me return to him either.

"I haven't seen these people in eighty years."

"Either way, your powers are far beyond mine or anyone else's around here. It makes sense why they had the military birds fill the castle before your arrival. They're afraid of you." He says turning the map examining it, "How did you bypass the Pulse Blockers?"

"This feels like a grand invasion of privacy." I blurt out turning the subject back to him. He doesn't need to know about my daddy and mommy issues.

"Because it is." He scrunches his face and pauses as he remains focused on the map, "I wanted to know who I'm working with. These Ropes have helped me make initial decisions on who I want to be friends with. They've helped me stay alive many times in the past. I trust them more than anything. That's why I know that even though you contain all this power, you're harmless. The Ropes have different colors for different people and how willing they are to cause harm. Your energy was teal like the normal color of Ropes, so I know you're a good person. I was surprised to see it be that color. Since I've arrived on Barretta, I've checked the colors for everyone I've encountered and not everyone has been a friendly color. Numitor being the most frightening."

"I already told you. Vesta is hiding something. She's barring you from seeing the Siren Cannibals location for a reason." But there's another reason too. I can sense it. There's another reason I can bypass the Pulse Blockers. It's just not coming to me right now. It has to be stuck in a memory I removed.

"But why let you bypass it?" He asks.

"I don't personally think they're letting me bypass it. It might be something they didn't account for. If I had an explanation, I would tell you. It's probably one of the powers and memories I don't remember right now. Can't explain Vesta's line of reasoning for keeping it from you. But what I do know is that there has to be a mole in the castle."

"What makes you say that?"

"Withholding information. Blurring the facts. Spewing propaganda to comfort the masses. Tell me, how would Barretta act if they knew a mole was among them? They'd be paranoid. They wouldn't trust each other. Paranoia creates community in-fighting. And when soldiers can't all work together, then it makes the community weak. There is no unity in paranoia and distrust. All you really need is for an enemy that was once a friend to topple that trust and the society collapses. So, here I am, a common enemy, and stranger, for everyone and guess what? It unifies Barretta. It distracts from the real enemy still at large."

"So, you're saying Vesta is spreading propaganda?"

"Yes."

"But why would she do that? Vesta isn't like that."

"She's a leader. She has to control the masses. Even seemingly good rulers can spread misinformation and lies if it means we prevent societal collapse."

Cassius stays silent. He wants to ask a million questions. His mouth opens and then closes. None of them come out.

"Can you see people's Ropes without projecting?" I ask.

"Yes. But maps like these give me headaches if I do not project them out of my body." He looks at me concerned as if trying to figure out a dilemma.

"What's wrong?" I ask trying to fish it out of him.

"As you slept, I checked all your Ropes. For a person who has met many people in his lifetime, you have very few remaining connections in this universe. But the few that you do have are rather strange, that's why I was wondering why your color was teal."

"What are you getting at?"

"Do you know who your parents are?"

"Yes." As Time Absorbers you never meet your parents. It wasn't always like this. Or at least, not with my grandpa, Titus Kronos. Kairos never wanted the parents to get too attached to their children because if they did, they wouldn't want to get separated from them at such a young age. The earliest they take children away from parents is seven. Getting too attached also meant feeling pain when they would alter your child and send them out for who knows how many years. Kairos had the technology to de-age Time Absorbers for however long he needed them. There was no cap to how long they could live. There was no cap to how long Kairos could keep them. So, Time Absorbers just have children and release them to the Templite government. Most Kairos Loyalists are okay with it since they are firm believers in Kairos's Cleansing Ideology – the idea to eliminate all mixed-race children from the galaxy. But those who weren't okay with it were usually arrested for trying to break their kids out of the Revival Unit Building.

I know my parents are May and Vakander. Though my grandfather, Titus, focused on raising me.

Cassius sighs, "Well, what about this one?" He focused on a bright crimson red twine strand and drags his finger to the far end of it. It takes him awhile to get to the end of it. At the end of it lies Tempus. He unlocks his jaw, "This is the Rope I'm most concerned about."

I'm not surprised.

Cassius zooming in on a throne room at the very top of an hourglass castle. A damaged Kairos sits staring blankly as he gives a command to his men in a spiraling tower with vast open windows overlooking Tempus.

"You are Kairos's nephew. You are the heir apparent to the Templite Throne. The future Time Lord."

CHAPTER 20
THEA:
TAMASHII

A GOLD ALTAR *in front of the throne temporarily holds the newest wolf of the kingdom born in autumn.*

My mother presents him in the candlelit ceremony, "We welcome our newest wolf, Tamashii. A wolf born half in life and half in death."

"We welcome you, Tamashii. Strengthen our pack with your soul. Grow into a rooted tree. Build a life of pure beauty." The citizens chant.

———

Five-year-old Tamashii changes in to his small wolf form and pretends to tackle me. I pretend to be overtaken and shout, "Oh no, my enemies have captured me."

"You make fun of my abilities. You let me tackles you."

"Did I?" I tickle him as I taunt him.

———

"What if he's a Time Absorber?" My father asks my mother in a royal meeting.

"What makes you suspect Tamashii is a Time Absorber?" I ask them both.

"He asked us when he gets to shadow travel."

Only Opaques can do that.

"Your first task as a newly appointed queen will be to train Tamashii." My mother informs me.

"Why would we train the Time Absorber?" Jimmy asks, "So that he can know how we fight and beat us when the time is right?"

"We have intel that he is the heir of the Templite Throne."

A BIRD SURGEON *stood over me. Darius smiled, "She's responsive Alejandra."*

The hologram of Darius and Alejandra was to my right. Blinding lights reflected off the oxygen mask on my face.

"Where are you?" I asked Alejandra.

"Debriefing with the leader of Barretta. We barely made it..."

———

Jupiter did that foot tapping thing she did when she was nervous. I stirred and faced her. My entire body sore and bandaged up.

"You're awake." Jupiter cheered and rushed out the door.

I didn't want to move again. Everything just fucking ached. Every slight movement hurt.

Jupiter returned with Alejandra. Alejandra dropped to her knees and kissed my head over and over and over again.

"I thought you were dead." Alejandra cheered.

"Bitch that fucking hurts."

I pushed her away.

"Glad to see she's fine." Darius stood in the doorway. "As soon as you can, we need all of you in the surveillance room."

"She just woke up."

"And I'm happy she's okay. But this is war and they need the remaining leaders of Venus to show face."

———

Televisions, with footage of the attack recorded from street cameras and drones sent out by the Tsunami Pods, replayed everything.

Elementals were killed by the red figure. Reanimated corpses overwhelmed the city. Tsunamis flooded the streets. The purple tendril injected something in to the planet. Rogue Robots migrated to the Ship from all over the planet. Avi searched the building we were last in. He demolished it in hopes to find us.

Avi placed a hand on our home planet and purple tendrils, the size of tree roots, exploded from the ground infecting everything around it. The water turned the color of ink. He retreated and guided Rogue Robots in to the Ship.

"Venus held ten billion citizens at its peak." A bird in a Barretta Committee kimono said, "Your city held one billion of the remaining survivors. Your rescue pods salvaged almost every single person. Not counting the thirty thousand Elementals felled by the reanimated corpses and Avi. How did your city do it?"

"That sounds condescending." Alejandra retorted.

"Not to be taken that way. I do apologize for my frankness."

"How can we understand you?" I ask confused.

"During your time healing, we administered Lingua Viles and Vida Viles to every single one of your surviving citizens."

"How did you extract us?" I desperately needed to know. Why was I here and others gone? I'm glad we're here and breathing. I'm grateful to have survived but watching all the Elementals on the screen die makes me feel like a failure. My people died and we just escaped. I know in their hearts this is the way they would have wanted to go. To go down fighting any attackers. But, maybe I could have done more.

The bird tapped a screen and blew it up so it can be viewed on a larger scale.

One Barretta Ship sent missiles at the Tendril distracting Avi as another Ship entered orbit. The Secondary Ship scooped up the entire Tsunami Pods fleet. Both Ships sped off in to space's orbit. "Avi's priority was the tendril and the Rogue Robots. By now, the poison has reached the core of the planet, and it is currently starting to die. His secondary priority was Jupiter."

"Why me?" Jupiter asked.

"You contain a crystal inside of you that Kairos is looking for."

"What kind of crystal?"

"It was a piece of a crystal created by fairies for the former time lord, Titus Kronos. Eight centuries ago, when he died, he dispersed seven crystals amongst the stars. The crystals found their homes when the new crystal child was born and it imbedded itself next to your heart. These crystals are a failsafe put in place by the previous Time Lord. They prevent the universe from being destroyed by Kairos."

That's why the red figure was aggressively coming after us. He had a target. And that target was Jupiter. We weren't crazy for assuming he was ignoring everyone else. If it hadn't been for his secondary mission to protect the purple tendril, we would have been captured or worse dead.

"I don't feel a crystal inside of me." Jupiter added.

"You don't but it's there."

"So, he was willing to destroy a whole planet for a crystal?" Alejandra asked in her irritated-as-fuck tone.

"The problem with fail safes is that they can be misused. Lest a crystal be removed from the holder, which we didn't know it could happen until the fairies told us it could, the power of the crystal can be used to take over the universe."

"What makes it a fail safe?" Alejandra interrogated

"It means that if Jupiter dies, the crystal starts to deteriorate and the universe collapses with it. The crystals are woven in to the Threads of the universe. So, our main priority is keeping her alive." Darius responded.

"Didn't seem like a priority when you gave us two fucking hours to evacuate." Alejandra snipped.

No one seemed to be addressing the real concern. Besides the universe and the crystal, the Rogue Robots left with Kairos and his Ship.

"What about the Rogue Robots?" I asked.

"Our intel tells us they're being transported to Lykos." The bird says, "I can only assume they will be used to police the citizens."

"What are you going to do about that?"

"We can't spread ourselves too thin. We are here, now, and we can't house all of the remaining Venus survivors. Epsilon has agreed to take them in. In exchange for border protections and mandatory military witch training. Your people will be fine."

"Why are you making it sound like we won't be joining them?" Alejandra prodded. Always the necessary pit bull. All the questions I didn't have the energy to ask, she did for me.

"The rescue on Venus came at a cost." Darius broke the news for the bird lady.

My stomach dropped. We have been stripped of our homes and of the comforts we held dear. All to be saved and traded. Nothing comes free in any land.

"So, we are being exchanged, for what?" Jupiter asked.

"For one, Jupiter will need to remain protected from Kairos." The bird lady said, "And, for another, we need your skills on Barretta."

"What about you?" Alejandra bit at Darius.

"I will be jumping back and forth from Epsilon and Lykos. I will be learning new spells and doing recognizance on the current state of affairs for Lykos."

Alejandra scoffed. She didn't ask him if they would see each other again. She didn't make any comments about their first kiss. She didn't bring up their life altering moment that seemed to have been shoved under the rug.

"Kairos is closing in on the Scorned Planets. And we have to stop him." The bird lady pointed to all of us, "you will see your loved ones again but now is the time for action."

"Can we see our families before we leave?" I asked exhausted.

———

Darius and Alejandra argued quietly in a corner of the surveillance room. Jupiter's younger siblings, Marcos, 18, and Ophelia, 19, hugged her tightly then shrugged it off with a few insults telling her how ugly she was. I love you was never a phrase in their love language. You're ugly was the equivalent to "I love you so much that I hope you don't die and make it back because you're actually cool people."

My mom burst into the room yelling at an officer in Melivian.

"Tu no me controlas hijo de puta." You don't control me you son of a bitch.

She pushed the officer off her arm and ran to me.

Her tears started flowing. Words of gratitude escaped her lips as she thanked her old gods for my survival. Her kisses plentiful and more than I've received in my entire lifetime.

"The waves were drowning me." Mom said, "Those machines picked me up and I went looking for you on the submarine. They told me you were fighting some monster and keeping the city protected. They showed me footage of what happened to you and I was so worried. I thought you were dead. They wouldn't let me see you and your fucking father said, 'Let them take care of her, they're healing her.' And even though he was right, they should've never kept me from you." She embraced me again and I squealed from the pain. I hugged her through the aches as if this would be our last time seeing each other.

My mom was the first to let go. Not fully. And not because she wanted to but because she was a chismosa and wanted to know information. Melivian mothers survived for entire centuries off gossip and insider knowledge.

"What happens next?" My mom asked.

"What do you mean?"

"Don't play stupid with me." Alejandra always took after my mom. Both of them were always too smart for their own good, and could read anyone's bullshit like a picture menu at a restaurant, expressive and to the point.

"They're taking you to Epsilon. That's the closest planet with the capacity to house the amount of survivors we have."

"And you?"

"Barretta." Darius eyed me from where he stood talking to Alejandra. I could hear his stare, 'Don't say anymore classified information.'

"Por que?" Why? Because the world is fucked. Because the world is unfair. Kairos is a dick-tator. Because my whole life I have never known peace. Every waking second has been some stressor. I worried for my people and what would happen to them. I worried about the waves consuming my home. Monsters attacking my people. And the end of my home. And now, that it's all gone. Now, that everything I was so afraid of would happen, happened, I was here parting ways with my only family unable to decide my fate. Men like Kairos don't ever have to live with stress. They barrage the people they watch over to remain subjugated. Anyone who opposes his perfect idea gets erased.

"It's the safest place for us. And they need us."

"For what?"

"I can't tell you."

"Don't make me use the Mind Link."

I block her out of my mind, "No, don't go digging. Please."

"All I'll be doing without you near me is worrying."

"Distract yourself. They will be training you Epsilon spells. Learn them. You said our family descended from witches at one point. Forget about us."

"I can not forget about you three. Even though Jupiter is not mine, she is still one of my own. I raised her. I raised you three. It will be hard to distract myself."

My mom embraced me again and whispered, "Take care of Alejandra. Es terca. Her mouth will get her in to trouble."

"I can't stop you. What makes you think I can stop her?"

My mom released me and my dad just stood there holding back tears. He hugged me and whispered, "I love you."

My dad let go after a solid minute and just stood there not saying anything. My mom always said my father impressed her with other methods besides words.

Mom and dad talked to Alejandra leaving me alone with Darius. I looked him dead in the eyes and said, "Protect them with your life. Check up on them. Keep them preoccupied. We can't have them worried about us."

"We will still all be worried. Besides, I already made that promise to Alejandra."

"Will Kairos come for Epsilon too?"

"Eventually."

"Did Barretta rescue our people so they could be soldiers in this war?"

Darius paused and shook his head before he responded.

"Jenny, everyone is acting within their own self interests. It sucks to be used right after we were rescued, but this is our best option. Kairos will only keep coming for everyone that doesn't fit his standard. More innocent people will suffer if we don't stand up and fight him. A repeat of what happened on Venus will happen again to others."

"So, you want me to be grateful when we're being used?"

"Feel how you need to feel. I'm not excited about this situation either. But direct your anger at that correct people. This is a really frustrating situation. We are all just lost our homes. We all are being separated from our families and loved ones. Be angry. But be ready to fight the real assholes in this fucked situation."

"WEAVING IS TEARING *your soul's energy apart slowly and combining it with another's. Every soul has massive amounts of energies stored in small fires called Wisps. These Wisps hold our memories, personalities, and powers. By splitting Wisps with another person, and when done right, the souls complement each other. For example,"* Calliope signs and steps up to the oceanid, Serena. They grab each other's hands and slowly start to unravel their beings. Strands of blue and green peel apart from Serena and Calliope intermingling to create a bright yellow. Their combined energies create a gigantic, spherical Power Source between the two. *"Once the Power Source is created, by sharing energy, either person can send it out. It works better and lasts longer when one person uses the shared energy."*

"How is it different from Siphoning?" I sign and mouth my words in tandem.

"It is a form of Siphoning but instead of giving your energy away, you're recycling the energy between each other. Weaving allows for all energy exerted to return to the user. So, you can strike down an enemy and absorb the force of the strike to replenish all lost energy."

"My mother mentioned that if I do this wrong, I could end up melding with the other being to create a creature like the Barretta War Birds."

"Yes. While this is true, Nymph knowledge passed down, from me to you, will allow you to learn the correct way. There will be no room for error because there will be no errors."

"That makes no sense."

"It will. Now let's begin with baby steps."

Calliope spends the next few minutes explaining how I need to release my Fairy Dust and act as if I'm going to open a hole in to the Fourth Dimension. Instead of unravelling the threads of the universe, she orders me to unravel one hand at a time.

I swirl my Fairy Dust around my hand and focus on unraveling the Threads that bind my hand to this physical existence. Thin Wisps of smokey purple tendrils emerge from where my hand once was. I feel no pain.

"Reform the hand by Weaving the universe back together like a sewing needle to torn garments."

I follow her instructions and my hand returns to its regular form.

"Why was that so easy?"

"You've been doing a form of Weaving every time you travel through the Fourth Dimension. Weaving Wisps is no different than opening a rift. You tear yourself apart to meld with another and become stronger. You just need the right guidance to know how to continue."

For the rest of the day, Calliope has me repeat the same hand until I'm exhausted.

The day after, she lets me do both hands.

The day after that, she allows me to do my feet and hands.

Each day, a new limb is added, and I practice Weaving from sun up to sun down.

At one point, I became an unraveled purple shadow. The entire day, Calliope had me tracking one of her wives without getting caught. I successfully followed two out of six times. The other four were too aware of my presence and knew Calliope would be training me on Shadow Walking. Usually only shadow walkers and opaques could travel through shadows. I didn't question if I needed these skills or why I needed them. I just trusted Calliope. While mother and father seemed like they were stumbling through life, Calliope was so confident in herself and my abilities that I never had room to question anything she asked me to do. It made me feel bad that I respected her more than them. I still loved them. I just always felt in the dark with my parents. Like with this marriage that was sprung on me. It was never a choice they allowed me to make on my own. The irony of it all makes me laugh. Because without them forcing me to be with Calliope, I wouldn't have found a person to put my full faith in.

Calliope has me return to my fairy form.

"Well done. Soon you will be able to spy on others and use your shadow form to attack and evade enemies."

———

After a long bath, Calliope waits in bed for me. I lay down next to her in a sheer nightgown. Calliope wears nothing. Completely naked from head to toe. It's hard to keep my eyes from roaming her body. I have to keep reminding myself that she is my wife. I can look at her like this. Right? Is this okay? Am I being a creep?

Calliope smiles, *"What's on your mind?"*

Her scent sweet like warm milk and cookies on a rainy day.

"I just think you're beautiful."

Her right hand reaches slowly up my night gown lifting it over my head. Meanwhile, her other combs my loose, green hairs. Her fingers tease my opening. Her thumb massages my clit while her fingers gather my wetness as lubricant. Her gentle fingers play my body like a prodigy violinist. I press my lips against hers trying to suppress a moan. Warm lips leave my mouth and trail down my neck, collar bone, and down to my nipple. Her tongue circles around my nipple while suctioning her lips around it. She changes the suctioning pressures. Whimpers escape me. My fingers claw at her skin.

"Don't... you want me to do something for... you." I get out in between moans.

"*Cum for me.*" She signs with her free hand and switches nipples.

My entire body is overwhelmed with ecstasy. Tension swells throughout my entire body. I'm close. Everything seizes up. I'm about to cum when Calliope slows down. My climax stops. I look down in to her eyes and she grins, "*I said cum for me. But I'm going to make you earn it.*"

Her tongue trails down my belly. It circles my clit replacing her thumb. Our bodies start Weaving apart turning in to Wisp ribbons of green and purple. We turn in to a dark gray cloud. Somehow, in this gaseous form, Calliope continues to edge me over and over and over again until finally when I cum we slowly start to reform. Our bodies become our own again. Her glowing green and mine glowing purple but now a gray Power Source lies between us. Calliope licks up my cum and wipes up the excess.

Did she do this just so we could create a Power Source? Was this the easiest way? I lay on the bed naked staring at the gray spherical Power Source between us. It slowly starts to turn invisible but I know it is still there.

"How long will it last?" I ask her.

"*As long as we remain in sync. At any point, we can absorb the Power Source back in to our bodies.*"

"Did you do that..."

"No." She interrupts, "*I wanted you since the day I met you.*"

"Do your other wives get jealous?" I... I want her all for myself.

"*My other wives have relationships amongst each other. My bonding to them was a power move. Just like ours. They acknowledged a long time ago that this was a business venture but it could also be fun. If we allowed it to be.*" She massages my face, "*Are you the jealous type?*"

"I think I can be."

"My territorial darling. I love it." She sighs, *"Are you territorial of me?"*

No. Maybe. This was fun. I loved this experience. And I think she's absolutely beautiful. But our connection feels half business, half pleasure. An odd tense mix of responsibility and lust.

"Do you want me to be?"

"I like a little jealously. It keeps the relationships fun. But no. I want you to be fulfilled. Enjoy the moment. We all have a finite amount of time to enjoy life. We can live forever but that does not mean our entire existence will be enjoyable so... have fun."

I sneer, "So, are you going to have to eat me out in the middle of a battle field in order for me to create another Power Source?"

"Hopefully not. But I will do what I must. Even if it means tasting you on my lips before entering a battlefield."

Calliope caresses my face and longingly stares in to my eyes. I laugh and kiss her forehead. My arms wrap around her body as she snuggles in between my breasts. Her body absorbs my warmth through out the night.

My mind loves the idea of Calliope. But a gut feeling tells me this isn't my puzzle piece. She won't be the final one in my bed. Our love making matches but our energies are in different places. I sleep enjoying this moment knowing this won't be my last.

———

I wake up remembering Calliope. Sweet Calliope. I miss her and our weird situationship.

I sigh as I stare at the ceiling partially blinded by an ominous glow at my bedside. I turn to Marina and find a magenta Power Source in between both our beds. Wisps of purple smoke leave my arm as red leaves Marina. I stare at the Power Source confused. I've never created a Power Source without merging energies before. Marina tosses in her bed and squints at the light coming from the Power Source.

Marina jumps out of bed startled, staring at the smoke leaving both our bodies. She frantically points at the Power Source. I wave my hands for her to remain calm.

I start to draw step by step pictures of how Weaving works. After I'm done, I show a replica of Marina and I sharing energies until we become one and create the Power Source. She shakes her head. Her hand massages her forehead. The more she studies the pictures the more the message reveals itself. She points between me and her and then the Power Source. I nod. She shrugs, *What is it for?*

———

I lead her out behind the castle to a patch of grass where soldiers usually train. Barretta guards watch over us. They escorted us here and I had them translate everything to Marina. A few words were lost in translation, but they said Marina got the general gist from the pictures.

Marina forms red spherical orbs using the Power Source between us and the orbs change to magenta. She releases it on a nearby mountain. The magenta orb creates a cavernous hole almost taking out the entire peak. The energy of the blast returns to the Power Source as if it never left Marina.

Marina cheers in witch language.

"She says that is the most powerful she's ever felt. The power is beyond anything she has ever felt. How did you combine the energies?" A bird says in a monotone voice.

"Tell her, I don't know. I had an Ancestor dream. They're known to be very powerful. I must've initiated the Weaving while I was dreaming."

Marina cocks her head and speaks back to the guard.

The guard repeats, "Why would it work for us?"

How do you say, 'I find you very attractive and want to make sweet love to you,' to a complete stranger after knowing them for such a short amount of time?

If anything, this proves we are one hundred percent compatible. Or I'm delusional.

"I don't know. It happens to people who have strong connections."

Marina blushes and nods. Why did she blush?

Does she...

Does she feel...

No.

Stop.

She is just a really nice friend.

She talks to the guard.

"That's interesting." He replies for her.

I nod and absorb some of the Power Source. I release the Fairy Dust and it levitates me higher than usual. Neon purple tendrils of light tremble under my skin. I release a Fairy Dust cloud, and it coats the mountain tops. The Fairy Dust wants to go further but I reel it back in. This time it went further than ever. Further than when I was with Calliope too.

Ethereals, if you can hear my pleas, let this beautiful goddess destroy me.

———

Marina and I sit in the grass waiting for breakfast time to roll around. The guards chat amongst themselves speaking in hushed whispers about the Templite boy. They stay at the ready observing past the field to ensure no one is trying to sneak up on us.

I pick at the grass and peel it in pieces.

Marina sighs irritated. She wants to ask a question but she doesn't want to interrupt the guards.

I draw on my notepad a question mark.

Marina scribbles an arrow pointing at a drawing of Barretta with a question mark next to it.

She points at me three times then the picture.

Why am I here?

Kairos ruined everything. I had to flee. How does one translate that they had no choice in their current state of housing?

Calliopes screams crawl through my body like spiders.

Her wives facing Kairos and Avi just to be poisoned by his purple tendrils.

Salem....

The memories make me dizzy. The Power Source re-emerges and starts to glow. Images of the attack on Flounce play on the spherical Power Source. Wisps of smoke leave our hands dissolving in to the orb.

"What are you two doing?" The guards chase after us.

"I don't know what is happening."

Marina doesn't try to stop anything. She doesn't argue or fight.

My legs go first, then my body, and lastly my eyes. They meet Marina for a slight moment. Her eyes remain my anchor as I almost panic.

This is not the worst that can happen. Her voice reaches me. Her real voice.

We become nothing. Nothing but Wisps and smoke.

———

I open my eyes.

I'm floating in a training field with Calliope and a version of me before the Kairos attack.

Calliope stands in the training arena behind the Crystal Palace explaining to me.

"There is one more power besides the Weaving that is forbidden. It is magic stolen. Appropriated by thee Kairos and his Time Keepers from a dead group of fairies called the Guerreros. Titus and his followers protected the Guerreros while they were alive and prevented them from going extinct. Titus fell in love with a beautiful Guerrero and she gave birth to a girl. Titus's daughter fell in love with her broth-

er's vampire best friend, Vakander. And they created the heir to the Templite throne and grandson to Titus. An heir to the Templite Throne that took all the genetic attributes of his mother and nothing from his father. Kairos was born out of a Lycan affair that Titus later regretted. Kairos sired two children and hid them away from his enemies."

"Why do I need to know all of this?"

"History is not just to learn from. It is to track the demise of a people. To scour through the origins of power. The Templite Heir is the only other being, that I know of, with the ability to harness this forbidden magic. You have practiced a form of it your whole life without knowing its origins."

"What kind of forbidden magic is it?"

"Guerreros were multifaceted like most magic beings. Their forbidden magic included but was not limited to erasing entire time-lines, using memories they had in their past and hide them away for later in Artifacts, and even collapse entire universes. With so much power, they could do what Kairos had always wanted."

"Why didn't they?"

"Power in the wrong hands breeds death and destruction. Power in the correct hands maintains the balance of the universe. Kairos used the Guerreros to cut seven timelines. The Guerreros intimidated Kairos and he forced their mass extinction. They were the first beings Kairos destroyed when he took power."

"How did we know they could erase timelines?"

"Before Kairos took power, Templites, loyal to Kairos, would try to travel the cosmos through black holes but it would have negative effects on other universes. The black holes would cause havoc, swallow everything whole, and destroy planets. Wars between timelines were set off by Kairos and his soldiers' need to master blackhole travel. They thought that being able to be anywhere and everywhere could provide a great advantage during battle. Once enough casualties came from The Inter-dimensional Wars, all thirteen timelines signed treaties to never travel through blackholes to each others' lands ever again. Titus,

Kairos's father, was forced to clean up after his mess. Fourth Dimensional travel was the only approved form of travel between timelines."

Calliope sighs, *"Titus enlisted the help of the Guerreros to teach curious Templites loyal to Kairos how to travel through the Fourth Dimension. Templites struggled to learn how to navigate the Fourth Dimension without getting lost. Black holes for them were always easier to navigate but messier to use. When Kairos realized his loyalists would never master Fourth Dimensional travel, he decided to cut seven timelines of the thirteen timelines. This would create an empty space of travel that could be accessed with only using black holes. So, they used the Seers among them to calculate which timelines would most likely survive from a mass dictator who would enslave all. They scooped up all the individuals from those timelines that could repopulate their planets and brought them here to ours to be used as slave workers."*

I'm scared to continue. I ask, "What about the rest of the people left in the timelines?"

"They were erased. Key members of all seven timelines were removed from existence. They essentially cleared pathways in the cosmos in order to create Limbo. With Limbo's creation, Time Keepers could now travel all over our universe by haphazardly opening up black holes called Pulses instead of harnessing the craft of Fourth Dimensional travel."

"What happened to all the displaced individuals?"

"The beings were evenly distributed to planets they would best assimilate to. Evolution took control as races mixed together. Wyvern creatures became dragons over generations as their species intermingled with fire breathing leviathans. Fae and fairies created a new type of fairy for Artemis to rule over. With overpopulation and Kairos propaganda, food and resource scarcity created contentions among the natives and the displaced. Mixed-raced children and the displaced were seen as less than. Harmful laws were created to limit the amount of mixed-race children that could be had on certain planets. The Scorned Planets were opposed to these types of laws. Although, Kairos

tried to lead a task force on Lykos to rid all mixed-race wolves. He also failed. The Neutralist Planets were split amongst the laws. And the Kairos Loyalists leaned heavily towards these discriminatory laws. Titus and his followers struggled to push back Kairos's influence. Once the father of the Templite Heir, Vakander, united his vampiric forces with xenophobic Templites and Lycans, they toppled the Templite Empire and Kairos took control of what is now known as, Tempus.

I stayed quiet that day.

"What the flying fuck." Marina shouts. Wait... I can understand her.

"I can understand you."

Marina remains gobb-smacked. She asks me directly, "How? Was it the Power Source or the Weaving or Both?"

"Welcome to the Power Source you two created." Artemis' body-less voice emerges from all around us.

Her red, green, and black threaded body rises from the ground. The scene in front of us erases.

"We Weaved this together?" I ask Artemis.

"Yes, you did. You found the perfect match. Someone who can match your magical abilities and strength. The Power Source leveled you up. Your Wisps are your memories and can be shared through the Power Source. But so can the energies and knowledge you two have. Calliope could only teach you the basics. Marina here is meant to give you the support you need for the next stage of your life. This is an unlocked ability that you possess when you have access to a Power Source or Siphon all the energy from a being. Power Sources are accessed through the realm I have dominated in death."

"So we're in the Fourth Dimension right now?" Marina asks shaken.

"Yes but not the one you were trapped in."

What does that mean?

Marina tries not to hyperventilate. Artemis struck the right chord. Tears well in her eyes. Her chest heavy.

"The Fourth Dimension is all around you. Hidden pockets of the universe stowed away unless seen from a different angle. There is no need to fear it."

"Does this have something to do with the Templite boy that arrived at the castle?" I ask.

"Everything is connected. Weaved together in a perfect tapestry. He will see this one day. But you created this so you could speak to Marina. You wished to show her your life before all of this. And here we are."

————

The scenes all around us change.

I'm walking down the aisle getting married.

Salem talks to me about fighting for my people.

My mom officiates the wedding.

Calliope and I are making love.

Our history lesson on the universe.

————

Calliope and I sit in the training arena.

Night has fallen on Flounce. The crystals from the palace refract various shades of purples, blues, and pinks as moon beams strike it from all angles. Calliope cries in to my hallow arms.

It's been a month since our marriage and I already feel us drifting apart. Who knew marrying a stranger would lead to an unhappy union? And not only that, a stranger who saw impending doom.

Calliope stares at me as if we're no longer together.

"What happened?"

"*We can't stop him. The Nymph seers ran through various scenarios and we lose Flounce in all of them.*"

I stay silent. I don't know how to console her. How do you fight the future if it's set in stone? How do you decide that the fate you can't escape from will happen?

A Templite Ship emerges from thin air like some awful magic trick.

I jump back startled. It hangs in the air immobile.

My stomachs twists, it's happening now. I can't stop it. I can't stop it. I trained for this. How do I go up against a Ship that big? All the stories do the size of the Templite Ships an injustice. It blocks out all stars and moons. The light from the heavens and the castle are gone. The Ethereals can't protect us. Now, we're left to fend for ourselves.

"*I need you to absorb the Power Source.*" Calliope orders me. She repeats herself forcefully. I hesitantly absorb the Power Source and Calliope cuts the Weaving ties between us. Our shared power connection disappears. Our knowledge no longer shared between each other.

A purple tendril crashes in to the middle of the training field. The dirt debris tosses the ground in to the sky. Debris smacks Calliope and me off our feet and throws us across the training arena. My chest screams in agony. Red blooms from my shirt. Calliope lifts on to her elbows with chunks of bark missing from her arms and legs. The purple tendril pumps a liquid in to the ground. The ground quakes with the aftershock of the impact. Purple tendrils that look like veins bury themselves in to the dirt and speed our way.

I pick up Calliope and run towards the exit of the arena. The purple veins build fake tree formations across the field. The trees shoot out liquids from the tree tops. Purple viscose liquid hovers above us. Right as it is about to hit us, Calliope builds a tree bark shield with her arms. The liquid scatters all around leaving a slight path for us to keep running. Trees start sprouting all over the field around us preparing to shoot more liquid into the air.

"We have to keep moving."

Calliope screams in agony. I turn back to see the purple veins have consumed her entire body stemming from the bark shield.

"Can you change in to your shadow form and separate yourself from the poison?"

Calliope tries to start unweaving her body. But the tendril veins keep her restrained. Her neck snaps, legs break, arms twist at odd angles. Her arms, legs, and body elongate. The wood beneath the bark glows neon purple. Horns sprout from her head. A spiked tail slithers out of her buttocks. In a matter of seconds, she is a gigantic beige and purple demon. Her body rises in to the air at least eighty stories tall.

She is kinda hot but... fuck she is scary. Scary hot... literally. I can't be getting horny when I'm about to die.

"What the fuck."

I turn in to my shadow form. My shadow travels through the ground. Calliope bellows an ear piercing roar. Her feet stomp above me scattering more of the poison across the planet.

My shadow flies in to the Trinity of Trees. Once I find Salem on the top floor of the trees, I reassemble my full form. They stand with Calliope's six wives beside her. Fairy and Epsilon soldiers stand all over the Trinity of Trees at the ready. Their powers all ready to attack the Ship but they're ignoring the tendril.

"They're poisoning the planet." I shout across the expanse. But why aren't they attacking with soldiers? Every story I've heard contains endless Pegasus riders annihilating beings left and right. What is different about this time?

Not one peep from the Ship other than the tendril.

Calliope's six wives scream in unison. Their bodies dissolve in to smoke and rise in to the air. The six clouds of smoke fly directly at the tendril thinning out completely until they evaporate in to the tendril.

"What's happening?" Salem hold red orbs of light in their hand.

"They're turning the Nymphs against us." I tell Salem. "Calliope forced me to detach my Power Source from hers before she got poisoned."

The tendril releases one wife-turned-demon at a time. They all look like Calliope except in their respective colors. Blue, green, white, brown, gold, and teal.

Calliope and her six wives hover over the Crystal Palace and Trinity of Trees.

They bellow in unison, "We are here to take control of Flounce. Submit peacefully and none of you will die."

"We have to get you out of here." Salem grabs my hand, "I don't know what their plan is but you're the last heir to the Flounce Throne. We can't recuperate this planet without an heir. It'll be lost to Kairos."

"You act as if we lost."

Salem frowns, "Not yet." Salem spins the red orbs in a circle and shoots it at my feet. Salem's orbs speed up around me binding me to the circle with Threads of the universe. I thought only Guerreros and fairies could do this. I resist against the Threads fighting to stay and fight alongside my people.

"Noooo. You have to let me fight for my people. You told me I get to die for my people. That it would be for the best of my society."

Salem strengthens the binding circle as I try to shift in to my shadow form. They weave my body back together counter acting my powers. Calliope didn't train me for this. She didn't train me for the moment I would try to shift and someone wouldn't let me.

The ground below the circle opens up in to the Fourth Dimension. Salem slams their hand against the wooden sky bridge and I fall in to red, green, and black darkness. My hair flails in front of my face and eyes. I try to reach out and resurface myself to the hole in the tree. A red power yanks my arm downward. From the hole, I see Calliope and her six wives unleash their abilities to poison the planets. Salem closes the threads of the universe below them.

"Noooooooo."

Let me save my people. Let me save them. Please.

My body crashes like a comet against a field of grass.

———

A sharp kick startles me awake.

Barretta guards point their arrows at my head and everything comes flooding back. I quickly get up and spin in a circle. How do I get back home? Barretta is not too far from Flounce. What are they doing to help my home? Where is Salem? Calliope? Her wives?

Birds point arrows at me closer but it does nothing. It means nothing. Mom. Dad. My kingdom. All under attack. And I'm here still alive. Why am I alive? Why me? Why? Are they alive?

"I need to get home. He attacked my home." Tears flood down my face and the birds don't respond. Their stoic faces remain unflinching.

A female bird in a kimono greets me, "Ashley of Flounce. Heir to the Flounce Throne. Picked by the ancestors to carry the power of your people for generations."

"They need help. Get me back home."

"I do apologize but that can not be done. You were sent here for a reason and I cannot allow you to return."

"Flounce is under attack. You need to help them."

"Our armies are preparing for war on Barretta as we speak. We cannot lose numbers now saving another planet. Epsilon will send reinforcements."

"You fucking cowards." I charge at her in my shadow form. Cassius steps out from the tunnel leading to the castle and Weaves me back in to one piece.

Fuck. Two for two. Why didn't Calliope teach me how to defend myself against this?

"Execute her or send her to the Orphanage?" Cassius asks.

"We do not execute queens here. Bring her inside and make her feel at home."

"Let me go. I'm not supposed to be here. I'm not supposed to be here." I thrash against my restraints but I can't move. Mom. Dad. Calliope. Salem.

Marina and Artemis step on to the field and the images blur into oblivion. I'm dragged in to the castle by Cassius. Until the image of me fades in to the tunnel. The tunnel remains.

We are back in the Power Source.

"Did you ever find out what happened to Flounce?" Marina asks.

My voice chokes on tears and anger, "No. They've kept me in the dark about everything."

"Would you like to know?" Artemis offers.

"No."

I can't handle knowing. Not right now. I can wait for the truth. At one point, I wanted to know if my mother and father were safe. I wanted to see what Calliope was able to do in her poisoned form. The destruction and harm she brought to Flounce. But that was merely curiosity.

"As soon as my new body is ready, I can name you my Successor and bestow my power on to you. In that time, train with each other and make each other stronger. As an Ethereal of Artemis, you can fully channel the Fourth Dimension, travel through the past and in the future, and help the cataloguing and preservation of mythological creatures. You can use your Power Source to travel to past wars and observe battle strategies."

"That's why he killed you. You could change the tides of battle by seeing common strategies used. And Kairos's seer abilities and Seer advisors allowed him to see the full extent of your power and find the best possible way to kill you." I tell Artemis.

"In part, yes. I will not stay dead for long. We will destroy Kairos. And all the revenge we want will be ours. Souls on this side are at your beck and call. I have a leader of my army ready to serve you. She too was killed by Avi and her people by Kairos. I will give you the army to gain Flounce back."

"Flounce is not completely lost?"

"Sick but not lost. Kairos did not employ the same methods for Flounce as he did other planets. Your people can be cured."

"That's why Vesta said there will be an attack on Barretta. Lykos,

Epsilon, and Flounce. They're trying to take out the Scorned Planets one by one. What about the Neutralist Planets?"

"Vakander is pushing back with his vampiric soldiers and clearing Templites. But he can't clear them all. Kairos knows his odds of taking out the rest of the universe are stronger if he can gather forces in the Loyalist areas and corrupt enough beings with his poison in the Scorned Planets. Infecting beings with his poison powers will allow him to use them as his loyal soldiers."

"Vesta didn't tell us any of this." Marina breaks her silence looking more relaxed than before, "they know he's coming."

"The increase in Barretta soldiers weren't for the Templite boy. They were for an imminent attack from Kairos. In due time, everything will be told to you all. There is a mole Vesta has been trying to fish out. This is why she could not tell anyone."

"Who?"

"Not for me to disclose. Patience. And all will be revealed."

"Vesta knows about his plans."

"She can only predict so much. But she is close to guessing right. She planned everything strategically. The crystal wielders, Exile, and Kairos's plans. She is covering all bases and stretching our reach as far as possible."

"She wasn't lying when she said she couldn't help Flounce." I sigh hating the truth.

"You are never alone, my dear Ash. You may feel helpless and defeated but a warrior rises the highest after a terrible fall."

Our bodies dissolve in to smoke and the field re-emerges. Artemis waves goodbye as her image disappears. The field returns and the Power Source stands in front of us blinking multiple times. It shatters like glass and floats away in to the atmosphere. Our Power Source used up and gone.

Marina tries to speak and the unknown language comes out.

Damn. Not again. I was just getting used to the sound of her voice.

The guards stare at us confused. It's only a matter of time before they tell Vesta everything.

Marina and I push past them and head to the showers to get ready for our day.

CHAPTER 23

THEA:

WHY MUST *we train in the mountains?" Tamashii asks as we trek the snowy peaks. We stay in our hybrid forms to keep warm.*

Because mother and father are scared of you knowing too many secrets. They want you training as far away from the castle to gather as little information as possible. Tamashii is just a boy. What do they have to fear from a boy? If we can guide him in the right direction, then it won't matter how much intel Kairos gathers. The boy will fight against him.

"To train you of course. Ice can be melted by fire," I start making an excuse up, "But our elemental magic is heat. Fire is a part of heat but melting snow and boiling it can also be a weapon. Flames being the primary source of heat, boiling water is our secondary source, what would a third source be?"

Tamashii takes a moment to think.

His eyes go wide, "Heating the air."

"Yes. We can heat the air or stars in our hands. Our skin is resistant to the heat of stars and supernovas. While many of our ancestors have died on different planets due to supernovas destroying their worlds, our species survived by adapting our skin and always carrying portable oxygen masks."

I hold out the oxygen mask device in my hand for him to see. It is a contraption that adapts to the face and can keep oxygen flowing to the user for as long as it on their face. It becomes ineffective once taken off.

———

I finish tying Tamashii to the fire pit. Purple flames engulf my hands.

"Ready?"

Ten year old Tamashii's eyes widen at the fire.

"Do you really have to light me on fire to see if my skin is fire resistant?"

I set his shoes on fire.

"Wait," Tamashii panics, "I didn't say I was ready."

"If you can talk, you're ready."

Tamashii screams and thrashes violently.

The flames consume Tamashii's entire body flowing in a circular tornado. His innocent face drops. A warm calm seeps through his entire body. The bindings fall off in the flames.

"After five years of training," I sigh disappointed, "You still don't trust my teachings."

"I am sorry, master." He marvels as the flames match his movements. Tamashii twirls the purple flames in his hands. "How can we do this?"

"Years ago, Kairos had the power to end worlds with his eternal fire. Since he has acquired life threatening injuries, he has relied on his poisons to kill planets or take control of them. Our Universe consisted of thirty-eight planets. Today we only have..."

"Twenty-four."

"Very good. In the span of one day, Kairos used his eternal fire to burn two planets down at a time until the Ethereals finally cut him off of all of his powers. The Ethereals grant us our abilities. The Lava Ethereal, Agni, grants us his heat powers. Should we make him unhappy, he can cut all powers from our physical forms. The only one Ethereal that still supports Kairos is Pan, the Forest Ethereal. They

worked together to crumble the fourteen planets they killed in our solar system."

"Why can the Ethereals cut off our abilities?"

"They are the scales of the universe. They ensure not one side goes too far astray. They are the checks and balances of the galaxy."

"So are you a good person only so that the Ethereals don't take away your abilities?"

"I am not good or bad. I will do what I need to do for my friends and family. But I do good because life works as a ring would. An action, good or bad, commits to venturing in to the world in a circle. So, when it's time to return to the sender, it will return the energy you gave it in the first place. We fuel this ring everyday we make decisions. The bad ones create ripple effects. Violence poisons and splinters in to branches of hatred. While good decisions heal the world and are less noticeable."

"Are you only a good person because you're scared the ring will bring you evil if you act bad?"

"No. As I said before. I am a not a good person. I exist to protect the ones I love and to live a full life."

"What if Agni were to take our abilities? Would you spite him?"

"If Agni deems the need to stop my actions, then so be it. My actions must be stopped."

Later that night, as we settled in to our campsite worn from the day. We have sleeping bags set side by side. Tamashii asks, "What if someone were to kill an Ethereal?"

"Are you looking to kill one?"

"No, I'm asking because I want to know what would happen to their soul, their powers, and their abilities to cut off powers? What would be the result?"

"Ethereals usually pick Successors before they die like my mother and father have me lined up to be the queen."

"Yes. I understand all of that. But worst case scenario, what if they just die? Where do they go?"

———

I didn't have an answer. I turn my flame body to Beelzebub, "Where do Ethereals go when they die? What happens to them?"

"We are just like anyone else. We are born, we are chosen, then we crossover to the Fourth Dimension or the Cataclysm Realm."

"You were an Ethereal?"

"Yes, child."

"I've never heard of a Beelzebub. I only know of Chronos, Cthulhu, Agni, Artemis, Pan, Ukko, and Madame Destiny."

"I was called a different name before. I miss my old name, but this one suits me more."

"Will you ever tell me?"

"Maybe, one day."

"So, you're trying to find a physical vessel like Pan took mine?"

"Yes."

"Why?"

"Kairos is trying to build his army again. He will do anything to complete his mission in Cleansing the universe. His plan is to kill all the Ethereals so he can have access to his full powers again. The day I died, he was granted his Ground and Moon abilities back."

"Can he wield all the Ethereal powers?"

"Yes."

"For a man with all the power in the universe, why does he need to wipe out entire beings?"

"Ideologies, money, material gains, and prophecies. An ideology can corrupt a soul until it makes it its mission to complete it. They'll justify the murder of million to get their way. Eisboler was a prominent religious leader, who still worshipped a long since dead eighth Ethereal, on Lykos before The Great Migration of beings to this timeline. He united quite a few planets under his belt for Kairos. Kairos fell for his rhetoric as a teenager and became an advocate for removing refugees from Lykos, formerly known as Necropolis. Years later, a group of refugees were blamed for Eisboler's untimely death. Everyone

around Kairos knew he had done it. They didn't speak up on it. Kairos became greedy and Kronos saw this too late. Present day, the Prophecy has gotten him paranoid. A child of two or more races would take control of the Templite Throne. Kairos is scared his nephew or another being may produce an heir worthy of taking him off the throne."

"Why not kill his nephew?"

"Because two is better than one. Two fully powered beings who could harness all seven Ethereal abilities could take over the entire universe. Kairos is trying to sway Spike to remain on his side so that his bloodline can continue. Not only that, if Kairos can use Spike as a vessel after his physical body dies, he would have all of Spike's abilities and his own."

"Who needs that much power?"

"There was a time an eighth Ethereal lived. He controlled the dead. His name was Muerte."

"What happened to him?"

"Us, seven Ethereals killed him because he grew lusting over the excess killing of innocents."

"What happened to his soul?"

"We assume we destroyed it, but I guess he was hidden somewhere in the Fourth Dimension."

"So, the real Kairos died at some point like I did?"

"Not exactly. Kairos and Muerte share a body. A vessel and the spirit. You could've stayed with Pan in your body. But I opened the door for you to come here. He did not have the power to drive you out. At one point, Kairos must have preformed a ritual to bring himself close to death in order to bring the soul in to his body. When Ethereals want to live again, they'll do anything to find a way out of the Fourth Dimension. And once they find a vessel, they'll do anything to keep it. Pan is probably pretending to be like you as best as he can be."

"So, who is really in control? Kairos or Muerte?"

"Kairos is using Muerte as a Power Source. They are both weak beings who need energy to sustain their reign. Kairos always acted of his own volition. I think they are working in tandem. Any corrupt *leader will work with those they need in the moment until they no longer need them. Muerte could not control the Fourth Dimension. Kairos could not control his timeline. Together they have enough energy to continue killing the masses which they both want. The dead feed energy into them both. And as their powers replenish, soon, they will no longer need each other. At that point, they could continue working together and create an army that will obliterate our timeline. Or erase each other trying to become the one true leader. But if Muerte returns, we would be dealing with planets full of undead working against us."*

OF COURSE, I knew that. But when your uncle is known as, Kairos, the Mass Murderer of Planets, you don't really share this information with everyone you meet.

"How do you know I'm his nephew?"

"The Ropes are made from different materials for different relationships. Steel for lovers. Your Rope to Jimmy is steel. But I'm guessing you won't elaborate so I'm not asking. Moonstones for motherly connections. Jasper gems for fatherly connections. And so on and so forth. In this case, twine for nephew or niece. You have a power long enough and you learn the subtleties." Cassius bluntly prods, "Why do you think Kairos has kept you alive for so long?"

"The most obvious reason would be to continue his legacy. He wanted me to be his right-hand man. His power and forces alone couldn't win him the Scorned Planets. With my strength, he could take over every planet in our universe and in other timelines that ever went against his beliefs."

The truth is Kairos can't kill me. Not yet at least.

"Why do the birds need me?" I ask him.

"Let's say we overthrow Kairos and kill him. And we have no one to take the throne. That leaves a vacuum of power. Not all his followers will accept our way of ruling immediately either so with no ruler of Tempus, they can self-appoint one or a well-organized group can swoop in and take power. If he still has soldiers alive to fight us, they will come for the throne and take over before we could find a worthy candidate. You being the heir makes the transition of power more palatable even if they don't necessarily agree with your rulings. You banishing and killing all Templite leaders who committed Clensing could set an example for all the planets working with him. They need to see someone of greater power rise to the throne."

The good guys need me to lead. The bad guys want me so I can help take over the galaxy. I just want to live a normal life. I wouldn't mind being the ruler of Tempus, but when you're the ruler of anything, there's always a target on your back. I don't want to live in fear for the rest of my life *...again.*

"My uncle hates me. Why do you think his people would bow to me?"

"Your uncle has modeled you in to a Templite lovable prince. His propaganda makes you a star in your world. Though you look different from your Templite form."

"How do you know about me?"

"Vesta has us study prominent leaders that need to be killed in Kairos's cabinet of murderous assholes."

"And I made an appearance?" I'm taken aback but I really shouldn't be. I knew Vesta was playing a game.

"Yeah. We study Templite propaganda and how they corrupted the Loyalists." Studying propaganda but not being able to see Barretta's propaganda, but okay, "How they feed artificial stories to their populous in order to keep them controlled and loyal to them. They brainwash them with cult tactics. Leaving means you disrupt their way of life and everything they know. Makes them easier to control."

"And Vesta never cleared up that I'm not on his side."

"That's the lesson we're still learning. Are you on his side?"

Frustration burns through me. Do all other Scorned Planets learn this too? Am I just on everyone's shit list across the galaxy because

I'm related to him? The gears turn slowly with a realization. Kairos wanted it this way. He wanted my image tarnished throughout the galaxy. He wanted his propaganda to show that I was the poster boy for the Templites. That way I had nowhere to run to in my real form or if people found out who I was. I was never safe. Not just being a Time Absorber but anywhere people knew I was his nephew.

Cassius pauses with a puzzled expression.

"Can I ask you a question?"

"I can't say no."

"Do you remember much from your last lives?"

"Yes and no. It depends on what you ask me about."

"Do you remember how the Last Time Lord died?"

I try to forget. But his voice clouds my brains. In every lifetime, it's the one thing I remember pretty quickly.

I love you, my little, Spi.

"It happened when I was a teenager. I lived in the Templite Castle when he died. All I remember is that time stopped for a few seconds. Beings could move but it felt like when white noise abruptly dissipates. A void of sound that used to be there replaced by an uncomfortable nothingness. There was no order in the universe. You could feel the millions of universes within our timeline chipping away into pieces each second someone wasn't in control of it. Existence crumbling in on itself. Then, it snapped itself together, but the foul feeling of emptiness didn't go away. It lingers to this day. I knew nothing of war at the time. Picking sides wasn't on my mind. All I knew was that someone I considered a father had passed away. My mother was picking up the pieces my father and her brother caused throughout the galaxy. Kairos forcibly took my grandfather's place, and he adopted me as his own son for years until he decided I should be a Time Absorber. My life has felt like seconds since then. I have no sense of when things happened. I just know they happened. And as I grew older, I saw a darkness festering in Kairos growing larger by the day. I had been trying to escape Kairos for so long. It is not fair when you are forced to choose your survival over your home. Being forced to leave good memories because political leaders decided they no longer could keep their dicks in their pants. Their dick size contests were more important than leaving people in peace and harmony. And on top of all of that, Kairos tried to take all my memories too. But they clung on to my soul and wouldn't let me forget who I was. It may take me awhile to remember but the memories always come back."

"The Old Time Lord was murdered over six hundred years before I was born." Cassius informs me, "And we are still fighting their war."

"Kairos tried to control me. He had me married off to someone he wanted me to love. A political marriage birthed out of greed from my uncle's and Avi's parts. But he also grew power hungry, as most men do. It didn't take long for Kairos to implement the Cleansing. And when I refused to bow to him and allow him to commit war crimes, for eight hundred years, I was silenced. Forced to become a Time Absorber. He couldn't kill me, so he kept me frozen in time."

Cassius sighs after a moment of taking everything in, "This... is a lot. I guess Tempus's history is more complicated than what I've been led to believe." He shakes his head looking frustrated, "Follow me."

"Where are we going?"

"To take a shower. You smell like ass. It's time to get ready for training."

CHAPTER 25
SPIKE
TOMMY, BRODY, AND THE TWINS – DAY 2

CASSIUS GUIDES me up two stories of spiraling staircases before entering a hallway that splits into four.

He stops.

"Male-identifying beings on the left, female-identifying beings on the right. Center left is for non-gender specifying. And center right is for specialty care for reptilian, avion, amphibian, etc. Once you're out of the shower, there will be clothes waiting for you at the dispenser in the center of the room. Don't take too long getting ready. I need to show you something before we go out on the training field."

"Is it a good something?" I smile and cock my head to his groin. "Going to show me how you tied up that one girl?"

"Something to help you in the future." Cassius lashes out.

I nod walking slowly into the left room followed by Cassius and up a small flight of stairs. At the top, stalls line the walls in a circle each one teaming with steamy conversations. Seven-foot marble dividers reach up to the ceiling allowing for privacy. All the stalls are taken so I stand there waiting for one to open. I grab a fresh white towel at the circular laundry machine dispenser at the center of the room. I nosily wait peering into everyone's conversations.

Near the back, a boy is rapping with the person in the stall next to him.

Cassius yells over them all, "Hey Tommy, you getting under the foreskin? Or are you too busy rapping?"

"Shut the fuck up, Cassie." Tommy's voice raises in pitch angrily.

"I'm just worried that your fellow soldiers will run away if they smell smegma."

"It has a very cheddar-y fragrance to it, so it adds to my natural musk," Tommy says so confidentially that now I'm worried if he's going to clean under his foreskin.

Cassius smiles charmingly, "Vesta doesn't think you smell too good. And I know how you like your foxy older birds."

"She told you personally?"

"Of course. We had an entire meeting about how it needs to be fixed. Now fix it."

Tommy pulls back the curtain and is quite handsome. A semi-muscular pale body appears with armored scaly skin. Long hair on top of his head arches up and reemerges along his beard. The sides of his hair shaved to the skin. A militaristic look that suits him. He catches me staring and smirks, "You're a quiet one. I bet you I can make you squeal with pleasure."

Gross. Guys who can make you squeal with pleasure never have to say it out loud.

"Spike, meet Tommy. He'll fuck anything from any planet."

"Pansexual, you fucker," Tommy protests, "Get it right. I have refined tastes."

"Nice to meet you, Tommy," I say calmly ignoring both their comments.

Tommy walks over with his towel wrapped around his waist and leans on the wall next to me, "We should wrestle sometime on the battlefield."

"He's your new trainer. Watch how you speak to him," Cassius informs Tommy.

"Oh, I... I'm sorry," Tommy stands up straight, "I didn't mean to offend you. I just thought you were another refugee." In doing so, his towel falls, and a brick meets my eyes.

Noted. I'm keeping an eye on him. I mean... not like that. Well, scratch that.

Tommy leans into one ear not bothering to pick up his towel, "But if you want to... you know... later after training I won't tell anyone."

I don't say anything. I would do it, but Cassius is staring daggers at me.

But if I accidentally hit my head on a brick... it wouldn't be my fault. Right?

"So, no?" Tommy asks. His eyes squint for a second. Recognition just like Numitor and his wife. He clears his throat, "You have very pretty eyes." He pauses confused, "Have we met before?"

Cassius smacks his head, "Go, get ready you idiot."

"You're just jealous of me," Tommy boasts as he walks to the center of the room. His green Gamma-2 inspired battle suit drops in to his hand from the laundry machine dispenser. His chest leads the way out of the room. His brick flopping around ready to knock someone out.

"He's a douchebag but he's useful," Cassius grins, "He grows on you."

I bet. I bet he grows inside people too.

Just then, a curtain opens beside the shower Tommy left. But there is no one there. Wet footprints appear on the floor and stop in front of me and Cassius. The shadow of what Tommy looks like swivels on the floor beside the footsteps.

A body-less voice comes from silence.

"He has his redeeming qualities. You'll eventually come to see. I'm Brody."

"You're a shadow person from Opaque." I say remembering my files.

In my eight hundred years, I was never good at staring at shadow people. Imagine hating eye contact and then not being able to see someone making eye contact with you.

"One hundred percent. Tommy and I have been friends for years. He isn't a bad person just weird. Plus, he knows that anything he does. I do. So, it's as if he has a guard always watching his back."

Brody pats my back unexpectedly and I jump.

"Glad to finally meet you. Cassius told me a Time Keeper was coming to train us. Your energies are very nice. Your shadow is sad. Did you lose someone too? A lover? Lovers? A daughter? A son to the cosmos? Is he still alive? Vampire son? This is very odd. You miss your instructor. Thea?"

I've had Shadow People read me before. They always have difficulties reading Time Absorbers since most of our lives are lived being reincarnated. They can never pinpoint exactly where in time things happened to us. Vakander used to call them powerful psychic bastards since they can read energies and tap into memories from the past, present, and future. Powerful beings to have on your side during war especially when they could read every last one of your thoughts or implant hallucinations.

"Tommy would be very willing to have some fun with you. I wouldn't mind it either. I'm more of a voyeur anyway, but you're not bad looking." Brody continues, "You know Jimmy. I miss him. Your paths crossed for a moment, or two, in a past lifetime."

Cassius turns to me and speaks.

"The rope that led us to the Mansion on the Lake. So you have met Jimmy before?"

"More than met. It's complicated."

"More complicated than Tommy?" Cassius jokes.

"Just as complicated as Tommy." Brody adds.

Cassius's face stops mid sneer.

So, he knows.

If Cassius can hide things about himself, I will too. He doesn't need to know about my past relationship with Jimmy. He doesn't need to know that our love story ended abruptly on Lykos. I jump in to Tommy's empty stall and leave Cassius's jaw on the floor.

———

Once I finish cleaning myself, I change into an armored orange and black one-piece fitted suit. It is an Epsilonian male battle-suit. **SPIKE** is etched on my upper right bicep. This outfit makes me feel naked. I'm not the skinniest person either. Being shy of two-hundred and twenty pounds makes an outfit like this highlight both the good and the bad. My ass being the good and some jelly rolls being the bad. Luckily the armor is adaptive cloth. It fills in the uneven parts of me that make me want to run back to my room and never come out.

"The suit looks good on you," Cassius compliments as we both have differing opinions. His suit looks like mine but better suited to his physique.

"I'd rather be wearing a sock."

"I have a few in the room that we can sew together if you're being serious." Cassius jokes. I stare daggers at him. You can joke about my entire life being a joke but not my appearance.

He sighs when I don't respond, "I'm trying to be nice. If we have to work together, the least we can do is try to get along or pretend we're friends."

"Now you wanna play nice after being a dick for almost two days. Did your heart grow all of a sudden?"

I leave the air stale and awkward.

I follow him closely down the stairs and into the hallway. Cassius guides us up more spiral staircases. Exercise in this place never fucking ends.

"Why do these suits have to be so snug?" I complain. "They're as bad as your attitude."

"They're mobility suits. You move right, left, up, down and the suit moves with you. This adaptive cloth is different than what you're used to. Where on Tempus it automatically knows your body type, here we're a bit more archaic and the cloth has to feel your muscles moving to adapt."

"Is this what we're wearing to fight on Exile?" I taunt him knowing this suit wouldn't last a second against a Siren Cannibal.

"Yes. The suits have micro-armor underneath that senses when you're in battle or danger and it deploys immediately. You'll see what I'm talking about once we're out there." He smiles, "We have tailors on hand to add any adjustments to the suits."

A girl and boy with purple hair march downstairs almost in sync. Their Lycan humanoid facades are visible to a trained eye. The longer I stare the more I can see their real forms. Their skin black with a purple mane and fur. Large black head with wolf teeth prominent enough to crush an enemy's head. Seeing past the mask creates a headache and I stop trying. This used to happen with Jimmy and Thea all the time. Lycan and Barretta children always came in pairs because of the Imbarasi Viles women were given to repopulate after their mass casualties. These Imbarasi Viles ensured every person who gave birth did so to at least two children, and, sometimes, more would come out. Lykos were administered the Viles after it was colonized by Kairos and given the name change from Necrpolis to Lykos. Barretta administered theirs shortly after Kairos decimated their population. It's rare to see Lycan or Barrettan children to be born as an only child.

Both beings have purple suits and crazy long voluminous hair. She holds on to his arm with one hand and with the other uses her cane. The girl's arm reads: **CELESTIA**. And the boy's reads: **EMORY**.

"You're going the wrong way, Cassie." Celestia scoffs.

"I'm dealing with a personal matter, Celestia. We'll be there in a second."

"Thea's gone for two seconds and you're already hooking up with the new recruits. Shame on you, Cassius." Emory sneers. "Don't see nice buns like that every day. I don't remember Vesta opening a walking bakery."

"He's your new trainer. And why does it matter that Thea is gone?" Cassius says visibly frazzled, "I'm a free man with free choices."

"Oh, C'mon, Cassie," Celestia puts her hand on his chest and Cassius smacks it away, "We all know you've made love to her... in your dreams." She pauses to look at his hand, "And possibly pretending she was your hand."

Celestia's movements are like that of a snake. Irises redder than blood and stuck on no one. She is trying to intimidate me, but I like her already. She's serving absolute cunt and exuding bigger dick energy than any guy I've ever met.

"Hey," Emory points to me, "You're the one everyone's been talking about. The reason we have all these new guards and curfews."

"They think I'm a threat." I confirm his statement, "Maybe I should be afraid of myself."

Emory smirks, "If you ever give us any reason to fear you, we'll just cut out that pretty little brown neck of yours. Celestia and I love raw meat especially when it smells like that of a Time Keeper."

Emory knows what I am. How interesting. It seems like everyone else is reading me more than I've been reading them. Distrust is heavy here. Vesta has her claws in everyone. They think they're viewing me from a microscopic lens, but I can see through everything. Their intimidation is born from a fear of the unknown. What else isn't she telling them?

On Tempus, the citizens were always too afraid to rebel. Backstabbing Kairos was never a thought, at least not a rational one, or his armies because of their power, so, in turn, we all trusted each other. Paranoia was never an issue since we had no doubt in anyone's loyalty.

"Good thing, I'll never give you a reason to do so," I say.

"Get going both of you. We don't need any more distractions," Cassius tells them.

"We're excited to get to know you more, Stranger." Celestia stares in my general direction and tosses her hair in my face.

Once they're out of ear shot, Cassius tells me.

"Troublemakers. Their Rope connection is the strongest I've ever seen." Cassius sighs, "You also might want to stay away from Tommy. Emory has a thing for him. They're not tangled by Ropes but by sheets. I don't need you mulled and discarded by the Twins."

"Was it that obvious that I was staring?"

"You weren't being coy by staring directly at his dick."

AT THE TOP of the stairs, we round a corner and walk into a glowing hallway. We're so high up we have to be in one of the castle's attics. The arched, attic door buzzes with harsh blue beams of light blinding the air around it. The sound of a heartbeat hazes our ears. A heartbeat symbol appears like a scar around my wrist constantly changing. Everything around us is otherworldly. Someone is trapping the attic in a Pulse. All of time fractures inside of the room. It's a Time Prison. To put it simply, the moment I step in to that room all time used inside of the room will not be consumed by the external world. One minute in there means no time passes in the real world. All aging slows as well.

"What's going on here?" I step back from Cassius.

"We're not going to trap you inside of the Time Prison. May told me you were stripped of almost all your powers by Kairos. You usually have time on a different planets to relearn them over a span of years. But we don't have years to fight our enemies. Our mission to Exile is in a week. Maybe you can't learn all your past powers but if you can relearn enough of them, then we have a higher chance of surviving."

"You really did your research on me, didn't you?"

"I thought you were my enemy. Templites and Time Keepers have been given a bad name across the galaxy because of Kairos. I did everything in my power to learn how to snuff you out if need be. I didn't want to underestimate you in case I had to protect my friends."

Cassius opens the door to the Time Prison attic. The attic has high ceilings and large round glass windows at both ends facing the sunrise and sunset. A desk sits by the sunrise window. On the other end, rows of books are pressed in a tight corner by a green window nook. A chair with a rug underneath is propped in front of the mini library. The ceiling slants up in one direction and possibly never ends. My eyes travel down from the ceiling to the center of the room.

My soul leaves my body. For a few seconds, I'm not here. Unease creeps into my limbs. In the middle of the room, twenty cement pedestals surround a round empty space. On each pedestal lies a worn Artifact. A piece of bloody clothing, a pair of glasses, a mansion, a bracelet, and sixteen others.

I recognize them. Mementos from my past lives.

I walk to the pedestals to touch the Artifacts. A teal tentacle stops me from grabbing them. It is one off Cassius's Ropes.

"Not yet," Cassius says, "Once you touch it, a Memory Pulse will open up and it will send you for a moment back to that specific time period."

Nostalgia grips my heart. Every soul I ever encountered trapped in the memories of these Artifacts. I should have been the one to retrieve them. It should have been me who went and found these.

"I know that but... I'm more... How did you find these? I kept them hidden."

"Vesta had the idea to find them. Thea saw you in her visions and watched you hide the Artifacts all over the universe. May, Thea, Jimmy, and I have been traveling to different planets to acquire all these memories. The Barretta Committee barely approved this. They didn't understand why we would want you to regain your memories, or, for you to become a little more powerful with each Artifact. They realized that they needed an equally powerful being to go up against

Kairos in the event he ever regained his abilities. Getting all twenty wasn't easy."

I rotate in a circle trying to remember glimpses from my past lifetimes. Blocks remain clouding my brain hiding past abilities, information I learned on my abilities, and the powers I created in those worlds. The pain each one caused to forge is fresh. The heartache of being ripped away from a beautiful life. My eyes stay on one Artifact in particular. The Mansion. We were at peace for a moment. Jimmy, Tommy, our daughter, and I. A mesh of the past, present, and future. In a future that never existed or has yet to be created. The only peace and ease I have ever felt. I remember being killed that one last time. The end of my twenty-fifth incarnation. I knew the moment I was Activated on Venus that I would die. That it was the end for me. And, the next thing I know, Vakander and May are saving me from Tempus.

Cassius snaps me back to reality.

"We're only missing five. We have been doing this for the past four years. Kairos was catching on. And I guess some other beings are too. The past few missions have been us fighting off Time Keepers and rogue mercenaries."

A realization hits me. That's why Cassius hated me when he first saw me. This was all my fault. He's been risking his life for my ungrateful ass. Not just his. Thea's as well.

"You couldn't get to the Artifact on Exile?"

Cassius nods. His face droops. A dark cloud comes over him like if he isn't here at all. His eyes are blank. Many eyes in my past lives have carried this expression and I've never liked being on the receiving end. I want to console him, but I don't know how. How do I console a boy I just met?

It takes him a moment to gather himself.

"May Pulsed us to the front of the mansion. May and I were tasked with killing all Siren Cannibals outside of the mansion while Thea and Jimmy went and stole one of the Artifacts. They were captured by their leader. He used his luring song to hypnotize them."

I wonder what else his Ropes can do if he was tasked with killing Siren Cannibals. He continues, "We were overwhelmed. These side missions to retrieve the Artifacts were done under the condition that no Barretta soldiers would need to assist in bringing us home or helping us find them. So, with no one to help us, May extracted us. Since then, they have upped their security around the mountains. Pulse Blockers block every point of entry. We haven't been able to Pulse back in there with reinforcements. They must have placed Pulse Blockers all over the mountains."

Pulse Blockers were invented and distributed throughout the galaxy by Vakander to stop Time Keepers from coming onto every planet. They are a barrier first and a blackhole dissipator second. Since they were created, many have been stolen his idea and placed them all over the universe. Black markets have replicated the design and created traps for Pulses which can injure or kill Time Keepers and Time Absorbers if they walk onto the wrong side of the galaxy.

Pulse Blockers being on Exile means Vakander had to drop them off there at some point. If Exile has them, are they trying to keep me out? Or are they trying to keep Kairos out? May? But anyone one of us can walk through the force field a Pulse Blocker creates. No Pulses can be made in or out but it doesn't stop people from walking through them. There has to be some sort of strategy behind this.

Cassius crosses his arms, "They know we're coming back. But, now that I've checked your Ropes, we have the knowledge of Exile we need. We know how many Siren Cannibals we have to deal with. In hindsight, it was idiotic to try and get your Artifact without knowing how many of them there were. Regret is pitiful inaction."

His mopey eyes make me feel bad for the dude. Especially since it is technically my fault Thea went to find my Artifact. But my mind nags me about Vesta lying to us. I'm pulled in two directions. I'm not trusting Vesta. But Cassius digs the knife deeper by sniffling a little and restraining tears. Damn, he's a simp.

"We will get her back." I say to stop him from barreling into another depressive episode. "I will do everything in my power to get them home."

Finding her will help us get one of the last Artifacts.

Adding Cassius's version of the story to the mix makes me understand why he has been looking at me like a conspiracy theorist. Maybe it's just my trust issues. Maybe I'm just the problem... Maybe the Siren Cannibals have evolved in to madness and are devouring the lives of innocents.

Or maybe two truths can coexist. Vesta is up to something and so are the Siren Cannibals.

But what? What game are they playing? Or... am I becoming susceptible to Vesta's lies?

No. I can't be, not me.

But if I am, damn, Vesta has one stellar PR team.

EMORY GUIDES me to the dining hall after our morning chat with Spike and Cassie. We sit at the usual table we always sit at with Ashley and Marina. I hear Jupiter's beautiful curls bouncing in to the room. She passes me trailing behind the scent of raspberries and lilac. In my lustful dreams, flowers cloud her naked body.

I'm too gay for this shit. Emory complains through our Mind Link, *I'm blocking your thoughts out. I'd rather not picture Jupiter in such a intimate erotic pose.*

They sit at their usual table quietly discussing the previous day's events. I turn towards them.

My wolf hearing enhances to focus in on them.

"She's staring again." Jenny teases.

"She's cute but looks high maintenance." Alejandra harshly comments.

Emory's taunting from before plays in my head. I could initiate. I can do this. It doesn't take much, right? What do I have to lose if she rejects me? Just the crippling embarrassment that is sharing the same space as her every morning. Fuck it. We could all be dead tomorrow.

I jump up.

"Celestia?" Emory interrupts my endless thoughts, "What are you doing?"

I ignore him and release my walking cane and start heading over to the general direction of Jupiter's voice. My legs are lead but moving at a stuttering stumbling pace.

I want this. If I want something, I should go for it.

I hear Emory and Ashely frantically speaking to each other.

"She's going to actually do it this time." Ashley says surprised.

"She better not chicken out." He knows I can hear him.

You got this. Emory Mind Links to me.

Do I though?

Jupiter and the girls have gone silent the only sound coming from her curls swaying back and forth. Her heart is beating just as fast as mine. We're in sync? She wants this too. Just as much as I do. We're both nervous. I sneer. I got this.

My cane hits the edge of the table and I stop. I want to send out Vibrations to see her reaction, but I don't want a headache so early in the morning. I can see her general shape as a shadowy figure. That's all that matters. All three of their blurred shadows stare at me.

I jump right in.

"Hey Jupiter," I manage to get out without choking, "I was wondering if you wanted to hang out later tonight?"

Jupiter stays quiet for a second, "what would we be doing?"

"We can have a picnic on the rooftop of the castle. Or we could just hang out..." My words fall off.

There is a silence that rearranges my brain. I come back to my real body and realize how crazy this was. I only did this to prove to Emory that I could. That I could do this. I didn't need to do that. I could've just...

"I would love that. What time?"

"Right after training."

"Works for me."

"Well, I'll see you then."

"See you darling."

I slowly make a confident walk back to the table with Ashley, Marina, and Emory. I sit down and everyone starts whispering loud enough for everyone in the dining hall to hear.

"She said yes." Emory cheers.

Jupiter hears Emory and her heart relaxes.

"Yeah." Is all I can say.

"Wait, are you two getting married tonight? Can I be the flower girl" Ashley teases to break the tension.

"Can I be the flower girl's assistant?" Emory asks jokingly. "No, your wedding planner/best maiden-that's-a-dude/brother/best friend/god father of your future babies."

"You two are ridiculous."

"Isn't that how lesbians work?" Emory taunts, "They just get married when they meet?"

"Usually." Ashley adds, "at least from what I've seen. Any baby names picked out? I think Aurora would be nice. It means new beginnings."

"I'm glad you two are enjoying your selves." I spout.

"So, what are you going to do on this date?" Ashley asks.

"I told her we could have a picnic on the roof or hang out..."

"Hang out is code for fucking. You know that right?" Emory asks.

"No, I didn't. I wouldn't have asked her that if I knew."

"Already too late. Dust off the cobwebs sissy. And show her your best moves."

"I can help." Ashley adds, "With the picnic portion of it, not the fucking. She's all yours."

I'm doing this. I'm really doing this.

"What do I talk about?" I ask.

"Let it start naturally." Ashley says. "She obviously thinks you're attractive. Get to know each other. If it's awkward, then just do as Emory says and skip the wedding. Get straight to having fun."

Marina adds, "That girl has been eye fucking you since I could remember."

"That's a good thing?" I ask.

"It means you shouldn't be worried." Marina sneers, "She's ready ready."

"For what?"

"Celestia," Emory's smacks his head, "How are you not understanding? Have fun. Enjoy yourself. She said yes for a reason. You did the hardest part. What could go wrong on this date?"

———

I wait for a shower to open up. After breakfast's excitement, I just need to wash off the nerves before our training day starts. Refugees from the planets of Venus and Gamma stay here. Lines drag down the hallway for the women's restroom come late morning. I'm closer to the front of the line now. A curtain pulls slightly open. I hear Jupiter's hair bouncing beyond the curtain. She whispers under her breath, "Come here."

"Me?" I say loud enough to sound like a cough.

"Yes!"

I remove my clothes and wrap a towel around my chest. Walking stick guiding me around the laundry dispenser. I sneak in to the shower. Jupiter closes the curtain.

"I don't want to wait for tonight." Jupiter says with lust in her voice, "I want you right now."

Jupiter gently kisses my lips. I kiss back making the kisses aggressive. She turns the faucet on. I remove my towel. Jupiter digs her nails in to my lower and upper back. I lean in to the shadow of her neck and suck on it. At first soft and gently then a little more forceful as she starts to silently suppress moans. As she squirms more, she bites in to my shoulder to stop anyone from hearing. My mouth trails from her neck to her large, round nipples. I use one hand to play with her beauty and I massage her nipples with my tongue. I switch to her other breast before kissing down her beautiful dark stomach. My mouth trails until it reaches her clit.

My mouth teases her clit. My mouth alternating from it to my version of heaven incarnate.

Her legs tremble. She bites in to her hand to suppress any whimpers. Jupiter abruptly stops and I pull away.

"Are you okay?"

"Yes." Jupiter kisses me on the mouth for thirty seconds. The best thirty seconds of my whole life before she adds, "I wanted to save more for later when we *hang out*. I want you to have an appetizer before we get to the picnic."

Cruel temptress. I smile frustrated but happy. Jupiter leaves the restroom by giving me one last kiss.

Maybe Emory is right. Maybe having a little fun is okay.

CHAPTER 28

THEA

"WHY SHOW *me all of these memories?" I ask Beelzebub*

> *"All dead beings must accept their deaths. But only those that come to terms with it and have no left-over resentment can cross over to a peaceful afterlife."*

"I can accept the idea that I died, but I am not ready to crossover." I think about my planet and my brother. Tamashii turned Spike. And all the innocent lives lost with Kairos's attack. Where did they go?

> *"They came here first. They talked to me. Some accepted their deaths."*

"And the others?"

> *"Are waiting for their leader to bring them home."*

———

Beelzebub takes me to a balcony five stories off the ground level. Below, an army of wolves all made of purple flames bow for me. They rise in unison and howl.

"They do not respond to me. When the time is right. You will lead them back in to the physical world and exact your vengeance."

"My people."

My flames shake. How can flames cry? They are not capable of that so we must show them our pain. Show them how we suffered. Show them our tears through scorch marks. Burn the idea in to their heads that too many have suffered already.

"What do I have to do?"

———

Beelzebub takes me to an endless cylindrical chamber.

"The next stage will be growth..."

She disappears and leaves me alone. I roam the chamber for hours looking and looking for an exit. I start to panic and scream trying to reach a wall just so I can break through it. I give up frustrated.

"Thea?"

A familiar voice calls me. The voice echoes in the chamber over and over again.

"Why him?"

My mother's voice. It echoes and echoes until it's booming through the chamber.

"Why him?"

"Why him?"

"Why him?"

"Why him?"

"Why him?"

———

I'm back on Lykos in my physical form. We walk across an elevated balcony on the rear of the castle. An endless series of arched windows to our right. A cool floral breeze fills the humid air coming from the jasmine trees staggered in between the arched windows. Under the balcony, a waterfall on the side of the castle feeds in to the moat and the lake below.

"Why Cassius? Do you not see the bald spot on his head?" My mother jokes, "You are very pretty. You can do better than him."

"Maybe, but do I have to love him for how he looks physically?"

"No. You do not, but a Venus humanoid boy?"

"Not again ma. Not you with your subtle interplanetary racism. Grandpa married grandma and she was a witch. Then, you were born. Did you have a problem then?"

"I do not have a problem with my birth if that is what you are asking."

"Then why are you so worried about Cassius and I being together. Isn't that what Kairos has a problem with too?"

"Do not compare me to a genocidal maniac."

"But little ideologies and issues create bigger issues."

"You may be right. But that bald spot is glaring."

"I can just give him some of my fur if he gets cold at night."

My mom laughs. "Very accommodating of you."

We walk through arched canopy rows of jasmine vines growing around wooden frames. Each of them providing shade to the balcony. Little petals cascade leaving their floral perfume everywhere.

"Are you ready to be queen?" My mom asks.

A silence follows. I'm not. I never wanted to be queen. I grew up with the knowledge that Jimmy would be king. One day he decided it would be too much work and gave it up to me. In the past, a new ruler would be picked by pitting both royal siblings against each other in an arena and having them duel to the death. My mother was the surviving sibling. Jimmy probably didn't want that for us.

"I do not expect you to be ready now. But one day you will be." She sighs, "I'm glad Jimmy did not subject you two to a duel. You were

both born with so much potential. I was scared it would go to waste in a duel."

"Why did you duel your sister?"

"The time came, and we were both very young and stupid. We assumed being Queen would bring fame and riches and boys, and while it has, being queen is a lot of responsibilities. Your grandfather wanted the best to survive. He was following laws put in place by our twisted ancestors and amplified by Kairos when he ruled Lykos. Your grandfather's reign and all those before him were of proving your worth. Truth is, I wish I had broken that cycle. Your aunt and I were both on the brink of death. And she did the unimaginable." She stares at my unwavering face, "She killed herself to save me."

Finding out this biting family lore startles me.

"Why?"

"Because she did not see his rules as fair. She did not want to rule on a throne that would continue the wheel of violence. 'When does the violence end?' were her last words. I didn't understand them until Jimmy gave up his throne for you. So the question I ask you is: "When does the wheel of violence end?"

"What do you mean?"

"Being queen is about carrying traditions and practices. Ruling in order to keep control. But what rules can you do away with in order to finally stop misery from infecting everything." Tears well in her eyes, "I miss my sister every day. More than my mother and father. She was my protector and guidance in to this lonely cruel world. I do not want that for you and Jimmy. I want a better future. One where children do not have to duel for a throne. One where children can live freely." She cups my hands in hers, "Thea, do what you must to break the cycle. But never let anything come in between you protecting your kingdom or your family. Love the bald headed boy and live a wonderful life but live it with joy."

———

I return to the endless chamber and the echoes stop. My mother is gone. Jimmy is gone. Cassius is gone. Everyone I love is gone. But they don't have to be. I can still fight for them.

I was never supposed to find a way out of the chamber.

I push my flames out as far as I could push my powers when I was alive. Flames extend in all directions for hours. Pain leeches to my core. Agony seers through my being. I ignore all of it. Because none of it matters. Nothing matters when you have nothing to lose and everything to gain. Nothing matters unless you push. Push until the pain is no longer there. The echoes start to reverberate in the room. I push them back. They have no place here. Hours and hours of pushing the echoes back until I'm hitting the barriers. The walls start to fissure all over. Cracks start to collide in to one another. And I push harder. Harder. The pain starts to subside. It doesn't exist. It only hurts because I think it hurts.

———

There is no pain, no feelings, there is nothing here. The Fourth Dimension is what you make of it. It can be the entry to all worlds and universes. Nothing can bar you here from doing what needs to be done.

My body splits and escapes through all the cracks...

In one universe, I'm a scientist.

Here, I'm the queen that killed Jimmy.

· · ·

Kairos has conquered the universes in this one.

Humanoid robots have taken over every planet.

Pan is the king of all planets.

Peace has been achieved here.

I slip through all the cracks and all the Threads. A never-ending chamber of Threads that open up to endless realities. Threads upon Threads. My flames soar and soar and soar and...
A purple blinking Thread leads me home. Back to Beelzebub.

————

Beelzebub reels me back in with a green Thread wrapped around my waist. I have a waist. I have a full corporeal form again. Not physical. Just flames with hands, feet, eyes, and a mouth. My hair no longer falls but floats to a narrow peak of flames.

"How does it feel to see the grand scope of everything?"

"Freeing." Nothing binds me to this reality. Nothing keeps me here. Only I choose to do so.

"It is nice to see the possibilities and know that you have choices. To see that in any given lifetime you can save your world or doom it. It's up to you." Beelzebub

unties the Threads from my waist, "What will you choose to do? Did you still want to fight for them, or would you rather roam the universes freely?"

I am not tethered here. I choose to be here. It is no longer my duty to protect my people. But my choice.

"I'm ready to destroy Kairos in this universe and save my kingdom."

"GLAD TO FINALLY SEE MY two favorite boys working together," May's voice erupts from behind us. She must have come in quietly while we were talking, "Our team grows stronger with you by our side, Spike. You've had twenty-five lives to try and escape Kairos on your own. You are no longer going to fight him alone."

Unnecessary jab but cool.

"You couldn't save me sooner." I tease.

"I wish I could've saved you sooner. When Kairos rose to power, he stripped me of my resources. I had to build myself from the ground up. So, while you were being sent from planet to planet, I was trying to stay under the radar. I jumped from planet to planet looking for help and safety. Back then, it was easier to garner support for Templites because everyone associated us with Kronos instead of Kairos. They saw us as fleeing refugees of Kairos's totalitarian regime. The name Templite didn't have as much of a stigma."

"I spent the next few centuries fighting back Kairos's armies on different planets. At one point, Vakander was tossed out by Kairos, and he joined our side. My primary responsibility was stopping my brother from causing the maximum amount of harm. I feel like I never did enough. He always had more man power. I ended up on

Barretta after Kairos pitted Gamma-2 against Barretta. He forced the Gamma-2 armies to eliminate Barretta. Of course, the Barretta armies were stronger and with their advantages of War Birds and aerial attacks, the Gamma-2 soldiers were captured or taken care of. I oversaw the reconstruction of Barretta with Vesta, Cassius, Celestia, and Emory. Celestia and Emory were training to be soldiers at the time, but the Royal Lycan wolves wanted them to learn about politics early on. It was around that time that the Royal Lycan Wolves sent us a message that they assumed a Time Absorber was among their midst. Thea sent us messages that the Time Absorber was drawing the Templite Throne, pictures of Kronos, and asking for people he once knew. We assumed it was you, but we could not accept a high priority Templite refugee. Barretta could not fight off Kairos if they knew we took you back. You were safer on Lykos with the wolves to protect you. The Barretta armies grew gradually as the population naturally rose again. The dead were memorialized, and War Bird statues were erected beyond the mountains where our highest civilian populations took a hit. No one lives there now. Dallies grow in full bloom and every year we celebrate those that passed in that horrific mass genocide."

"The Royal Lycan Wolves had plans to extract you in your Lycan form to Barretta. Our plans meant nothing. We should have anticipated an attack on one of the largest armies in all of the Scorned Planets." The Scorned Planets were the twelve planets against Kairos forming armies to dethrone him. Some of them enduring the brunt of the Cleansing. "You died on Lykos and were taken back to Tempus. Jimmy helped us track you down to Venus a couple years later. We all thought he was going crazy when he said he could smell you on Venus. Barretta was willing to supply the Crafts that would extract you under the condition that no Barrettan lives were harmed. So, Vakander was permitted temporary stay on Barretta to make an extraction plan. Our original plan included us taking you from Venus. Vakander with more knowledge of Pulses and their Placenta Pod accompaniments advised otherwise. The Placenta Pods send a

Data Link to The Library of Souls. The Library of Souls is a massive artificially intelligent room. It holds a holographic diagram of the entire universe that Kairos can access Time Absorber intelligence from. The Placenta Pods act as a tether to all Time Absorbers in the universe. From the Library of Souls, Kairos can track on the map where the Time Absorber last used their Pulse through the Data Link. Breaking you out meant breaking out your Placenta Pod too"

"The knowledge Vakander had was the reason Kairos tried to have him assassinated when he rose to power. He did not want any secrets of Tempus or Lykos to be released to the world."

"Three components went in to saving you. One: breaking in to the Revival Unit. Two: stealing your Placenta Pod which Avi gave me hell for. And three: having vampire armies in Limbo ready to fight off Templite soldiers."

"How many causalities in order to save me?"

"Saving you was our top priority. Barretta expected us to return alive or else..."

I interrupt her, "How many did you sacrifice to save me?"

"Seven thousand wounded. Five hundred passed on."

Fuck me. No. This is what I tried to avoid every time I tried saving myself from Kairos.

"There are vampire soldiers on the front lines right now constantly pushing Templite soldiers back from the Neutral and Scorned Planets. Every day a few die so that the Scorned Planets can prepare for war. Thousands are born so that more can enlist in the future. Vakander has his vampire breeding farms pushing out as many soldiers as possible. Barretta knows that one day it will have to throw its full force behind every other planet against Tempus. Kairos has been attacking the Scorned Planets to debilitate their armies because he knows we're coming. I made Barretta a promise. That you would be the new Time Lord one day if we saved you. I'm not the Barretta Committee. I don't care if you become the new Time Lord. My goal is to keep you and the Power Crystal safe."

"At the expense of everyone else's safety?" The more people I meet, the more people I feel like I'm leading to their deaths. I've been in this story before. I don't want to grow attached to these people. I care about my life but I'm not ready to have these people lay their lives down for me. Or have my presence be the reason Kairos kills them for hiding me away.

But I don't want to be alone.

"Whether you're here or on Gamma-2 or Exile, Kairos will hunt everyone in this universe down that doesn't match his description of universal perfection. He will eventually come for the Scorned Planets." She pauses to gather her thoughts then continues, "Look, everyone here in this castle and the galaxy has lost something because of Kairos. Those who haven't have seen their friends in agony or have joined our cause because they believe in what we are fighting for. Since Kairos was young, my brother was a determined one. He would do absolutely anything to get what he wanted. You've seen it yourself. He is scared a mixed-race child will overthrow him even though he is one himself. So, what does he do? Kairos sets out to purify the galaxy's races. In doing so, he slaughters trillions of children. You're safer anywhere in the galaxy than every other child. He needs you alive. You are one of his keys to regaining ultimate power."

All this information causes my brain to short circuit. Confusion muddles my thoughts. Forgotten memories try to cleave their way in to my skull. They push for me to remember. It's right there. Gahhhh-hhh. Fuck, this is so awful. I just want to remember this one fucking thing.

"I can fill in the blanks. I know you don't remember everything. I know that you remember certain things. The Artifacts will help you remember everything you have forgotten. And until then, we don't expect you to know everything. It must be frustrating to be in this current position. We're here to help. Everyone in this castle is here to help. Everyone we have met so far serves a purpose," May explains, "Let's start at the beginning," May heaves and holds back tears, "Titus, my father, died because Vakander and Kairos attacked him in a mutiny. Kairos planted this foolish idea in Vakander's mind that they could rule the galaxy as kings of the galaxy with unlimited power. Behind my back, Kairos seduced Vakander and used him for his vampire armies. The plan was to strip Titus of his power and split it between themselves. As Vakander already had influence throughout the galaxy, he found it an inciting offer. But my father didn't die because of his wounds. In his final moments, he stopped Time for one second."

Some distant and forgotten part of me remembers this story. A shadow of a memory like deja vu. I lived through it. Why can't I remember all of it? It's the story of why Kairos could never really kill me. Not all of it comes back to me. All of this feels like blacking out after a joyful, mindless night of drinking. My anxiety surges. I can remember glimpses of every life shortly before everything faded into a teleporting fog. Going from place to place without the knowledge of how I got there. My body decides when I'm actively awake participating for a short moment until I wake up the next day in a stranger's bed with a piercing, not remembering how I ended up naked. I remember chopped up pieces. Though a fog blocks the memory of everything in between.

"Relax." May rubs my back as she sees me struggling again to remember minor details. I start scratching at my scalp. Frustration stabs my overloaded brain. My anxious foggy brain grasps at endless nothings of memories trying to piece a life I once lived together. Gibberish mixed with nonsensical bullshit.

"One second was all he needed to prevent his unlimited power from falling into the wrong hands. In that one second, he ripped his Power Crystal from his heart and placed the first crystal piece inside of you. Then, Kronos tasked one of the Epsilon Coven members to place the other six pieces inside of six selected beings across space and time. The Power Crystal keeps the universe and everything in it alive. Without it, the universe would crumble and implode in on itself. Your grandfather saw you and six others as worthy successors to the Templite Throne. For those that weren't born yet, the crystal remained under the care of Salem until they found the right being.

Ever since, Kairos, has been trying to figure out how to pull out the Power Crystal from your body. You were the only guinea pig within his grasp. Every time, he has done so, he has almost destroyed the entirety of existence. There was no way to track the individual Power Crystal pieces until they were merged in to a being's body. Eventually, the individual crystal pieces merged with the souls of the selected beings. At that point, the seven Crystals mixed with the destiny of the beings involved and were able to be tracked through Seer visions. Kairos used to be a Seer until Madame Destiny revoked his ability to see the future. So, Kairos has been using Time Absorbers to kidnap Seers across the galaxy to help find the seven pieces of the Power Crystals."

"The only way to overthrow, Kairos," May adds, "is to unite all seven Crystals and use their power to kill him, before he finds them."

All those centuries living captured by Kairos. Most Time Absorbers never lasted as long as I did. They were allowed to retire but not without new beings taking their place. There was always a retirement segment in every Time Absorbers life where they could raise an entire family. These kids would in turn become the new Time Absorbers. The worn-out Time Absorbers were always allowed to die and disappear into star dust as they were consumed by the universe. But he kept me. Experimented on me. Chased me down, killed me and revived me all for a Crystal. His armies attacked me viciously to recapture me every time. Never allowing me to live a normal life like everyone else.

"There is a way to remove the fragment or else he wouldn't have tried to keep me incapable of rebellion for so long," I assumed he was after my abilities. I could feel it in my core. That's why I hid the Artifacts. That's why I removed my abilities and scattered them across the galaxies. I always told myself I was hiding my abilities to prevent him from getting stronger.

But the real reason I did it was because Titus asked me to do it. The half memory lingers as a whisper to the void. All I can remember now is his voice. I don't remember what he looked like. Just a bodyless voice like my subconscious.

Never let him see all your strength. Hide away your powers. Not for me, but for those that can't defend themselves. Remember to always be a spike in his side. And never forget, I love you, my little Spi.

May continues, "Kairos has been sacking planets for the 'Essence' Artifact for decades since he found out it contains the answer to his dilemma. His search must have triggered a Seer memory for Thea which led us to most of the other Artifacts. We think it is a power that can help remove the Crystals. If he takes the Crystals from the people holding them, we're screwed."

Hesitation clouds my mind.

All beings experience their past lives in dreams and daydreams. Some think they are nightmares. They are recovered as lessons for how to survive. Artifacts are stronger versions of these memories. These Artifacts help channel past lives. My grandfather and I intended for them to one day help me gain my powers back in the event I escaped Kairos. I just never expected to escape Kairos. I never expected to be here today. Alive and breathing without a prison to keep me in place.

———

As I enter the circle, I touch the black glasses with my fingertips, and nothing happens. Cassius and May are confused when nothing happens.

A voice in my head calls to me, *Mijo, put them on.*

His delicate voice. Titus Kronos Guerrero. My grandfather.

My untrusting finger shakes as I open the pair of glasses and place them on my face. A blue line emerges from the first pedestal forming a clock around me...

Myst's Sky Ships
Piper's Cottage Colony
Piper's Cottage Colony
Esmeralda's Castle
Knox's Hidden Forts
Queenie's Castle
Rae's Hidden Tunnels
Avery's Aviaries
Salem's Cathedral
Reyna's Necromancer Temple
Wren's Aerial Temple
Thorn's Cavern Homes
Grave's Cavern Homes

BOOM.

A roar of gravity erupts like a volcano. The floor is ripped from under me. My body free falls like a broken elevator speeding to its doom. I watch the attic sink miles away into stars, gases, and planets.

You are in Limbo. All Time Keepers and Time Absorbers travel through Limbo to access different points in history, dimensions, part of our universes, and timelines, Titus speaks to me.

I'm sucked into an invisible object and excruciatingly spread out like spaghetti and then put together again. My body shoots out of the Pulse and into a horde of galaxies. All around me planets are reforming. Exploded stars are putting themselves back together. The planets are rotating in reverse.

I blink...

———

Purple and red clouds fill the Epsilon atmosphere. I point with my sepia fingers at the red and purple clouds.

"Why do the clouds look like that?" I ask my mom.

Mama Amanda picks vegetables from her garden to make dinner.

"The elements in the air create the redish glow. We use the purple as an atmospheric shield to block out any people that wants to harm us." She replies.

"Why do we need protection?"

"Witches, warlocks, and warwicks are always preparing for a battle even if one will never happen. I love you. And I would do anything to protect you." She caresses my face. Her hands waft an herby scent up my nostrils. I'm hungry already. "You're young and with training you will one day protect yourself. But as you get older and more people enter your life, you will see how far you will go for the ones you love."

I'm only thirteen and can't train with the mages until I'm nineteen. I'm six years away from that day and I can't wait. Time needs to hurry up.

Mama Amanda grabs my hand, and we walk in to our grey stone, two-story cottage. It isn't a big house but it's cozy.

"Go take a bath, Axel." Mama takes off my emerald winter cloak and hangs it on the coat rack, "Mama Reyna and Simon are coming over. I don't want you scaring them off with that smell."

———

I swim in the ten-foot deep and three-foot-wide porcelain tub. A circular window lights up the room with three of the thirteen moons of Lykos concentrated on the woods. Trees reaching to space cast monstrous dark shadows on the brown floorboards. Black candles are perched on every counter dripping endless wax everywhere. An orange glow dances with the moonlight while mist steams from the tub.

My familiar, Lavender, dives underwater transforming from a cat to a mermaid with a cat head and body. I laugh and dive in after it. Her light purple mermaid scales dance through the bubbles and swishing water. We chase each other playing around for another ten minutes.

Once my fingers prune over, Lavender drags me to the surface by my ear. Her mermaid tail and gills return to a full feline body in order to jump from the water on to the floor. Mama Amanda pulls me out of the tub and wraps my naked body in a warm towel. She swirls her finger in circles at the tub draining the water.

"They're here. You spent a little too long swimming."

"I always swim this long."

"We have guests. So, hurry." Mama seems more anxious than usual.

———

My mom dresses me in a suit and tie. Very formal for our usual evening dinner. We walk down the black obsidian staircase in to the kitchen on the right. Our amethyst table is in the shape of a triangle. Mama Reyna sits on one side. The dining room, with dark green wallpaper and floral pattern prints, is circular. A black chandelier hangs over the table. Our walls are covered in spiraling tree branches and darkened leaves coming through the floor boards and in to the room. Mama Amanda is expected to sit on the longest flat side. Meanwhile, I'm sitting next to Simon. Simon's brown skin shines in the candle light. He shifts uncomfortably trying to adjust the itchy suit. It's the same spot in the back by the tags that bothers me. Mama Reyna probably ignored his pleas to wear normal clothes.

Before I sit down, I shift the shirt by two inches on the side and rip the tag from his neck collar. Mama Amanda swishes in my direction with her red lace dress and gives me the side eye. I smile pretending I don't know what I just did. Simon's shoulders sag in relief.

"Thank you." Simon whispers.

Mama Reyna sports a billowing white silk dress that swallows her appearance completely. Shoulder puffs reach higher than her head. A black silk shawl covers her back with gloved hand inserts. Her face is both old and young. Not quite forty but maybe thirty. But one can never tell with de-aging spells and Vida Viles. She could be thousands of years old.

Mama Reyna turns to me after a long period of me staring at her and winks. Her polite way of saying I'm staring. I turn to Simon. His eyes are already on mine. How long has he been staring? My brown face turns red. Sweat starts forming on my head.

Simon smiles awkwardly.

"Everyone sit." Mama Reyna commands.

Food appears floating from the kitchen on to the triangle table.

Mama Reyna and Mama Amanda talk for hours about wars going on in the galaxy. A few Epsilon armies have been dispatched to aid innocent planets being attacked by Templites. Apparently Lykos has one of the strongest armies followed by Epsilon and Barretta. Then someone else. I stop paying attention because Simon stumbles through small talk. It sounds mechanical coming from him. Like it hurts him to say everything he is saying.

A slight headache starts forming at my sinuses. His words a blur.

"I heard you're already training." I switch up the conversation.

"I am. I have been for a year now. They are going to have me train you if you end up in Mama Reyna's group."

"Really?" I ask excited. "No way."

"Yeah. Is that a bad thing?"

"No. I can't wait."

Daydreams cause a headache. My eyes cloud completely white.

An older version of Simon is fighting someone...

A man stands over me and him. Simon is dying. I'm not liking this. I want it to stop.

Get me out of here.

The man kills me next. The white leaves my eyes.

Mama Reyna caresses my face, "What did you see, mijo?"

"I had a bad daydream."

"That was no daydream." My mom adds.

"Then what was it?" I ask confused.

"You possess the Sight." Mama Reyna turns to mom, "Do you have Seers in your lineage?"

Mama Amanda shakes her head, "I'm just as surprised as you are."

Reyna sneers at the response.

"Do you think..."

"I gave birth to him."

"Templites can implant an embryo and have it grow up inside you. Time Absorbers grow up like normal beings."

Mama Amanda stutters gibberish, "But... How?" Tears of horror well in her eyes.

"Nothing they do makes sense to me either." Mama Reyna adds. She stares down at me, "Do you remember who you are?"

"My name is Axel."

"That was not the question I asked."

"What's going on?" Simon interjects.

"Seers can only be produced by having someone in their lineage who was previously a Seer. Seers are rare to have among Epsilonians. Either he's a miracle child or a mole from the Templites. Now, what are we going to do with you?" Mama Reyna threatens.

Mama Amanda steps in front of me, "He's a child. Please leave him alone."

"I will leave him alone under one condition."

"Name it."

"If he becomes a threat..."

"I will personally kill him."

The room stays quiet. As it should considering they just said they'd be willing to kill me if I betrayed them.

"We are no better than *him* if we kill him."

"You are right." Mama Reyna says after a long pause, "I'm taking him to the Coven."

"What if they vote to have him executed?"

"You will uphold your promise."

———

I stand in the center of a dark cathedral with chains on my hands, legs, and waist. A spotlight blinds me to the thirteen silhouetted shadows peering straight at me. The thirteen Coven leaders stand in a circle surveying me. Five witches. Five warwicks. Three warlocks. As I spin, my suit shifts with the tag digging far in to my side. I pull on the chains to scratch and can't reach. Great.

"Esmeralda. Queenie. Piper. Reyna. Amanda. Knox. Avery. Salem. Wren. Rae. Grave. Myst. Thorn." Mama Reyna recites the names of the Coven, "We have all been gathered here today to determine the fate of Axel Wraith. He is suspected to be a Time Absorber living among our people. Although he is a child, his presence can be the demise of our world considering the ongoing war with Tempus."

"This is all a bit much. All I saw was a daydream." I state to everyone.

"A vision of the future?" A woman, with dark ebony skin, blonde waves, and a full body leather outfit strapped with knives on thick thighs, is the first to speak.

"That could be beneficial to our cause. We need a Seer to combat Kairos." A man in layered dull grayish fabrics states.

"Sister Esmeralda and Brother Grave. What if he gives *them* information?" Mama Reyna asks.

"It will be an equal exchange unless they can somehow hack in to his mind. Control him remotely and have him kill all of us." Grave responds.

"They cannot." A warwick with a bald head and feminine features announces. They have tattoos covering their entire body. Their red dress made of lace like Mama Amanda containing their immense presence. Pointy black nails like claws click rhythmically. The dress's skirt flowing all over the floor making them appear to float. "I worked with Templites before." Their femininity and masculinity both prominent in their presence. They say plainly leaving no room for speculation, "His Placenta Pod Data Link will send this conversation to Kairos. Any visions are blocked out from Kairos by Madame Destiny. She started blocking his Seer powers when he started killing people relentlessly."

"Chaos Salem. With your expertise, theoretically" Mama Amanda asks, "How could I give birth to this child?"

"It is the playing of God. Kairos and his strategists have a map of the entire universe with everyone that exists on it. Two Elder Seers are constantly feeding it information of everyone that lives in the galaxy. The two Seers are placed in a state of life and death where they are being sustained by machines that keep them alive. This state of half-life and half-death bypasses Ethereal permission to use Seer abilities. Every month, the strategists and Kairos meet to figure out where to plant their new informants. Once decided, Time Absorbers are de-aged, turned in to the being of their new planet, and they are transported on to Templite Ships. Their de-aging can go as far as a sperm with the ability to grow like a being from that planet. A Templite ambassador is then sent to distribute the Time Absorbers wherever they are needed."

"But how could they get so close to make me have him?" Mama Reyna asks bewildered.

"They usually land on the planet in a desolate area. From there, they disperse Time Absorbers camouflaged in the skin suit of the beings from that planet. They can disperse them in multiple ways. They themselves can implant the sperm in to their bodies and deposit it in to a native being. Which could have happened to you. They can drug you and implant the baby while you are sleeping. Or they can slowly integrate the Time Absorber in child or adult form as a lost soul in need of help."

Mama Reyna and everyone else look thrown off by everything they just heard. I'm definitely a little weirded out. I'm just a science experiment. There has to be word for seeing your existence stripped to the bare bones and realizing you're just a tool for someone else to use.

"It can happen to anyone." Salem reassures, "I will say. Seer bloodlines in Time Absorbers are never seen. Time Absorbers are reconnaissance tools. They wouldn't send a Time Absorber with Seer abilities out to an enemy that can benefit from it."

"You think they made a mistake?" Esmeralda asks.

"Yes, and I think they are keeping him away from Tempus for a reason. As it will grow, it will start to remember its last life. It is the one defect of a Time Absorber's soul. The Wisps remember. Both always remembers." Salem ends their statement.

"Put it to a vote. With the information provided by Chaos Salem who here wishes the boy to be executed?"

Reyna, Myst and Thorn raise their hands.

Salem says the next part, "Who wishes Axel to be given a chance to prove his innocence in our society?"

The remaining witches and warwicks raise their hands.

"It is settled," Reyna states a bit scared, "We will keep him alive. For now."

"Who will mentor him when the time comes?" A burley, pale, lumberjack giant asks. He crosses his rock-like muscular arms.

"I will take him under my guidance," Chaos Salem volunteers, "I will train him. And shall he betray us, I will do the honor of disposing of him. Of course. I will allow for others to bid to be his teacher."

At least we know there's no lack of volunteers ready to kill me.

Why is everyone always so happy to kill me? What if I throw a temper tantrum one day? Can I no longer be hangry whenever I want food? Why do they make clothes with tags in annoying places?

The candles in the cathedral burn brighter illuminating the entire room. A kaleidoscope of colors engulf everyone. Stained glass windows shine brightly with all the colors of the rainbow. Simon looks relieved in the elevated tiered pews. A few other witches, wizards, and warwicks file out of the cathedral. I didn't even know they were here. Someone must have blocked out all sound coming from the audience.

Simon runs over and hugs me, "I'm glad they didn't kill you."

"Me too." Mama Amanda hugs us both. They let me go as Chaos Salem walks up to us.

"I can't help with the Seer visions." Salem starts, "But I will try to help you learn how to master your warlock abilities. That is if no one out bids me for your training. I know what it feels like to be casted aside."

Mama Reyna grabs Simon and drags him away.

His touch lingers painfully one last time.

Salem's eyes stare in pity.

I wonder why?

CHAPTER 31

AXEL

SIX YEARS. For six years, I haven't seen Simon.

These years were pretty boring. Summed up to a few limited experiences and learning in a stagnant period.

Chaos Salem sent me home with basic reading materials to work on until I became nineteen. My task being to memorize every single word in all thirteen of the books given to me by Chaos Salem. Each one representing a Coven member and their tribes. Every day between my studies I wondered where Simon was. Mama Reyna made it clear I was a threat. Warlocks and witches surrounded Mama Amanda's cottage never letting me leave. I was a prisoner trapped for six years in the cottage with only my familiar, Lavender, and Mama Amanda for company. One day I was tired of it all. I would look for a solution to escape the cottage in the books. As I would go to perform them, the spells would vanish and move to another area of the book.

Six years of solitude. I cried, screamed, lost all sanity, and rebelled in every which way.

For example, one day, when Mama Amanda went to teach her students, I burned the house down. I let Lavender loose before it happened. She was my main priority. But they had to let me out and let me leave if there was no cottage. Right?

The fire was snuffed out by Mama Reyna in two minutes. Every charred wall and furniture piece restored. Black fumes dissipated to clean forest air.

I burnt down the house five times.

Mama Reyna scolded me each time. She would tie my feet to the highest branch of a tree for three days and leave me there hanging.

Mama Amanda finally convinced Mama Reyna to let me have a few days to wander around before I did it a sixth time.

That didn't stop me from doing it a sixth time.

The same punishment was dished out though.

My first night out, during my sixteenth year, I used it to explore the woods. I missed fresh air. The creatures. Nature. Lavender guided me to her clan of familiars nesting grounds in a circular meadow. At the bottom of each tree trunk, a hole leading to the nesting tunnels. They showed me the underground tunnels beneath Mama Amanda's Forest leading to Salem's cathedral and we stopped before we reached one of Rae's underground hubs.

They allowed me out once a week. The cats started guiding me around Rae's tunnels. I took advantage of the situation and mapped as much of Rae's tunnels without getting caught. They showed me hidden entrances to Thorn and Grave's cavern homes across the western section of the planet. I would pack a whole day's worth of food. Travel around for half a day exploring as much of Epsilon as I could through Rae's tunnels. And the other half of the day, I would use following cats back to Mama Amanda's cottage.

One day, the fun ended. The cats showed me Rae's headquarters at the center of the entire planet. A map on the wall of the tunnel displayed the headquarters being the return point to all tunnels and blocking access to all other tunnels on Epsilon. Which basically meant, the half day it took for me to reach this point would take longer to get to any of the other destinations on the map. That isn't even accounting for how stealthy I would have to be to make it through the hive-shaped headquarters to access the other tunnels.

I drew the map in a pocket journal I used to map the tunnels in the first place. I ripped out my map and overlaid it on the new map I copied. It matched pretty closely if I do say so myself. The bummer of all of this exploring was realizing I'd never get to explore the other areas of the map. Not until I was nineteen at least.

I still traveled in to the tunnels from time to time, but the idea of never seeing anything new made it boring. My curiosity craved new information. At times, I would ask myself: is it me that wants to know this information or Kairos? Do I have any real thoughts or emotions or ideas? Or does he fabricate my reality? A puppet commanded like a dog to their owner's will. Or a curious sixteen year old curious as to what mysteries live beyond his cage?

———

Every witch, warlock, or warwick is assigned to a member of the Coven to train with on their nineteenth birthday. The Thirteen bid for their picks. The Coven member with the highest seniority in the group would get their pick of students.

Six years later, I am cattle-called into the Kaleidoscope Cathedral with three hundred other potential students that come from all over Epsilon. Three hundred of us share the same birthday. Three hundred of us turn nineteen today and our lives will change forever.

I want Chaos Salem. I don't want the others. My anxiety peaks. What if Mama Reyna picks me so that she could somehow bully me and withhold information? That thought quickly gets brushed under the rug once I hear the other's conversations.

The mages that are expected to be the top students automatically will go with Mama Reyna as she is the oldest and wisest. Others gossip, "Those kids have been training since they were born. Mama Reyna had a magical regiment for future commanders that she puts specific citizens through. The magical regiment follows them from infancy to adulthood creating the strongest offense and defense warriors in the Epsilon army."

The Thirteen Coven members silence the chatter and begin.

Mama Reyna and her twenty picks file out the room.

Two hundred and eighty candidates left.

Esmeralda and Queenie are next as they were the first to join Mama Reyna's side in Epsilon's previous wars. They each take fifteen and go.

Two hundred and fifty candidates left.

Thorn and Grave.

Thirty-five and thirty-five split.

My anxiety starts to ebb when I realize that I'm basically contagious to be seen with. If these children gossip as much as they do, their parents must be worse. And what would it look like to have an accused Time Absorber be a part of your team? As insulted as I am, I don't want them either. Chaos Salem stood up for me when I needed them too. I need a trainer like them.

It still kinda stings to not be picked.

One hundred and eighty candidates left.

Piper and my mom, Amanda.

My mom skips me as I am a conflict of interest.

Thirty, thirty split.

One hundred and twenty candidates.

Myst.

Sixty for one instructor? Damn.

Sixty candidates left.

Wren.

Thirty out.

Thirty candidates left.

Rae.

Ten out.

Twenty candidates left.

Avery

Ten out.

Ten candidates left.

Knox.

Nine.

One candidate left.

I stand in the cathedral alone with Chaos Salem. Their heels click on the colorful mosaic floors.

"I guess it wasn't as hard as I thought it would be to get you." Salem cheers.

"That's all good. I didn't want them anyway." I add. "Where do we go for training?"

"Right here." Salem motions to the cathedral, "This cathedral is mine. It is the center of everything. I am the thirteenth Coven member. My place represents numbers one and three. One for new beginnings. And three for community. Thirteen on its own is a sacred number. Each member of the Coven is given an area to house and train their students. Reyna has the Necromancer's Skull Temple at the edge of the forest. Esmeralda and Queenie have their castles. Thorn and Grave use their cavern homes. Piper and Amanda have their cottage colony they have set up in the forest. You grew up in one of them. Myst lives in the Sky Ships protecting the planet. Wren lives in temples across the mountains providing aerial support and training soldiers that can survive in icy cold conditions. Avery built large aviaries all across the planet to train levitating mages and to help them control small birds. Knox built secret stone forts across the planet that can only be accessed by his students and Rae. Rae trains her mages in the interconnected tunnels below ground. They connect to each area above. All of us combined create unity. A working body with different cells, atoms, and limbs all doing its own function to thrive and evolve. There is no survival without community."

"Will we visit all of the other areas?"

"Only if we are called upon. Certain times throughout the year, Coven members cross train in order to simulate the counter attacks an enemy force would pose. Speciality attacks that can only be passed on from one coven tribe to another."

"When would we be called?"

"When the Threads of the universe come in to play."

"Is that what you teach?"

"Specifically, Thread manipulation. All Coven members know the basics of Thread manipulation but they rely on their natural born abilities. Natural born abilities are easier to use as they come from your core. They do not always require permissions from the Ethereals to use. But you will learn everything. Although, beings obsessed with the idea of evolution has always been my primary interest. What will beings do to evolve to their highest form? How much would they sacrifice including their own community members? Their obsession with a superior form intrigues me." Chaos Salem pauses to catch their breath. "Each week I will teach you a lesson. At the end of the week, you will be given a Task. For every Task you pass, we move on to the next lesson. If you fail, I will stop teaching you what I know."

"Are we trying to prove something to the other Coven leaders?"

"We have nothing to prove to them."

"Then why threaten me to stop teaching me."

"It's an incentive. All the other students will be pushed to their limits during their Tasks. The Coven lives under the belief that through evolution we can gain the highest forms of beings. Even the weak can prosper if they are pushed far enough. While I don't fully agree with that statement, I must adhere to my colleagues teachings to be on equal footing with them. The idea I agree with is: A being does not grow if they are stationary. A being does not grow without knowledge. A being does not grow without adversity. You and the other students must prove to yourselves that you want to live more than the monsters you face."

"That's cruel."

"And necessary. It is a cruel world, Axel. This world is only fair to those that want to survive and even then some still die. We are called upon as a Coven to protect each other and defend those that can't."

THE NEXT MORNING, Chaos Salem dresses me in charcoal mage robes, a brown scarf, and a black shirt and pants. We meet in the cathedral again. This time, they are in a matching outfit like mine. Heels have been replaced with brown combat boots.

"Our magic works off the manipulation of the Threads that make up the universe. We Weave the Threads in to…"

They wait for me to respond, "Shapes."

"What are the six cardinal shapes a mage needs to survive?"

"Hexagon, Squares, Triangles, Stars, Circles, and Diamonds."

"Why these six?"

"They wield the most successful results."

Chaos Salem draws six red lines in the air. They slowly bring them together.

"Hexagon is used to stop objects, people, and time. The number six represents harmony. Six years of solitude. Six years of learning. Six years of learning everything you need to know about the world before the world tries to devour you. This will be your foundation for all magical spells. To pull the Threads of the universe, you first need to ask the universe to bend for you. Hold out your hand and act as if you are going to pinch someone."

I hold it as they ask. At first, nothing happens. Chaos Salem just stares at me smiling. The mischievous smile that demands a little trust. A red ripple passes through my fingers as if the air was made of water. Slight resistance crawls under my fingers and I instinctively squeeze. A red taut strand pulls away from me. I don't let go. I create my first line. It stays hovering in the air. The next five are easier. And like a needle with thread, I Weave the strands together. The hexagon spins counter clockwise. A wind pushes past us stopping Chaos Salem for a second. The wind returns and time starts again.

"How did that feel?" Salem grins proudly.

"I stopped time."

"And you will do so many times in the future."

"I stopped you."

"I let you. A student cannot move forward without practice and making mistakes. I expect both success and failure from you in these practice sessions. Use the practice sessions to fail as many times as needed because in the Task you will be afforded no such luxury."

———

I spend the rest of the day watching Salem form the remaining symbols around the hexagon. Three squares make up the center of the hexagon. Squares are used for equal distribution of power. They can be used to share strength with another mage. Squares are the structure to the foundation. We add two lines above and below the squares to make six triangles. Three above the squares and three below. Triangles are used to work in tandem while amplifying abilities. When mages use the same spell at the same time, they can create a tsunami of energy hurled at an enemy. Six triangles are placed along the flat side of the hexagon to create a star. Stars can be used for explosions. They are the evolutionary result of smaller pieces and cogs working together to create a large whole. The result of a community's energies being used for good or bad. A circle encompasses the tips of the eight triangles. Circles are the innovation, progress, and protection one is awarded after they've worked as a team. Each circle provides protection against an outside force or keeps someone in. Four lines brush the circle to create a diamond. Diamonds are the final phase of the cycle. They represent a new foundation. Through all the iterations of innovations, a new idea will emerge whether this is a new invention, new way of doing things, new way of treating people fairly, or new way of working cohesively. The final goal is always to reach a diamond stage. Diamonds are also the hardest form of magic to create. This final pillar of the universe requires full body movements to create diamonds. The only ones to ever individually achieve a diamond have been each of the thirteen Coven members.

———

"I want you to create a diamond by the end of this year."

"You just said it was nearly impossible to do them."

"Impossible things happen when you apply care instead of fear to action. Through near death or practice, you will end the year knowing how to perform a diamond."

"You know it was easier to learn shapes when I was a toddler."

"Then pretend that you are a toddler if it will make it easier." Chaos Salem retorts.

———

Once I have mastered hexagons, Chaos Salem gives me an amethyst gemstone with smooth sides and the schematics to Esmeralda's castle.

"Your first Task will be to deposit this in Esmeralda's bedroom and return without being caught. This will be simple."

"They will think I'm the enemy if I get caug..." I trail off.

Chaos Salem sneers at me.

"Don't get caught. Got it." I sigh.

"Precisely."

———

Chaos Salem gives me climbing gear, a granola bar, and a small flask filled with nothing. They drop me off at the edge of Esmeralda's castle and wish me luck.

Esmeralda's castle is a fifty-story white building made of opaque quartz. A moat surrounds the main building with guards in white uniforms protecting the exterior. There are four entrances in to the castle that bypass the front door. The security quarters, the escape channels underground controlled by Rae, the receiving dock at the other side of the moat, and an aerial entrance for Wren and their paragliding soldiers.

Two entrances aren't currently viable. I can't fly and Rae protects her tunnels to certain places with heavy spells.

That leaves me with the security quarters and the receiving dock.

I spend an entire day trekking around the castle to where the receiving dock sits. By midnight, I make it to the rear of the castle having not rested all day. Minimal guards protect this entrance. The moat is the deepest here. A spell makes the waves erratic. The schematics made the waves seem tame. These monstrous waves move according to the movement and noises around them. They roar in defiance of any intruders.

I think the granola bar was meant to get me across the water.

I tear apart the wrapper and split the granola bar into six different pieces. This will give me one shot across the moat.

I come close to the edge of the raging water, enamored and terrified of the colossal waves. They roar at my footsteps matching my screaming adrenaline.

Fuck.

I sigh and toss two pieces of granola on opposite sides of the waves. The waves near me rapidly split in different directions. I form six walls comprised of hexagons to create a lengthy fifty-foot chamber. The waves return smashing against the hexagonal chamber. They stop for a few seconds affected by the hexagonal spell. I jump in to the transparent, red chamber hovering over the clear, deep water. Reptilian creatures, with long claws and round, slimy, greyish-green heads, and huge eyes, stare up at me smiling. They extend their neck and head fins in a threatening motion. They wait on the moat's floor swirling slowly to the top of the water.

My heart starts to palpitate.

Chaos Salem definitely did not tell me about them.

I toss the next two pieces of granola and the waves part again. I build a new chamber crossing in to it and returning the energy of the old one to my body. I'm seventy-five percent across the moat when the reptilian creatures start scratching at the hexagons ripping the chamber open in certain parts. They start to screech. Why isn't the spell stopping them?

Guards round the corner to the castle.

I repeat the process. Throw the granola. Build a faulty chamber. Run across. And tumble through empty air. I belly flop on to the shipping dock. Air knocked cleaned out of me. The reptilian creatures climb on to the hexagonal chamber chasing after me. I'm off the ground racing across the dock's creaking wooden planks. Guards shout at me rushing from my right where their guard quarters are at. At my rear, six more reptilian creatures climb on to the dock screech ing. I start forming hexagons as the claws trail at my feet. I build two hexagon walls behind me. Creatures thud against the barriers. The guards aim their spears tossing them at my head. I duck and it takes out two of the reptilian creatures chasing me.

I keep running until the dock ends with a huge area for holding supplies unloaded from Crafts. I trip on a piece of fabric but keep running. Behind the holding area are stairs that lead up to the servants' quarters, the main castle, and, at the top, Esmeralda's room. I climb up the stairs two at a time heaving every inhale and exhale. My breaths take up all the noise in my ears. That's when I notice the reptilian creatures feasting on the guards that were following me below. Their bodies are mangled. And eyes lifeless.

Fuck. That was my fault.

But why did the moat creatures attack their masters?

The creatures finish eating and return to the water. The erratic waves crash under the hexagon's expired spell.

I return to the dock and strip the clothes off the shortest man.

———

"Help!" I run in to servant's quarters covered in blood. "I was attacked by a moat creature."

An older man scurries to grab me a healer. With his back turned, I knock him over the head with the climbing gear.

———

I ascend the stairs to Esmeralda's bedchamber in the servant's uniform with a food tray in hand. Climbing gear wrapped around my waist under my pants.

Esmeralda stirs in her velvet-four-poster-king bed but doesn't wake up. I put the food on her light purple dresser slowly crossing over to her bed. She tosses again. I wait to see if she's awake. Still asleep. I creep over and deposit the amethyst stone under her pillow in a jagged slot.

A purple glow shines from under the pillow causing Esmeralda to stir.

What the fuck is that about?

She groans startling me, "Go away, Fred. I am not hungry."

I anchor up the climbing gear to her bed frame. Loud clambering footsteps pound up the tower causing Esmeralda to awaken even further. I remove my outer layer of clothes and deposit them neatly folded under the bed.

I climb on to the window's ledge in full gear and propel myself down the tower.

My legs groan in pain as I haphazardly try to rush down the side. My knees lock and bend flimsily.

I'm three stories off the ground when the guards peer over the windowsill and start to cut at my chord. I won't survive that drop. And if I do, I'm fucked, obviously. I slide down the remaining rope burning my palms. My feet hit the front entrance landing as the rope snaps overhead.

My palms are raw and cut open. Stinging pains sear from my hands and up my arms.

I run towards the bridge in front of the castle ignoring all the guards' arms trying to grab me. Guards blur in my peripheral. My adrenaline pushes me over, under, sideways, and up obstacles. A large man stands in front of the exit across the moat. I throw the flask at his nuts and slide under his legs. They start to lift the bridge that hovers over the moat. I run up it until the incline forces me to pick at holes and edges. My hands screaming in pain. I toss myself on to the flat edge of the raised bridge, bend my knees, and jump across to the grassy field.

I land on my stomach again with my legs dangling over the edge. All the air has been knocked out my fucking body. I see stars, planets, and fuck nuggets. My wheezing lungs clash with the serene, crisp breeze clearing the imaginary stars and fuck nuggets from my vision. I drag myself over the edge.

Chaos Salem stands over me and snaps their fingers.

———

"I got men killed." I guiltily confess to Chaos Salem once we're back at the Cathedral.

"They have necromancers working on them as we speak."

"Is it wrong what I did?"

"Depends on why you did it?"

"To survive. If they knew it was me, they would've found a reason to try to have you execute me."

"So, is your life worth more than their lives?"

I don't know the morally right answer to the question.

"How does one measure such a thing?"

"It is a conundrum. You versus them. Is your survival more important than their survival? You survived. That resulted in deaths. But you completed your Task. How does that make you feel?"

"Weird. I continued with the Task because I couldn't face the Coven again. I was scared of the idea of them killing me."

"You place two people in a room. One has an ill parent that is dying. The other person has a family to feed. But you must select one person to survive and the other to die. Who will it be?"

"Why can't both live?"

"That depends on you. You add meaning to the scenario. I can ask Mama Reyna this question and her biases would inform her decision. Her lived experiences will have her picking the family to feed because in her mind the community is more important than the dying individual. So, who would you pick?"

"Neither. Both deserve to live."

"So, let's add a stipulation. If you let them survive, you must take their place. What would you do then?"

I... I answered that question today. I would pick one of the two choices. I would pick me to survive. Yet, I can't bring myself to pick me to die in this scenario.

"I would pick me to survive and one other."

"Now why is that?"

"I can't help one of them if I am dead."

"Kairos will stop at nothing to accomplish his mission in life. I helped him to some capacity at a certain point in time. And beings will always make excuses as to why their mission in life outweighs the life of another. So, what breaks the cycle? What ends this tyranny of oppression? When do the excuses stop and we face the *monsters*? When do we take the action to save everyone even if it means our life is on the line?"

The way they say *monsters* tugs the wrong way. It veers me in to a line of thinking I don't like.

No. It...

"You placed those monsters in the moat."

"What makes you say that?"

"They weren't in the schematics."

Chaos Salem smiles, "And what else?"

"What else do you expect me to know?"

They laugh manically, "It was illusion magic. Esmeralda's castle was real. Your spells were real. But the guards and the creatures were," Red mists of dead guards being devoured by creatures hang in the air, "in the mind."

"How did I take a uniform off one of the guards?"

"I planted it there before today's Task. You tripped on it on your way in."

Salem was there for the first Task.

"This entire time you made me live with the guilt of their deaths."

"Yes. Because killing is not for the weak. It carries a heavy burden. I'm not saying to never kill. In order to survive this universe, you will have to stain your hands red. But be wise as to whose life you steal."

Chaos Salem grows quiet. In their silence, the Cathedral echoes. Slowly, tears in the universe lead to Fourth Dimensional souls screaming ear piercing wails. A pitch so loud musicians could study it and create new music theories from its existence. I shield my ears by cupping them with my hands. Cries leak through. Unavoidable and miserable. This goes on for thirty seconds before they stop.

"What was that?"

"Those are the unaccomplished dreams of the souls I helped reap when we cut the seven timelines." My jaw struggles to remain in place. I let them speak before I interject again. "They live with me for all of eternity. They follow me in the darkest rooms. They strike when I sleep. I will never rest peacefully for what I helped do."

"And what was that?"

"I created the Spear to end the seven timelines Kairos erased. I am the last known Guerrero in existence. The rest were killed off. I was near death when Mama Reyna rescued me and brought me here as a prisoner of war. The Coven saved me to protect an endangered species. They treated me like the animal I was. They taught me their magic and allowed me to be the thirteenth member in their Coven. They believed the mages were stronger with the enemy they knew."

"Why did you create the Spear?" My mind tries to piece together why they would help Kairos at all.

They stay quiet for a second, "The lesson that I want you to learn is that we were so scared of our own extinction, that we caused the demise of trillions. We were thinking about our own demise so much we disregarded everyone else. We believed Kairos would save us and, instead, we gave him the tools to topple entire timelines and destroy families and loved ones. He sowed division with the idea that ones' survival was more important than everyone else."

I take a moment to digest everything. My mind wandering back to the supplies I was given. I ask, "Did I use everything correctly to accomplish this Task?"

"Axel, you have all the tools you need to accomplish these Tasks. Everything I gave you was merely a bonus."

"QUEENIE'S CASTLE is the next Task." Chaos Salem hands me another amethyst stone. "By the end of the week, this will go behind her throne."

Another week goes by and we stay on the hexagon. Salem drives me insane with the endless repetition. They won't teach me anything else.

I spin the webs of the hexagon over and over and over and over and over and over again until my brain is on autopilot mush.

My hands following a repetitive motion until my eyes glaze to boredom.

To make matters worse, they have me doing all of this while carrying the amethyst stone in my hand. My arm goes numb under the weight of the crystal.

———

Each morning, I woke up, ate, showered, put on my clothes, and repeated the endless motions.

On the first day, we built a spiraling step ladder from the hexagons.

Day two, step ladder and inclined bridges.

Day three. Step ladder, inclined bridges, and stopping time for short increments.

Day four. All of the above while stopping time for longer periods of time and hanging upside down.

Day five. Salem gave me schematics of Queenie's castle. They expanded the size of the cathedral through illusions and built a mockup of her castle.

The castle has round spires. The main building of the castle is made of clear quartz. Inside of the throne room, pomegranate trees and various plants provide shade from the harsh solar rays coming into the castle. A cool humid environment fills the room with misty vapors. Black columns line one side and white columns line the other.

"Queenie sits and sleeps on the throne at the end of each day. The energy the plants receive from the sun recharges her." Salem informs me while projecting a holographic version of Queenie on to the throne, "Everything you learned this week will be to infiltrate the castle. You will spend the rest of today figuring out how the puzzle pieces I gave you fit in the castle."

Chaos Salem disappears leaving me alone with the illusion.

I spin the schematics of the castle every which way looking for the best possible entrance.

So far, the only reasonable entrance looks like it would be the student's quarters window. The window would match with the steps that lead to an inclined bridge reaching up to the throne room balcony.

I build the circuit Salem had me construct on to the layout of the castle. The circuit fits like the perfect puzzle piece to complete the picture. I run through it four times. I fail the first three attempts when Queenie and her guards spot me and throw me in jail. On the fourth, I turn upside down and drop the amethyst behind the throne.

That was easier than I expected.

———

Throughout the day, I run the course twenty times all with successes. Salem finally stops me.

"You think you're ready?"

I'm hesitant. I don't answer right away. In each successful simulation, it seemed too easy. There is something missing. Salem thrives on never telling me everything. They want me to reach conclusions on my own. What was that thing they said that I have all the tools to the answers in front of me, or something like that?

"The castle can't be mapped on schematics or in simulations." I point out.

"How could you tell?"

"The last twenty circuit runs I did were odd. Each one had a blurriness to it like it was hiding something."

"Queenie has hidden doorways to secret chambers in her castle depending on one's spatial position. The spells on her castle open doors to you if you are upright, sideways, or upside down. Each perspective leads to a different entry. Esmeralda and Queenie's tasks I expected to be easy. But, the next few tasks will require your maneuverability of the visible Fourth Dimension spectrum of this universe. There is a hidden Fourth Dimension that can only be accessed through Threads. And there is a visible one all around us that relies on changes in positions, angles, and perspectives to be seen."

"What does a visible Fourth Dimension look like?"

"My cathedral does not rely on the visible Fourth Dimension. It is illusion based. It looks smaller than it is because I will it to do so. Other Coven members use the visible Fourth Dimension to hide things in plain sight. I cannot explain it enough for you or show you in a simulation what it looks like. You must experience it for yourself. Hence, the need to hang upside down behind the throne."

"What is behind her throne"

"From this point on, I will no longer be providing you crystals.

You will need two sets of: two amethyst, two lapis lazuli, two aventurine, three moonstone, three citrine, and one rose quartz."

"Each set comes out to thirteen. One crystal for each Coven member."

"Yes. But, you must take double the amount. One for completing Tasks, and one set for casting shapes."

"Why?"

"Each crystal corresponds to a magical ability. Hexagons to amethyst. Squares and lapis lazuli. Aventurine and triangles, moonstone and stars, citrine and circles, and rose quartz and diamonds. The crystals can enhance your ability to use a certain shape or energy can be Siphoned from crystals to power one self up after a great battle. The strongest crystal and magical shape will be the hardest Task. The crystals channel the energy of each respective coven member if you hold all thirteen at the same time."

"Making it possible to eventually create a diamond shape if I train and carry all thirteen crystals."

"Precisely."

———

On the seventh day, Chaos Salem suits me in a student's uniform with an illusion of one of Queenie's student's faces. They snap their fingers and...

———

I wake up in the middle of the night in Queenie's castle beside a bunch of other students. Rows of individual beds fill a chiseled stone room with vaulted ceilings. Students are sound asleep undisturbed by my presence. I rush to the window and throw it open running through the first part of the circuit. I Weave the circuit from my mind letting the steps form around the castle and lead in to the incline bridges.

I run through the first portion of the obstacle course with no problems. I jump on to the balcony in front of the throne room. Guards walk back and forth behind the doors. I wait until they are out of sight to stop time.

I open the doors. A cool humidity strikes me. Two columns sit on both sides of a sleeping, Queenie.

I build up an inclined bridge, that flattens in to a series of hexagonal bridges between the trees and columns which ends directly behind the throne room.

My feet rush through the sky bridges between the trees and columns. I lean over the edge of the sky bridge hanging by my feet.

I'm upside down, but I feel like I'm standing on a solid surface mid-air. My legs don't take any of my weight. I'm suspended in this space by some invisible force.

A door appears on the back of Queenie's throne. In the center, pomegranates light up in neon reds and yellows. A divot sits in the shape of the missing crystal at the bottom of the fruit. I set the amethyst in the divot and a doorway behind the throne opens.

I throw myself through the door way and land on rib-vaulted ceilings.

The room groans and shifts.

I stand up and everything is upside down in this vault, but also right side up. The ceiling is now the floor and now everything on the floor is on the ceiling devoid of gravitational bounds. My mind is trying to make sense of everything. Piles of gold, crystals, and candles fill the cavernous room's floor hanging upside down like stalagmites. Desks lined with inventory counts and leather-bound books sit beside the piles of books. The arched floors make it hard to reach the treasure above. I build red hexagonal steps up to the upside-down crystal piles and upside-down desks above.

I grab a sack from my student's jacket sorting the crystals I need.

Two, two, two, three, three, one.

Amethyst, lapis, aventurine, moonstone, rose quartz.

My hands pick at the crystals in order of what I was told and stuff the crystals in my pockets. I go a second round for another set of thirteen making it an even twenty-six. I quickly start to head back down the steps once I'm done.

A throat clears the silence of the room. Queenie stands in the middle of an archway. Her long, brown braids cascade from her scalp to her thick thighs. She wears a white dress with leg slits and long sleeves that float. Her dark skin shines in the moonlight creeping in behind her. Her voice is sweet like honey to match her warm glimmering eyes. "The Templite becomes the first to break past me from this class of students. Salem is working hard with you. Every time we underestimate them, they surprise us."

"Did I fail the Task?"

"Your Task was to set the stone behind the throne. You did just that."

"Do all the other students share the same Tasks?"

"Yes and no. Salem apparently has you on an accelerated course. The Crystal Tasks are meant to be the final Tasks in a mage's training. From what I've heard, you've completed one of thirteen Crystal Tasks. Technically, you completed mine too so that makes it two out of thirteen. Be prepared to have the other Coven member's students going up against you through the Crystal Tasks."

This is all news to me. Again, Salem not explaining everything out right.

"Do you get anything from completing the Tasks before anyone else?"

"The first mage from their tribe to complete the Tasks becomes the next in line to be among the Thirteen Coven Members. No one has successfully completed Mama Reyna's trials. Their results led them to different placements among our community and armies. This year, we have her protégé son, Simon, who we all assume will be the next in line to be the Necromancer leader in the Coven. You and him will go up against each other. You are destined for great things in this Coven. Salem is really trying to ruffle some feather among the Coven leaders by sending you out so early."

"How come Salem didn't explain any of this to me?"

"I think you may have already noticed. Salem does not give answers so easily. You must earn them or figure them out mostly on your own. Their teaching style requires you to think for yourself and see everything that cannot be truly seen with the naked eye."

That's why Salem said they'd stop teaching me if I failed. I can't fail. They expect me to be their successor as their next Coven leader. So, if I fail, there is no point in teaching me everything they know.

"You think I can complete the Tasks perfectly."

"Nothing is ever set in stone," Queenie giggles at her play on words as she morphs the room around me. It starts to melt. Crystals falling towards my head. Books collapsing all over the room. I build steps out to the bridge outside of the doorway and rush out of the vault. Crystals knick me here and there. Books slam against the steps behind me. I leap through the doorway as it closes behind me. Time resumes. I hit the ground face first skimming against the rough stone floor. Queenie continues to giggle on her throne.

Guards see me on the ground behind her throne and rush at me.

I hear Queenie's fingers snap and I'm launched in to Chaos Salem's chest.

I'm back in the Cathedral.

"You did it." Chaos Salem cheers once they see what I'm holding.

"Eleven to go." I sneer.

Salem smiles, "Eleven to go."

———

The very next day, we start on squares.

"A square is meant for two. It builds off the idea that the individual should not do everything alone. They can accomplish a lot alone, but together their powers become stronger. Form three squares along the middle of the hexagon."

Salem and I work in tandem to feed off each other's energies. A purple satchel that contains the twenty-six crystals bounces on my thigh with every motion. I master the squares within thirty minutes.

Chaos Salem snaps their fingers. We appear at the edge of Mama Amanda's woods. She stands there looking around tapping her foot.

"I brought him." Salem speaks up.

Mama Amanda rushes at me and hugs me, "I've missed you so much, my darling child."

I snuggle in her embrace missing her affection. It's been almost four weeks since I last saw her. She pulls apart searching me for any signs of damage. She asks worriedly, "How have the Tasks been? They told me you completed two of the thirteen Crystal Tasks."

"Tedious. I didn't know learning magic would be this frustrating."

"The Crystal Tasks have never been easy. I almost failed mine three times."

"Why am I here?" I ask.

"Always straight to the point." Simon snickers stepping out from behind a tree. He wears an emerald cloak. His garments consist of dark green harem pants and a long, black sleeve with a green silk belt. He looks so damn handsome in his form fitting uniform. Muscles protrude from his clothes distracting me. I wonder if the clothes tags still bother him... or if he ripped off his shirt... I mean... if he ripped the tags off his shirts?

I run to hug him, and he embraces me back, "What the fuck are you doing here?"

I missed him so much. Mama Reyna took my best friend away from me. She took everyone away from me for six years. And now, he's here. His embrace grows tighter.

This is just what I needed. I needed a boyfriend. A friend that is a boy by gender. I'm just going to stop myself.

"Mama Reyna can't have me losing to you." Simon's words come out harsh.

"Ouch." I push away feeling like he gutted me.

"I mean... I don't care. I want us both to win these Tasks," Simon clears the air, "But she told me it would look bad to lose to a Templite."

"I thought the Crystal Tasks were personal trials to try and become the successor to a Coven leader." I state confused.

"Yes, they can be," Chaos Salem starts, "But, the Coven sees it as a competition and try to sabotage each other in order for the best candidates to complete all thirteen Tasks." That's fucked. "Their idea is that the Tasks should forge a war-ready Coven leader. Throughout the Crystal Tasks, Coven leaders can decide to form alliances to help their candidates reach the finish line."

"You agreed to this?" I ask Salem.

"I wanted you and Simon to come to a decision together. I will not force anything upon you two. But the remaining trials will need the magic of the square to complete them. It is around this time that Coven leaders make pacts and match up the best students. I wanted to catch them off guard. None of the other Covens have students ready to finish the Tasks, but that does not mean they will not try to foolishly send them out before they are ready."

Does starting with Simon mean I'll have to start everything all over again? Were the last two trials just a waste?

"What concerns you?" Salem asks.

"I completed two Tasks. So, are we going to have to run them again?"

"No. The Coven sees the square phase as the most crucial part of the Crystal Tasks. Every leader in all of space history has made alliances in order to grow their land or remain in power. With shared power comes shared lands, resources, and accomplishments. And if one person gets caught in the partnership, but the other completes The task, then they both succeed since one finished the Task."

My brain cells bring the pieces together, "That bitch. Reyna wants me because I already completed two Tasks and that would mean my partner would have completed them too."

Salem and Mama nod.

Mama speaks up next, "Parents can give their children advantages in the Tasks. Which Mama Reyna has afforded to Simon."

I turn to Simon, "What does that mean?"

"I completed the Thorn and Grave Tasks of my own free will, but she allowed me to win her trial without push back."

"She let you win her Task without trying."

Simon nods.

Fucking nepotism.

"If you agree to this partnership, between you and Simon, you will have five victories." Mama Amanda adds smiling, "And while I can't say overtly that I would do the same thing Mama Reyna did, you would be one closer to the end with my Crystal Task."

I look to Salem to see if they disapprove of this kind of talk. They turn from Simon to me.

"With two more wins, that would put you at seven, and you would only need six more Tasks to complete the Crystal Tasks."

Salem and Mama Amanda would just give us their wins so we could focus on the last six. Mama Reyna wins her wanted successor if Simon wins.

And Salem gets theirs.

And the Coven would be forced to take me in as their own.

"I agree to the partnership."

"Bind your magic together."

"How do we do that?" I ask.

"If this partnership is to work, your energies will naturally work together. Allow your magic to build in to his with the squares."

Simon and I build the hexagon and squares together, seamlessly binding us together with magic. The red glow of the hexagon and squares lights up our faces as we stare deeply in to each other's eyes. Simon smiles. The corners of my mouth lift a little.

I'm not alone anymore.

———

Chaos Salem and Mama Amanda let us run their Tasks without any pushbacks. Seven completed out of the thirteen.

CHAPTER 34

AXEL

THE EMPRESS AND THE EMPEROR

WITH COMPLETING two Tasks in one go, Simon and I have been given two weeks to study for Piper's trial. Mama Reyna has restricted me from entering her Necromancer Temple. So, Simon trains at the cathedral part of the week and the other half spends it at the Necromancer Temple. His guest bedroom is right across from mine on the second story of the cathedral. At nights, Simon and I go in to each other's rooms to read the training texts on Piper's mages. Candles and moonlight illuminate the floor to ceiling mountains of books.

Simon would never admit that he was stuck on me like adhesive. The people that divided us before no longer having a choice in our unity. It was partly why I agreed to have him as a partner. I could've completed the Tasks by struggling through them and barely making it out. But this path covered two bases: my completion of the Crystal Tasks and my love for Simon.

We take turns bringing each other snacks, drinks, food, and using the restroom. I have to remind him to take a shower between study sessions because his hyperfocusing drives him up the wall. Here and there, I usually end up distracting him and asking him questions. Simon gives me short answers so that he can get back to learning.

From time to time, I lean my back on his arm and read my book.

Simon wraps his arm around my body occasionally reaching over me to flip the page with his hand. After a few hours of studying each night, we spend the rest of the night looking out a round window in the ceiling towards the visible moons of Lykos.

"It's just weird. That out of all universes and out of all places I could be, I was born here." Simon says randomly breaking the silence.

"I wish I could say the same. Apparently, I was placed here with no real choice."

"Do any of us really have a choice in where our souls find themselves in the universe?"

"Do you believe in the Tesoro de Almas theory?" The Treasure of Souls theory was the idea that the moment soulmates passed on, the soulmates would spend their entire lifetimes looking for each other until they found each other again in another universe. A neon beacon would emit to where their soulmate landed and the other soul searching would go to it. Souls did this until they were destroyed or passed on to the Cataclysm Realm.

"Maybe. Do you think that's possible? For two souls to find each other after they died?"

I snuggle my book against my chest, "Even if it isn't real, it's romantic. The idea that someone loved someone so much in their lifetime that they created a hopeful dream. One in which you spend eternity with said person intertwined in each other's fates and chasing after each other."

"Who were we in a past lifetime then?" Simon brushes my cheek with his thumb repeatedly.

"I don't know. Maybe we were two ducks or two cats just wandering the universe together. Maybe we were specs colliding into nothing. Atoms on a microscopic level hoping to be more."

"I think I got lucky to find you again."

"Again?"

"Mhmm."

"You remember your last life?" I ask Simon.

"Here and there. I started having dreams of you. An older

version of you. You appear in a Venus body in front of me. Birds surround us. I'm in a Gamma-2 body. Oh, and they hate you there too."

Well, at least I know I'm hated even in past lives. Never having to be too worried about being popular.

"You think it is the past?"

"The alternative is a sub-theory to the Tesoro de Almas theory. We are inexplicably so interconnected that your visions are becoming mine. Our powers are transferring over to one another. Your visions become mine. My power becomes yours. A future with you is a future worth living." He cuddles half my body, "You are my beacon. You are the warm fire in a winter's night that I have been searching for. You are my home."

———

Each night, Simon and I would cuddle in bed. Simon's body runs like a furnace, so I have to turn away once his survival-heat turns insufferable. I miss his heat whenever he returns to Mama Reyna. She picks him up halfway through the week from the cathedral and gives me the death glare.

Chaos Salem gives me extra chores each day to keep me preoccupied. They try to fill my plate with more reading, but I have already read every book in the basic mage's curriculum. I had six years of memorizing every last word in those thirteen books.

I repeat the memorable phrases out loud as I do chores:

Templites rose from hatred. Kairos corrupted the masses. Many fell for his words of hope. While he continued to poison them and blame it on the new travelers from the different timelines.

The shapes are silly in theory but can save a life if overlooked. Our power relies on the universe bending to our will. The shapes are how the universe bends to us. To other beings, the universe will bend in other ways. We have to be well equipped in our methods of arming our children in order to fight wannabe oppressors.

El Tesoro De Almas or The Treasure of Souls can occur with only a true soulmate or soulmates. Each soul leaves a piece of themselves when they leave their physical bodies. Though, this may not be enough to revive a being, it is enough to know what their unaccomplished hopes, dreams, and desires were left behind. Faeries and Guerreros that can sew back the Threads of the universe can use the help of necromancers to piece together these mysteries.

I would have to ask Simon what that means later.

Once I'm done with my chores, I wander over to Salem in the main cathedral.

"I miss the boy." I admit to Chaos Salem, "I'm sorry if that is an overshare. I've just been so lonely for so many years."

"It is okay to feel. It is not something to be ashamed of. Just don't go burning down my cathedral, you hear me?"

I sneer, "I only did that because they kept me imprisoned."

"Are you free here?"

"Witches and warlocks crowded my house for six years and kept me trapped. I was a teenager, and they treated me like a criminal. I am of mage flesh and since been branded as the enemy. Hating me for existing is odd. Hating me for the decisions of colonizing extremists is unfair. The only one stopping me from leaving now to Tempus is you. And I don't want to leave here because out there I am the Templites' enemy. I have no true home to return to or memories of the past. Yet, I am shoved aside. You and Mama Amanda are the only ones who see me as me. So, yes I feel free here."

A puzzling look comes over Chaos Salem. They say, "He'll be

back in no time. Distance from loved ones can be healthy. Loved ones have tethers that bind them to each other. The Threads of the universe can be seen if you look hard enough. In the meantime, let's distract you. "

Chaos Salem gives me the run down on the next Crystal Task.

"Piper is..."

White clouds my eyes. Chaos Salem's words disappear beyond the vision.

Simon dies.

The child is hidden with Mama Reyna. They look like me and Simon combined.

A child is born of war.

War Ships enter Epsilon's atmosphere... Our son is at least ten years older.

The Spear that cut the timelines is given to me and Simon.

The Crystal Tasks are completed and a celebration with us on gold pedestals.

Simon is turned in to a vampire somewhere near the end of the Tasks.

The Crystal Tasks flash past me.

Piper sits on a throne like Queenie. Though she has clouded eyes like mine. The throne is made of moss, mushrooms, flowers, and tree roots. Her hands firmly grip the arm rests speaking in hushed whispers. Piper's ruby, frizzy hair floats in the air as if it has been electrified. Her albino skin is lightened with rouge lipstick and dark iridescent eyeshadow. A drowning purple dress hides the Coven member. Vines wrap around her body and throne.

"What are you doing here?" Piper looks at me directly talking to a million other souls at the same time. Her body duplicates into a million shadows around her.

"You can see me?"

"The ancestors are pointing you out. They are forming an image around you. Spike?" Her face splits in to millions of faces.

"My name is Axel."

"You have many names and many more names coming to you."

"I thought there were no other Seers on Epsilon."

"I am not a Seer. I am a Medium. I am the messenger between living and dead. Seers long past communicate with me still. Dead Seers are free to travel from the past, present, and future."

"So, I am the Templite boy they were worried about?"

"Heir to the Templite throne. Holder of a Power Crystal. Lover of Simon. Father to Simon Jr."

"Father?"

"You saw it yourself."

Out of my peripheral, I see the crystal pedestal at the top of the throne. Branches twist in the shape of one of the aventurine crystals I stole from Queenie. Inside of it, the crystal is missing.

"I don't really plan on having children. That seems like a lot of work."

"You are still young."

"Super weird to tell a nineteen-year-old they'll be a parent one day."

My eyes discreetly trail to the entrance to the forest holding her throne. A small opening from the base of a tree opens to the rest of the forest.

"I will not make this Task easy for you."

The white from my eyes retreats. Chaos Salem stands in front of me.

"What did you see?"

"The entrance to Piper's throne room. It is hidden at the base of a tree."

Chaos Salem summons a stone table with a snap of their fingers. They lay the schematics on the table. The forest is a labyrinth of tree roots, rivers, creatures, and paths that move every few hours. The map changes in intervals to show the path shifting every six hours. Four changes in one day.

"This is her throne." Chaos points to the end of the schematic where a ring of trees protects a throne.

I search the drawing for the specific tree. At the edge of the map, a tree with a thick trunk and a darker shade of brown stands out slightly from the rest.

"That one has the hole."

Chaos Salem uses their illusions magic to conjure a three-dimensional map with me and Simon working our way backwards from the tree. They incorporate the distance it would require traveling across the entire woods. The simulation provides Salem with a concrete plan, given the monsters can be slain, and adequate rest is given to each of us.

"The task would take approximately four to six days to complete."

"So, we have to have a week's supply of food and equipment ready. This is not what I expected from this Task. The last few were a breeze."

"From now on, each Task will prove your worthiness to the Coven. You already have a leg up on the other students with Simon by your side."

"Teach me the triangle."

"Why?"

"The square will not be enough. If I need to amplify his powers for any reason, we will need to know how to do so."

Salem nods. The next few hours, I struggle to form the squares in tandem with Salem's energy. That's odd. I wasn't struggling before. What changed? Around the fifth hour, we finally create the three squares needed to proceed to the triangle. My hands shake as I form the lines above and below the squares in the hexagon to complete the six triangles. Salem's energy is supporting me. It keeps me standing and prevents my wobbly knees from tumbling. But, the resistance is there. Our energies are not compatible. Salem and I repeat the triangles twenty-six more times before I can no longer try.

I collapse on my knees heaving. Sweat drips on the floor uncontrollably. A headache looms across my forehead and eyes. I rock back and forth.

"Wait for Simon to practice. You know how to do this. Teach him. It will work better."

My eyes go white again.

War Ships in the sky.

Dragons attack the initial wave of Ships.

"Make a deal with the dragons." Mama Reyna shouts at me, "Demand this of me. I will mock you and diminish you. But spite me. Force me to listen. Say whatever you have to say."

"What? But they are already here in the sky."

"Right now. Call Toxotes." Mama Reyna shouts at me.

Astrea and her dragon husband stand beside me. She cradles my face, "Axel, I know you and Mama Reyna hate each other right now, but, one day, that will all be resolved."

"Who are you?" My brain splits, "Astrea. What is happening? Why are you touching me?"

"You're having a vision but your eyes aren't white. You're split between here and back then. You're caught between your mirror visions of the past, present, and future."

"Where is Simon?"

"He went with the other dragons to awaken the Ancient One. But, we can't do that without the dragons. None of this future can happen without you. Do it for me and Simon. Do it for Simon Jr. and my babies." She starts to cry, "My wyverns are all gone. Please. They tried to combine their energy to defeat the Dark Pharaoh. They tried to create the Power Source and instead melded in to each other."

The ground rumbles below us. A tentacle from a Ship releases preparing to hit the planet. The planet splits where Rae's headquarters were as a weathered scaly gray dragon's face erupts. Her long body trailing on for miles. Spikes along his spine crack the planet even further.

The Ship's tentacle latches on to the Ancient One. The immense dragon snatches the tentacle out of the sky and crushes the Ship in her hand. More Ships appear in the sky adding reinforcements. My ears nearly burst as the dragon roars.

Time Keepers open Pulses around the dragon attacking her body. The attacked scales spin on the dragon's body flying towards the Time Keepers. Razors at the end of the scales split Time Keepers mid air. The scales fly up to the surrounding Ships destroying their control centers and engines. Debris descends upon the planet. Wren's paragliding soldiers take flight using shapes to redirect or obliterate the debris from civilians below. Myst's Sky Ships surround the skies creating forcefields over densely populated areas. Mages in the Epsilon Ships work to protect their people.

My eyes return. My mind is working on over drive. My body is shaking and I am sweating heavily.

"We need to make a deal with the dragons of Toxotes." I say as I try to relax my nerves.

"What do you mean?"

"Call the dragons. Call Toxotes. They are coming. War Ships are coming."

"When?"

"Eleven years from now."

———

"Why have we been called here?" Mama Reyna speaks first.

The entire Coven surrounds me. Shadows of faces hang ominously in the candle lit darkness of the cathedral. I stand in chains again. Déjà vu, mother fuckers. At least I ripped all of my shirt tags off since the last time.

"Eleven years." I speak up, "We have Eleven years until the War Ships arrive."

"Call the dragons, Reyna." Salem adds, "Call on Toxotes aid. The Ancient One needs to be awakened and Rae has not made progress. We need the dragons' energies to bring the Ancient One back to life. We need the Toxotes dragons to unite and connect their Power Sources to the Ancient One."

"What did the visions tell you?" Mama Reyna scoffs and asks me.

"You told me to tell you to call the dragons." I inform her.

"Are our reinforcements not enough? Are our Sky Ships not protecting us in this distant future?"

"They were dealing with the debris from the amount of Ships Kairos sent."

The Coven stays quiet. Everyone stares at each other in worried silence.

"How do we know Kairos didn't plant this vision in your head with the help of another Seer?" She retorts.

"Believe what you want. Your indecision will bring Epsilon's demise." Salem snaps. "You know Kairos will see our disadvantages and take them out."

Mama Reyna stays silent for a good minute, "Any other opinions?"

The Coven remains tight-lipped.

"Everyone in favor of ignoring the vision."

Not one Coven member raises their hands.

"All in favor of calling on the dragons of Toxotes?"

All thirteen Coven members raise their hands.

Salem snaps their fingers and I am teleported in to the crowd next to Simon. A multitude of families and students sit in the crowd behind a misty, translucent, black veil.

"Tempus is coming to Epsilon?" Simons asks.

I nod. "But we win if the dragons accept our call."

The thirteen Coven members move in unison drawing the shapes in the middle of the cathedral. They start with the hexagon, build the three squares in the middle, draw two lines above and below the squares in the hexagon, add triangles to each exterior side of the hexagon, draw a circle around it, and cement the call with the diamond. All the while, the shapes spin as they're being built. The multi-colored diamond spins counter clockwise blinding the audience. The colors of the Threads in the diamond cast a rainbow of light against the stained glass of the Cathedral.

The Coven chants:

We call on the dragons for aide,
Help us not fade,
Our lives are on the line.
Send our message through the divine.

The ancestors that I saw in my vision of Piper appear one by one in the room. Their specter forms a misty blue haze. Every ghost repeats the chant moving their bodies in the same way as the Coven members.

Ancestors be our bridge in this time of need.
Bring our query with dire speed.

The ghosts all add their own incantations before they vanish skyward.

Mama Reyna snaps her fingers.

We are teleported to Mama Amanda's cottage. Simon and I sit on the black, velvet couch in the living room. Salem, Amanda, and Reyna stand in front of us.

"Why eleven years?" Mama Reyna asks me.

"It is what I was told."

Mama Amanda speaks up, "The population of Toxotes has risen post Timeline Wars. Many soldiers that returned home missed their partners. They are facing overpopulation. We could help them. We have the room on Epsilon. We take some of their excess dragons. They help us with Kairos."

Salem adds, "On the same note, with a dragon's ability to reproduce in great volumes it will repopulate our armies. That way, we still have citizens and a planet to carry on our legacy once we are gone."

Everyone stays quiet at the implication.

"You think many will die?" I ask.

"There is no war with zero causalities." Salem states callously.

"You are the problem." Mama Reyna hisses at me.

"Then send me home. Get rid of me."

She is taken aback by the comment.

"Axel..." Salem adds before I interrupt them.

"No, if everyone is so worried about what I will become, throw me to the wolves. Send me to Tempus. I'm just as worried of Epsilon as everyone else. This is all I know. This is my home. Six years I was locked up for being considered one of them. I'm tired of being looked at like scum. I might be a Templite, but I don't remember that life-time. I don't remember anything about that boy or who he was. Epsilon is all I have ever known. And, here, I am worth nothing. So do it. Send me back. Murder me if you need to but that will not solve any of your problems."

"That is no way to speak to an elder." Mama Reyna snaps.

"You have no respect for me so I will treat you as you treat me. Just because you're an old bitch doesn't mean I have to respect you. Kairos is coming."

Mama Reyna slaps me. She turns to Mama Amanda, "Have you nothing to say about this?"

"Yes, I do." Mama Amanda stands between me and Mama Reyna. She pushes Mama Reyna back, "Figure your shit out. Respect is an equal exchange, not a matter of years lived. For the past six years, I have watched the witch I followed in to the darkness coated in blood and entrails treat my son as a criminal. Salem is keeping him on the right path. He has given us intel that will help us survive. It is a pity to see someone I respected fall so easily for the hatred Kairos infected the universe with."

Mama Reyna looks for someone to defend her. She turns to Salem.

"Don't look at me." Salem scoffs. "You barely tolerate me."

She looks to Simon.

"You partnered me up with him." Simon shrugs, "So, I'm on his side."

"Enjoy the company you keep." She turns to Simon, "Don't

bother returning to the Necromancer Temple until you successfully pass the Crystal Tasks."

Oh no, whatever will I do with Simon spending more time with me.

Mama Reyna snaps herself out of the room.

"I could offer you a room in my colony." Mama Amanda offers.

"I have a room at the Cathedral. I'll be okay." Simon responds.

"I'm sorry she refuses to take you back." Salem adds.

"Mama Reyna has taught me everything she needed to. She trained me with more knowledge than any of her other trainees. She wants me to complete these trials. She's just throwing a temper tantrum since she didn't get her way for once."

Salem smiles, "You said it."

"Thank you for standing up for me." I hug Mama Amanda.

"Anything for you baby. That vile witch needs to relax. She forgets we are all on the same side."

BACK AT THE CATHEDRAL, Simon returns to his room to wash up from the day. I want to follow him when Salem grabs my wrist and leads me towards the diamond burned in to the Cathedral floor. Red and green Thread benches form in the middle of the cathedral. They motion for me to sit on pews they created with their Thread manipulation.

They hesitate to speak and it has me worried. Their mood seems grave like if they have to throw up bad food.

"Are you okay Salem?"

They nod, "I am. But there is no easy way to say this. You know I helped Kairos create the Spear to cut the timelines, but that's not the full story. Before we continue your trials, I want you to know something. You may hate me freely after I speak, but I must say what I have to say."

"Does this have to do with the reason that the Coven despises you? The Spear?"

"Partially. Yes. I... I have many truths to tell you. You will ask me what people did to stop what happened. But the answer will be glaringly depressing. This story will be a juggling act. One that happens all at the same time and ends in disaster. Let me begin with the rise of

Kairos. Kairos was an influential charismatic man who promised his entire universe a better life. At the time, all thirteen timelines were free to travel and explore the galaxy through Thread manipulation. Time Keepers could hardly master the art. So only witches and fairies could explore the galaxy. They could escape to another universe if a totalitarian regime blossomed in their universe. Even when things were good, people who could manipulate Threads were thought to have an advantage over others.

"Political tensions across all planets were at an all-time high. Food was scarce. Medical treatments were costly. Billionaires needed someone else to blame other than themselves for the money problems they created. They couldn't take accountability for poisoning their citizens hydration sources, killed their clean air, censoring all media blaming billionaires, and raised their entire cost of living in the pursuit of capital gains. So, they started with a small idea. The idea was: remember a time when things were good. When money flowed freely. Wouldn't you want to go back to such a time?"

"It was a simple idea. Political leaders controlled by billionaires across planets were told to run with that idea. They campaigned with the slogan, "Return to A Better World." All while scheming. They needed to appease the general population so they fed them lies upon lies. But the populations were smarter than them. For a time at least. What the politicians needed was an enemy. Someone to blame for billionaires creating poverty. A tangible person, race, or being that could be the "real" villain and if they took those people out, everyone would be happier. A scapegoat is easier to blame and discard than losing profits and loyalty of the people you control."

"Now let's add context. Kairos was born in to the Lycan Lineage. Titus Kronos, the old Time Lord, conceived Kairos with the queen of Necropolis. He was a bastard. There is a tradition to the Lycan Throne. All children born to the Royal Lycan Family must either concede and give their throne to the next in line. Or all children must fight to the death and ascend the throne. Their antiquated beliefs thought that evolution brings the best leader much like Mama Reyna.

As a teenager, Kairos's mother and step-father died mysteriously. The Queen and King dead led to an investigation which came out inconclusive. All seven children, including Kairos, fought for the throne. But Kairos had an advantage. Kairos could produce black holes called Pulses. It was his secondary ability. So, he allowed the competition to weed themselves out. And when the last one left standing decided to charge at Kairos. He sliced the wolf in half by opening a Pulse at his center."

"Kairos became King of Necropolis that day. Many historians pinpoint that day as the day everything went sideways. But I think they're wrong. I think everything went sideways when he was born. Kairos changed the name to Lykos because he wanted a name that told people who they were. They were wolves and the universe needed to remember that. He wanted them to remember the power they wielded."

"I digress. Kairos as the King of Lykos was loved by many for his charm and out of pocket language that wasn't restricted. He said whatever he wanted and came to mind without caring if he harmed anyone. The general population that sided with Kairos were tired of having to respect everyone. They craved an enemy to channel all their anger towards. And ironically, they were tired of the rich exploiting them. Kairos was a funny character. He judged the rich among his Lycan people while catering to the whims of the wealthy. The highest bidders threw all kinds of money and physical objects to keep him doing their selfish bidding. Any time a reporter or journalist would start to track where the money came from, they would disappear, be jailed, or be called crazy for spewing so-called false hoods and blacklisted from their careers."

"By allowing the billionaires to do as they pleased, Kairos gave them free rein to poison their waters, kill public figures as they pleased, pollute their planets, and amount wealth through taxing the poor. He figured if you can tax the poor and keep the rich tax exempt, you can keep a population of ethical slaves. They go to a job and clock-in for money, while they were given a paycheck where money was skimmed off the top and deposited to Kairos's rich friends' accounts. The same friends that are in turn not paying these people a living wage. Keeping them stuck in a helpless never ending cycle of poverty."

"To distract people from finding out what Kairos had done, he did what he had to to keep the blood hounds from tracking his scent. He gave the people an enemy."

"That's where my story comes in. I am a Guerrero. I am and always will be as long as I shall live. My people lived on Gamma-1 and Flounce. We had access to all timelines through our abilities by cutting through the fabric of the universe. We were emissaries for Titus. He sent us to other galaxies to find new and innovate ways of helping our people overcome dictatorships and oligarchs. Anything you can think of we brought back from our travels." Salem smiles, "I met many people and fell in love many times. There was one person I loved most of all and she lived in the sixth timeline Titus had me frequent. It was much like our universe with very similar beings. She was a divine work of art spun beautifully by the masters of the universe. Her name was Azra. She was from Earth. In our universe, we call Earth, Venus. And everyday with her was magical."

"There came a day when Titus used the information all of us Guerreros had gathered and started weeding out the rich oligarchs and their corporations. He started with planets furthest from Tempus and worked his way towards Tempus. Titus cleaned up after his son's mess for years. The Scorned Planets were easy to take care of except for Lykos. Kairos's grip on Lykos was strong at the time. They were blinded by the barrage of propaganda hitting them that the Sirens, Time Keepers and Guerreros were bad people. They painted Sirens, Time Keepers and Guerreros as the enemy. They had to be dealt with. Kairos led a campaign against the three groups among what we now know as the Neutralists and Templite Loyalists Planets. It worked effectively on the Loyalists but the Neutralists were not completely convinced by his charm. It didn't matter. Eventually, Kairos had amassed the support of half the universe. He convinced them that Guerreros and Time Keepers were the reason they couldn't afford to live. To half the universe, our travels were the reason their water sources were poisoned. Their food was so expensive because Guerreros supposedly consumed more of it on their journeys. Their lives were unlivable because of us. He convinced them that their taxes were so high because their taxes funded our exploration in to other timelines. Of course, it wasn't true but a strong lie never has to be. A scapegoat just has to be a scapegoat. A being to blame to allow others to delve in to their awful behaviors. On every planet, we had people who did not believe Kairos, but their voices were drowned out or they had to temporarily assimilate to survive the next part."

"History is gradual. It only seems quick in history lessons, like today, because a short period of time is diminished to a few sentences. Entire lives forgotten and not remembered through our short attention spans. Guerreros were brought front and center as enemy number one. They were hunted down and murdered. And when they could, the Guerreros escaped in to other timelines to survive. Guerreros went in to hiding. They disguised themselves as other citizens. People wanted justice for their supposed actions. They wanted Kairos to enlist the Time Keepers and use his father's influence to hunt down the Guerreros in our universe and other universes. Since we were the enemy, the people mutilated us, ate us, killed us slowly, tortured us, and used us as their punching bags."

"During all of this, Kairos ignited a civil war among all the Templite Loyalist Planets. Those in favor of Guerreros and those opposed battled it out in the streets with lasers and their powers. People killed each other for the rights and lives that were being stripped of the Guerreros. Funny how the only solution to wanting respect is to fight against a bigoted aggressor. The victor then scrubs history to their liking."

"A few of us Guerreros came to Titus for help. We needed sanctuary from all the murders. Your grandfather hid me in the Templite Castle. Titus saved my friends and family. It felt nice to be safe again for a few years. Until the unrest grew. Kairos gained more influence through the Neutralists and Templite Loyalists Planets. You see, Kairos never stopped helping the oligarchs. He just enabled them further in to stripping the rights of his people. So, while civil wars were going on to protect and kill Guerreros, the rich were profiting off our dead bodies through multiple avenues. Arms dealers. Hospitals. Food. Soldiers. All used for profit. And when people came looking for an enemy, Kairos presented us on a silver platter over and over again. The story Kairos portrayed said 'After the Guerreros escaped in to other universes, they left the economies of all planets tanked and politicians struggled to recover.' The people wanted blood. They were hungry. And the rich needed shields."

"Kairos came up with an outlandish plan: cut seven of the timelines Guerreros were known to frequent. To do so, he needed strong enough, self-hating Guerreros to create a Spear that could do such a task. Kairos had Guerreros that complied to his regime but they were weak. He needed me or one of my family members to make the Spear."

Salem stops speaking. They give me a second to digest everything and to come to my own conclusion.

But I don't like the ending. I know the ending. The timelines were cut. But what were the details?

"What did *you* do Salem?" I ask.

"It is complicated. Kairos wanted to cut the seven timelines to travel across our timeline more efficiently with Pulses. The Pulses were blackholes that would unexpectedly cut through timelines and kill hundreds of thousands of people where they were opened. Kairos would give tours of other timelines to his billionaire friends. And when the people of other timelines started seeing their people killed by our leaders and rich people, they revolted. They would kill anyone that would Pulse to their universe. The rich that liked to vacation in exotic destinations demanded Kairos and his Templite Loyalists fix this issue. The rich wanted the seven timelines, closest to us and most likely to kill rich people, to be eradicated. The rich needed a liminal space between their favorite timelines. Or, what we now know as

Limbo. They were tired of fighting timelines wars in order to get to their favorite destinations after a few "accidental" deaths. Pulsing freely was their goal. So, when the time came to do so, Kairos flooded so much propaganda down his follower's throats they were fully gagged and in support of his cause."

"Billionaires funded his plan knowing the blood that would be on their hands. Kairos started kidnapping and testing all Guerreros to see if their abilities could create the Spear he needed to cut the timelines. Any that couldn't were used for servitude or killed."

"Titus came to me and my family and asked us for a favor. He asked if we could create a fail safe for our universe. It was only a matter of time before Kairos turned on every planet. He would keep making excuses and scapegoating different beings until every planet was poisoned and destroyed. Until all citizens were killed or he killed other planets. Kairos wanted them subjugated or dead. The blood could never stop spilling or else people realized who the real bad guys were. I would infiltrate Kairos's Guerreros, create the Spear for Kairos, and then cut the seven of the thirteen universes myself."

"Why would my grandfather want you to kill trillions for Kairos?" I ask.

"Kairos would eventually kill those seven timelines so we wanted it done on our terms. Titus knew how to protect the seven timelines and make it look like I cut them." They answer. "I would solidify the seven timelines in to seven Crystals and tie their Essence to the structural Threads in our universe. The Crystals were free to move around our galaxy once I returned. But my job would be to distribute them to different beings across the Scorned and Neutralist planets. All seven Crystals combined made up the Power Crystal that would be implanted in Titus until Kairos committed to his mutiny. At that point, I would split the Crystals up in to seven pieces and scatter them to the cosmos. The idea was that if Kairos decided to turn on his people and start killing them at random, then he would commence the collapse of his universe if he accidentally killed a Crystal Wielder. Kairos would have the tools to revive the individual but not without damage and warping being done to the timeline. The Crystals themselves would be kill switches for our universe if Kairos decided he wanted to fuck around. This would essentially slow him down from killing the entire universe."

"What happened to the beings in the Crystals?"

"For those beings inside the Crystals, their lives are momentarily in stasis. The other half of them, that were useful to our universe, were transported in to our galaxy with the help of Templite Ships. They were eventually dispersed across our twenty-four planets and integrated with our citizens. Thus, the timelines were cut, Limbo was created, and now, Kairos had new people to call an enemy. So, what did you expect happened?"

"He turned his people against the refugees from the other timelines."

"Kairos did it so effectively. He had laid the blue print down with my people, the Guerreros. He practiced making us suffer so that he could perfect the suffering on the next group. Kairos was scared a person from one of the seven timelines would cause a rebellion against him for his decision to cut the timelines. He allowed for the species to intermingle across planets. As they grew up and their powers presented themselves, he had his new enemy. A child born of two or more races with powers hellbent on revenge. Kairos planted the seed in to the minds of his paranoid followers. They were all scared karma would be swift and the mixed children would exact revenge for their lost relatives. It was so easy to work off paranoid individuals. They wanted to hide their sins so bad, Kairos did almost no work to convince them to stay loyal."

"Kairos knew he couldn't start mass killing people from different planets if Titus was still alive. So, he convinced his followers to commit a coupe. He wanted to take out Titus once and for all. But Titus knew this would be his plan all along. He summoned me from Epsilon, had me collect the Crystals in that one second that he stopped time before his death, and had me split them in to seven separate pieces. He had you as the first Crystal Wielder. And Titus had his daughter, May, left to unravel any unrest Kairos created in the universe."

Salem pulls out their necklace from their robes. Six crystals remain on the necklace, "Those worthy of wielding the Crystals have yet to be born, except you. Kairos dropped you off on my door step as a threat. He came to find me. And see what I've been up to. He can know all this information because I know I can just disappear, if need be, to another planet or the remaining timelines if he comes for us, which I know he will."

"So, the reason I've told you all of this is because I know your Data Link will tell him every thing he needs to know. I want him to see how fortified we are. I want him to prepare as we will. He can know our moves and how we plan to strike back. But we can counter him. I wanted to answer the question as to why Kairos is attacking us. He is scared of you, Spike. He is scared of me. He is scared we will expose his secrets and live to tell the tale. Now, you can hate me. You can think that what I did was callous and unnecessary. I'm completely fine and I will accept you if you believe so. But work still needs to be done. Those beings in the Crystals can still be saved. The seven timelines can be restored. Now, it's up to you and the six others that I will pick. And *Kairos*, I may not live to see the day you die, but know your death will come from one of my seven Crystal children."

"Are you speaking to him or to me?"

"Both."

What the fuck. From afar, I see the picture they have painted, but up close, I hate it. I understand why they did what they did. I would have done the same. But all Ethereals, this is fucked. I know that I would have been no better. Yet...Yet, it feels weird to accept all of this. To agree with the reasoning behind my grandpa's plan. Salem's plan.

"This was the only way to save all those people?" I ask feeling everything and nothing. Pressured to know this has always been my fight to take up. My mantle that has been waiting for me to come back to.

"Titus and I came to the conclusion that this was *one* avenue."

"Were there any other options?"

"Allow people to die and hope that satisfied Loyalist's bloodlust."

"But it wouldn't have. Those Crystals. They are the end all be all."

"These Crystal Tasks were created by me. Each witch, warlock, or warwick had one chance to earn their place as the next coven leader. They had to prove they could do anything to save their people with only one chance."

"How did you get Reyna to allow you to do the Tasks?"

"The same way you convinced her to save her people. Reyna loves her people. You pull the right Threads, and she caves. Her heartstrings are the easiest to pull. Easiest to manipulate."

"That's why none of the others picked me. They knew that you would eventually have to confess all of this to me."

"Yes. And no. They knew my responsibilities to pass on the torch to you. But they are still very hateful towards Templites."

"You're crazy." I accidentally say out loud. "I mean, no, I would have done what you did but..."

Salem holds up a hand for me to stop. They continue.

"To save the universe, we had to play Kairos's crazy game. There is no real change without a little bit of crazy. Peaceful protests got the Guerreros nearly extinct fighting for their right to live freely. If we fought from the beginning and so did everyone else, there would be a lot more of us Guerreros around. On paper, my people are dead and I'm the lone survivor. But the Guerreros live on. Hidden and ready to take down Kairos. As do Templites that were from your time. Kairos waged a war on us and it is only fair that a Guerrero takes him out."

"And who would that be?"

"You."

"Me? How?"

"Your real mother was a Seer. And your grandfather was never faithful. He bore your uncle from the Queen of Wolves. And he bore your mother from the Queen of the Guerreros. Our queen was also a

Seer. You possess all of her gifts. Your lineage is equipped with all the tools to take down Kairos. More powers will develop as you grow older. My people had many unique abilities that have since gone extinct. Thread Manipulation was the number one reason our colonizers wanted us enslaved. They couldn't easily travel through the universe. They lacked the years of dedication it took to hone any skills. They lacked the power required to open and travel through the Fourth Dimension. So, they created their discounted version of our power that only knew how to destroy. Their false powers could only work through the subjugation and elimination of those that did not look like them. But they did not realize we hid our other gifts from the world. You, Spike, can very well destroy the universe with the power you will accumulate."

"Kairos will come for me. How will I hide them?"

Salem spins a web of Threads unravelling the world around them. They reach their hand in to a box-shaped hole they created and pull out a briefcase. They pop it open, "Does this look familiar?"

Twenty-five chess piece like figures sit in the suitcase.

"No."

"May, your real mother, predicted twenty-six lives. Twenty-five lived in service to Kairos. And one to bring him down. Predictions can change but we assume that is how long it will take to develop all Guerrero abilities. Then, your mission is to hide away your memories and powers in these pieces for Kairos to never find."

I'm going to die twenty-five times. This can't be real. This has to be a sick joke. I don't want to lose Salem, Mama Amanda, or Simon.

"Why do you need the Guerrero abilities?"

"Guerrero abilities can't be controlled by Ethereals. Have you ever wondered how they can go on allowing this behavior from Kairos? They are fickle beings. The Ethereals can take powers away from innocent people if they get angry at them or if the corrupt ones compensate them fairly. We have a few good Ethereals but most of them have just stood by as all of this has happened. Madame Destiny is the only consistent one that has been fighting on our side. A few others are predators and murderers. With no Ethereals or Kairos controlling you, you can put an end to all of this suffering. Guerrero magic grants you powers with no hurdles."

"And Mama Reyna is worried that if I gain too much strength I can use those powers to be worse than Kairos?"

"Axel, when the time comes, if you are worse than Kairos I will be the one to take you out. I made that promise. Neither of us is worried you will be worse than him. She is just worried you will end up on his side. And I have complete faith in you. Faith you will restore the timelines. I have faith you and the other Crystal children will be the ones to end this nightmare once and for all. Kill Kairos. Kill the Ethereals. And, Spike Guerrero assume the Templite Throne. Let's end them together."

End of Volume 1.

ACKNOWLEDGMENTS

This book took eleven years to be what it is now. For eleven years, I felt like I was in Limbo as I kept trying to write this book and life kept getting in the way, Spike was never satisfied with how I was telling the story, and my mental health was all over the place.

Thank you to my hubby bear, Javi, who bought me my laptop so I could format this book. It made life so much easier. May we find each other in every lifetime.

Thank to my alpha reader, Ander. You helped me revamp this baby and give her more life. You begged for more Ashely and Marina scenes so I had to extend their plot lines. Without you, Salem would never have entered the picture.

Thank you to my developmental editor, Allison Cherry. Your notes on my manuscript mirrored Ander's notes. It gave me the reassurance and confidence I needed to write the scenes I was most scared of writing.

Thank you to Andy Payne for my wonderful and gorgeous cover design. Even if you hate this book, you have to admit that cover is fucking amazing. Andy heard what I wanted and listened and made it a million times better than what I ever imagined. To you, I give you your flowers forever and always.

Thank you to my friends and family who kept asking me when id be finished with this book. If it weren't for you all I wouldn't have gotten my ass in gear. Thank you Jasmine, Jazmin, Nander, Maria, Amanda, Alyssa, Jeremey, and, again, Ander.

Can I say thank you to a character without looking crazy? No.

Well, I'll do it anyway. Spike. Thank you for coming in to my life. Your story looked very different when we first met. And every time I got it wrong, you forced me to change it. You told me to take breaks when I couldn't figure out how to fix a problem and you gave me the answers with time and sent signs from the universe to guide me. The scene you gave me while I was on vacation in Japan helped me understand the direction I needed to take in the final editing process. And crazily enough, it fit exactly with what Ander and Allison told me I needed to fix.

And, lastly, thank you mama. Thank you for saying "You can do it. Si se puede." For reminding me that we Mexicans always get the job done no matter how long it takes.

ABOUT THE AUTHOR

Noel Alvarado is a Mexican-Honduran mess in distress full of stress. He's a card holding member of the LGBT-QWUAH community. He serves the GAY agenda before anyone else. He writes gay books that are alright and makes B-level content on all video platforms. He has a cat named Luke Skywalker. He is a hot Cheetos girl inside but thot-a-saurus-rex on the outside. You can find him playing Dead by Daylight or Final Fantasy 7 Remake religiously. If it wasn't for his day job and wanting to write these stories, he would play video games all day.

instagram.com/leonplaysintheuniverses
tiktok.com/@leonplaysintheuniverses
pinterest.com/noelfloatingintheclouds
bookbub.com/profile/noel-alvarado
bsky.app/profile/trashpandaleon.bsky.social